How many million... ...future?

P9-COP-309

"Audacious and terrifying
uncannily believable."
New York Times bestselling author
LEE CHILD

It was a sound that made his skin crawl. Rotors.

The staccato hammering of the chopper's blades seemed to come from everywhere. Then he saw it. A quarter mile south. Coming in right out of the sun glare.

An instant later he recognized the flattened, broad profile of a Black Hawk. But not the standard transport model; it was some special variant with stub wings jutting off the fuselage.

And missiles clustered beneath them.

Travis turned and sprinted for the Humvee, screaming Paige's name. Screaming, "*Get out!*" over and over. He could see her through the heavy glass, seated in back on the side facing him.

She couldn't hear him.

He screamed louder, the soft tissue lining his throat going ragged.

In the direction of the chopper, high in his peripheral vision, white light erupted and something shrieked.

He was thirty yards from the vehicle now, moving as fast as he could move, screaming as loud as he could scream.

Paige turned toward the sound of his voice at last, centering her focus on it so perfectly that, for an instant, Travis forgot she couldn't see him.

She was looking right into his eyes when the missile hit the Humvee.

By Patrick Lee

DEEP SKY
GHOST COUNTRY
THE BREACH

PATRICK LEE

DEEP SKY

HARPER

An Imprint of HarperCollinsPublishers

HARPER

An Imprint of HarperCollins*Publishers*
10 East 53rd Street
New York, New York 10022-5299

Copyright © 2012 by Patrick Lee
ISBN 978-0-06-195879-3

First Harper mass market printing: January 2012

HarperCollins ® and Harper ® are registered trademarks of Harper-Collins Publishers.

Printed in the United States of America

Visit Harper paperbacks on the World Wide Web at
www.harpercollins.com

10 9 8 7 6 5 4 3 2 1

For Sue, Tom, John, Barb, Jim, and Chris

Acknowledgments

This last volume of the trilogy came to life with a lot of help from very smart and dedicated people. Great thanks to my editor, Gabe Robinson, along with many, many other people at HarperCollins, including Liate Stehlik, Seale Ballenger, Pamela Spengler-Jaffee, Megan Swartz, Adrienne DiPietro, Kristine Macrides, and Danielle Bartlett. Thanks also to Ellen S. Leach, for catching a large number of mistakes that slipped past me but would not have slipped past readers.

And as always, thank you to Janet Reid, agent extraordinaire. Before writing books I knew there was more to this job than sitting down and typing, but I couldn't have guessed how *much* more—and the incredible work you do is the reason I can do my part at all.

Definitions Established By
Presidential Executive Order 1978-AU3

"BREACH" shall refer to the physical anomaly located at the former site of the Very Large Ion Collider at Wind Creek, Wyoming. The total systemic failure of the VLIC on 7 March 1978 created the BREACH by unknown means. The BREACH may be an Einstein-Rosen bridge, or wormhole (ref: VLIC Accident Investigation Report).

"ENTITY" shall refer to any object that emerges from the BREACH. To date, ENTITIES have been observed to emerge at the rate of 3 to 4 per day (ref: VLIC Accident Object Survey). ENTITIES are technological in nature and suggest design origins far beyond human capability. In most cases their functions are not readily apparent to researchers on site at Wind Creek.

"BORDER TOWN" shall refer to the subsurface research complex constructed at the VLIC accident site, to serve the housing and working needs of scientific and security personnel

studying the BREACH. All signatories to the Tangent Special Authority Agreement (TSAA) hereby affirm that BORDER TOWN, along with its surrounding territory (ref: Border Town Exclusion Zone Charter), is a sovereign state unto itself, solely governed by the organization TANGENT.

PART I

SCALAR

CHAPTER ONE

No one friendly had ever lived in the brick colonial house at the end of the cul-de-sac on Fairlane Court. Which was strange, considering how many different owners had come and gone since its construction, in 1954. Nearly twenty of them over the years. They'd all been polite enough: they'd all nodded hello when appropriate, and kept the yard meticulously neat, and never played their televisions or stereos loudly—if at all. To a man and woman, the owners had all been in their thirties, single, with neither children nor pets. They had dressed conservatively and driven dark green or dark blue sedans.

They'd also never answered the doorbell, regardless of the time of day. They'd never hung up colored lights for the holidays, or handed out candy to trick-or-treaters. Not one occupant of the house had ever invited a neighbor for dinner. And though the place seemed to change hands every two to three years, no one had ever seen a For Sale sign on the lawn, or found the address in a real-estate listing.

Strangest of all were the moving days. Despite the apparent simplicity of the men and women who'd lived in the house, every single one of them had required at least four full-sized moving vans to transfer their belongings. Some had needed upward of a dozen. These vans always backed up so snugly to the garage door that it was impossible to see what exactly was being moved in or out. And they always came at night. Always.

Neil Pruitt knew all of this, though he'd never lived on this street, and had never seen the house until tonight. He knew because he'd seen others like it; there were *many* others. Nineteen more here in D.C., and another ten across the river in Langley. In and around New York City and Chicago there were just under fifty each. Most cities near that size had a few dozen at least. Los Angeles had seventy-three.

Pruitt circled the decorative plantings at the center of the cul-de-sac, pulled into the driveway and got out of the car. The night was cold and moist, rich with the smells of October: damp leaves, pumpkins, smoke from a backyard fire a few houses over. Pruitt glanced at the neighboring homes as he made his way up the walk. A big two-story on the left, all lights out except in an upstairs bedroom, where laughter through cracked-open windows suggested a slumber party. A split-level ranch to the right: through the bay window at the front, he saw a couple on their couch watching a big LCD screen. The president was on TV, live from the Oval Office.

No such signs of activity from the brick colonial. Soft lighting at most of the windows, but no movement visible inside. Pruitt stepped onto the porch and put his key in the lock. No need to turn it—the mechanism beeped and then clicked three times as its computer communicated with the key. The bolt disengaged, and Pruitt pushed the door—a solid piece of steel two inches thick—inward. He stepped from the flagstone porch onto the white ceramic tile of the entryway. While the outside of the house had been updated over the years to stay current with decorating trends, the interior had enjoyed no such attention. It was clean and bare and utilitarian, as it'd been for nearly six decades. It was all the Air Force needed it to be.

The foyer was identical to its counterpart in every such house Pruitt had been in. Ten feet by ten. Eight-foot ceiling. Twin security cameras, left and right in the corners opposite the front door. He pictured the two officers on duty in the house, watching the camera feeds and reacting to his arrival. Then he heard a door slide open, around the corner and down the hall.

"Sir, we weren't expecting a relief tonight." A man's voice. Adler. Pruitt had handpicked him for this post years earlier. His footsteps came down the hallway, still out of sight, accompanied by a lighter set. A second later Adler appeared in the doorway. Past his shoulder was a woman maybe thirty years old. Pretty. Like Adler she was a second lieutenant, though Pruitt had neither selected her nor even met her before. The name tag on her uniform read LAMB.

"You're not getting one," Pruitt said. "I won't be staying long. Take this."

Pruitt shrugged off his jacket and held it out. As Adler came forward to take it, Pruitt drew a Walther P99 from his rear waistband and shot him in the forehead. Lamb had just enough time to flinch; her eyebrows arched and then the second shot went through her left one and she dropped almost in unison with Adler.

Pruitt stepped over the bodies. The hallway only went to the right. The living space of the house was much smaller than it appeared from outside. There was just the entry, the corridor, and the control room at the end, which Pruitt stepped into ten seconds after firing the second shot. The chairs were still indented with the shapes of their recent occupants. He thought he could tell which had been Lamb's; the indentation was much smaller. A can of Diet Coke sat on a coaster beside her station. In the silence Pruitt could hear it still fizzing.

He pushed both chairs aside and shoved away the few pieces of paper that lay on the desk. Long ago, the equipment in this room had filled most of the nine-by-twelve space. Over the years it'd been replaced again and again with smaller updates. Its present form was no larger than a laptop, though it was made of steel and had no hinge on which to fold itself. It was bolted to the metal desk, which itself was welded to the floor beneath the ceramic tiles. This computer controlled the system that occupied the rest of the house, the space that wasn't easily accessed. Pruitt could picture it without difficulty, though. He looked at the concrete wall to his left and imagined staring right through it. On the other side was the cavernous space that was the same in every house like this, whether the outside was brick or vinyl or cedar shingle.

Beyond the wall was the missile bay.

Pruitt took his PDA from his pocket and set it on the desk beside the computer. Next he took out a specialized screwdriver, its head as complex as an ancient pictogram, and fitted it into the corresponding screw head on the side of the computer's case. Five turns and the tiny screw came free. Within seconds Pruitt had the motherboard exposed. The lead he needed was at the near end. He pulled it free, and saw three LEDs on the board go red. In his mind he saw and heard at least five emergency telephones begin to ring, in and around D.C. One of them, deep in the National Military Command Center at the Pentagon, had no doubt already been answered.

The response would come down on this place like a hammer. No question of it. But it would come too late. And those who responded would never guess his final intention. Not until they saw it for themselves.

He inserted the lead into a port on his PDA and switched it on. The screen lit up, the required program already running. It was one Pruitt had written himself, tailored for this purpose. The hourglass icon flickered, and then a password prompt appeared. He entered the code—a very long one—waited through another two seconds of the hourglass, and then saw the screen he'd expected. There was an input field for GPS coordinates. He pasted them in, having typed and copied them in advance, and pressed ENTER.

A second later the house shuddered. A heavy, continuous vibration set the floor and the desk humming.

Pruitt turned to the wall. He pressed his hands and then the side of his face against the concrete. Felt the animal waking up in its den.

Fifty-eight years ago the missile bay had contained a Korean-War-era Nike-Ajax. Pretty funny to picture it now, a weapon so simple and limited being trusted to defend the nation's capital against Russian bombers and ICBMs. The Ajax fleet had been swapped out for the Hercules in the early sixties. Definitely an improvement, though still probably not up to the task. Only in the late eighties, under Pruitt's tenure, had this program become viable—in his opinion—with the adoption of the Patriot system. A hell of a missile. But that wasn't what was on the other side of the wall now.

Pruitt absorbed the vibration for another second, then pushed off of the wall and stood upright. He took a slip of paper from his pocket and set it on the desk beside the PDA.

The paper had a single short sentence written on it:

See Scalar.

The intended recipients would know what it meant. Pruitt himself didn't even know. Or care.

He exited the room, leaving the PDA plugged in behind him. He returned down the corridor; where it met the entry, Adler's blood had formed a common pool with Lamb's, cherry red on the white tiles and nearly black where it'd saturated the grout.

Five seconds later he was out on the flagstones again, in the moist wind that smelled like leaves and pumpkins and smoke. He left his car in the driveway; already he could see the headlights of first responders, four blocks away and coming fast. He ducked around the side of the house and moved toward the backyard.

He could hear the missile from out here now. Louder every second. He heard dull thuds as heavy stabilizer arms retracted against the bay wall, and by the time he rounded the back corner of the house, the small basement windows at the rear had blown out and were venting steam into the night.

Pruitt crossed the shallow yard to the pines on the far end and stopped there, just inside them. He turned back and watched. He had to see it.

The house stood haloed by the headlights of the incoming vehicles. Tires skidded in the cul-de-sac and car doors opened and men's voices shouted. Fast reaction. Almost fast enough.

The roof blew. The whole middle span of it. Wood splinters and asphalt shingles scattered upward like confetti, and in almost the same instant a shape knifed up through the opening.

An AMRM Sparrowhawk. Advanced multi-role missile. In keeping with the military's crescent-wrench philosophy in recent years, the Sparrowhawk was a single tool with multiple uses. Specifically, surface-to-air and surface-to-surface. This one, stationed at this house, had only ever been meant for the defensive role, surface-to-air.

That wasn't the role it would play tonight.

The missile, as wide as a telephone pole and

almost as long, surged upward through the open roof, driven by a primary charge from the launcher below. Its momentum carried it above the treetops, maybe sixty feet higher than the roof's peak, and just as it slowed and nearly stopped, the missile's own engine engaged. For a third of a second it hovered almost still, like a Roman candle held upside-down. Then the flame beneath it went pure white, and the rocket screamed in a way that sounded eerily human—at a hundred times the volume—and a fast heartbeat later the thing was only a streak of light, climbing toward the speed of sound above Georgetown.

Pruitt watched it through the pine boughs. At two thousand feet its trajectory went flat. Its path defined a neat little semicircle in the sky as it hunted, and then it was gone, screaming southeast toward the ground coordinates he'd fed the PDA thirty seconds ago. The coordinates the Sparrow-hawk would reach about ten seconds from now.

Movement at ground level caught Pruitt's eye. The couple at the house next door had come out onto their rear patio, scared as hell and looking for the commotion. It was funny, in a way. Had they known, they could've stayed right on their couch, watching the live feed from the Oval Office.

That was where the show was going to be.

CHAPTER TWO

Every night Travis Chase took the elevator up to the surface and went running in the desert. It was usually cool, and always clear. Tonight was no exception. He could see the machine gun flashes of a thunderstorm in the Rockies, fifty miles southwest, but above him the stars were hard and sharp in the twilight. The scrubland was solid as asphalt and took no footprints. It crunched lightly under the treads of his running shoes, his footfalls setting the cadence for his breathing. He could do six miles now without getting winded. Not bad. Forty-four years old and he was in the best shape of his life. When he'd started running in the desert, more than a year ago, two miles had been pushing it.

His circuit brought him around toward where he'd started. The loop was seven miles total, so he could walk the last one. His cell phone had built-in GPS that could plot his path and tell him when he'd covered six miles, but in recent months he'd found he didn't need it. Habit and intuition were enough.

He slowed to a walk. His heart rate fell toward normal, and the pulse against his eardrums faded to the quiet of the desert night. This late in the year, whatever insects were native to Wyoming were long dead or dormant; there was no sound but the wind moving over the sand and dry brush, and the occasional, distant calling of coyotes.

In the trace moonlight Travis could see the low shape of the elevator housing a mile ahead. It wasn't much to look at, even in daylight: a decrepit pole barn surrounded by the remnants of a split-rail fence. Someone could walk right by it and have no desire to investigate—if someone could get within thirty miles of it without being stopped.

This empty landscape was the most secure piece of real estate on the planet. There were no roads within a forty-mile radius. No overflights by either military or civilian aircraft. Intrusions by off-road vehicles, which were rare, were swiftly turned away by people who looked like pissed-off ranchers. They weren't ranchers. They were something closer to soldiers, though not American soldiers. Strictly speaking, this featureless patch of eastern Wyoming was not American soil, and hadn't been since 1978.

Travis slowed further until his footsteps became silent. Now and then, when the wind faded, he could hear the distant rumbling of the storm. He was half a mile from the elevator when his phone beeped with a text message. He took it out, switched it on and narrowed his eyes at the bright display.

NEWS. COME BACK FAST. CONFERENCE ROOM.
—PAIGE

An intense chain of lightning unwound itself sideways over the mountains, illuminating the front range. Travis switched off the phone and picked up his speed to a sprint.

Two and a half minutes later, in the deep shadows of the pole barn, he caught his breath—a full-out run could still wind him. He faced the elevator doors, opened his eyes wide and waited for the biometric camera to find one of his irises. A quick flash of red skipped across the left half of his vision, and then the doors parted in front of him, throwing hard light out onto the concrete barn floor.

He stepped inside and faced the array of buttons. All fifty-one of them. Though he only rarely had reason to press the button for the deepest level, his eyes always went to it, drawn by his awareness of what was down there. Sometimes, especially in the elevator, he could swear he felt the Breach somehow. Maybe in his bones. A rhythmic bass wave, like an alien heartbeat, five hundred feet below in its fortified cocoon.

He pressed the button for B12, and the doors closed on the desert breeze and the darkness. The cab descended.

What was the news?

Not a new arrival out of the Breach. If that'd been the case, Paige would have directed him to the Primary Lab, where newly arrived objects—*entities*—were always taken. Not a new discovery about an old entity, either. That, too, would've probably taken place in the Primary Lab, or some other testing area.

The doors opened on twelve, and Travis stepped into the hallway. Like almost any corridor in the building, at any given time, this one was deserted. Border Town was enormous relative to its population: about a hundred full-time personnel. Spread over fifty-one floors, they didn't often bump elbows.

Travis turned the corner that led to the conference room, and saw Paige standing outside the open double doors, waiting. She had most of her attention turned inward on the room—Travis saw the glow of a television monitor reflected in her eyes—but she turned toward him as he approached. By now he could hear the ambience of a large number of people inside the room. Maybe everyone in the building.

When he reached Paige, she put her hand on his arm and left it there for a second.

"It's bad," she said, and led him through the doorway.

It was everyone. Standing room only. All eyes on the three large LCD panels on the right-side wall. Live news feeds: CNN, MSNBC, Fox. All three had aerial coverage of some structure on fire, surrounded by emergency crews. Travis looked from one screen to the next, seeking the clearest angle on the event, and after a few seconds the middle image pulled back and there it was.

The White House.

Burning.

More specifically, one of its wings was burning; the central portion of the house looked fine. Travis couldn't tell whether it was the east or west wing that was on fire without knowing which way the aerial shots were pointing. He finally let his eyes drop to the captions at the bottom of each screen, and understood. An explosion, very near the Oval Office, possibly inside it. He studied the image again. Only a gutted cavity remained of the president's office, all of it aflame despite two streams of water going into it from fire trucks on the scene.

"He was in there," Paige said. "He was on TV, live, and then it just went to black. About a minute later they started reporting on it."

The story resolved over the next two hours. Details came in, sketchy and then solid. The three networks must've had nearly identical sources—with each new piece of information, their chyrons updated almost in unison.

Twenty minutes into the coverage the secretary of state confirmed that President Garner had been killed. Vice President Stuart Holt, in Los Angeles for an environmental summit, was already in the air on his way back to Washington. He would be sworn in aboard the plane.

Travis found it hard to see Garner's death in its proper light—its global and historical significance. Garner had been a friend, and now he was gone. That was the only way Travis could feel it, for the moment.

He tried to stay focused on the coverage. The details of the blast had already begun to crystallize. There were dozens of witnesses who'd seen a contrail in the air at the time of the explosion, though it was unclear, at first, whether it'd belonged to an aircraft or a missile.

Then, five minutes after the official announcement about President Garner, all three networks cut away from the White House to a new feed— still an aerial shot, but at a different location. A residential street somewhere. A cul-de-sac full of more emergency vehicles, mostly police cruisers but also an ambulance and a single fire truck. The house at the end of the cul-de-sac was heavily damaged in some way that was hard to make sense of. Most of its roof had been blown off, and the debris lay scattered around it, but the walls and even most of the windows appeared intact. Nothing was burning.

Around him in the conference room, Travis saw sudden looks exchanged. He glanced at Paige and saw her focusing hard on the televised images. The house. The missing roof.

A man to Travis's left said, "Archer."

A few others nodded, Paige among them. After a moment she seemed to feel Travis's stare, and turned to him.

"Archer is an old Air Force program," she said. "Goes back to the fifties. Defensive missiles concealed in civilian areas. Supposed to be a last line against a nuclear strike."

Travis watched the implication spread across the room. President Garner had just been killed by someone in his own military.

It took less than an hour for rumors of the Archer program to filter into the broadcast coverage. Travis wasn't surprised. Secret as the program was, it had to require hundreds of people to operate it. Maybe thousands. Impossible to keep them all quiet in the aftermath of something like this.

By two in the morning there was official confirmation that Archer existed, and that it had been
used against the White House. CNN got an Air
Force general on the phone who addressed those
two points and then spent the next five minutes
saying nothing at all in a dozen different ways. No
word of a suspect. No word of a motive.

The helicopter footage remained the backdrop
throughout, mostly covering the White House but
occasionally returning to the cratered home on the
cul-de-sac.

Travis had an idea that no further news was
coming tonight, though the investigation had
probably made serious headway already. No doubt
there *was* an official suspect, dead or in custody.
Those working the case probably knew most of
what they would ever know. But they would be
very careful parceling out that information to the
public. The process would take weeks, not hours.

By 3 A.M. the crowd in the conference room on
level B12 had begun to thin. Paige looked at Travis
and communicated her thoughts without a spoken
word.

Five minutes later they were in their residence on
B16, under the covers, holding each other close in
the dark. Travis could think of nothing to say. He
thought about Garner. Knew Paige was thinking
about him too. Only platitudes came to Travis's
mind. Garner had lived a long and dignified life.
He would be remembered forever. His death had
almost certainly come without pain. Maybe without awareness, even—the blast had probably killed
him before he could see or hear it.

All of it true.

None of it helpful.

He kissed Paige's forehead. Pulled her closer. Felt her body relax as sleep came on. Felt himself begin fading too.

Paige's phone rang on the nightstand. She rolled, picked it up, squinted at the display. Travis saw by her reaction that the number was unfamiliar.

She pressed the button. "Hello?"

The caller spoke for a few seconds. Travis could discern only enough to tell that it was a man's voice. He couldn't make out the words.

"Yes, I'm in charge here," Paige said. "Who is this?"

The conversation lasted five minutes. Paige hardly spoke. Just quick affirmatives to let the man know she was still listening.

When the caller finally stopped speaking, Travis glanced at Paige. In the diffuse glow from her phone, he saw her staring at empty space, her forehead knitted.

Two more syllables from the caller. It sounded like, *Still there?*

"Yeah," Paige said. She shook off whatever she was trying to think of. "What you're describing doesn't sound familiar to me. I'll look into it here, but you should probably assume this is a dead lead." The man spoke briefly again, and then Paige said, "Thanks, I'll let you know."

She ended the call. Her eyes narrowed as if she was reviewing what she'd heard, committing relevant details to memory.

"That was the FBI," she said.

"About Garner?"

Paige nodded.

"Do they have a suspect?"

"Yeah. Commanding officer of the crew on duty at the Archer site—a man and woman, both murdered. Cameras inside the house caught it all; the officer didn't even try to hide his face. They're into his financials now, and it looks like he got a giant payoff weeks ago, and spent all the time since making it liquid. Getting ready to disappear. Which he's now done."

"They don't know where the money came from?"

"No, and they probably never will. They called here because the assassin left a note behind. The FBI seems to think it was addressed to us."

"But you think they're wrong?"

"No, I'm almost certain they're right."

CHAPTER THREE

P aige pulled the covers aside, arched her body across Travis's, and stood from the bed.

"Come with me," she said.

She crossed the room, naked, to the desk chair where she'd left her clothes. Travis stared at her body in the soft light. Some sights were just never going to get old. Then he stood and went to his own clothes, clumped against the wall, and began pulling them on.

"The guy on the phone was Dale Nellis," Paige said, "chief of staff to the FBI director. He read me the note—it didn't take very long."

She opened a drawer in the desk and tore a blank page from a notepad. Then she took out a pencil and wrote a single line:

See Scalar.

"That's all," she said.

Travis stared at it. He knew the word *scalar* as a mathematical term, but couldn't see what meaning it might hold in the context of the attack.

"The FBI ran the word through their computers to see if anything interesting turned up," Paige said. "A last name, an organization title, something like that. But they came up empty. A few small businesses have used that title over the years. A computer repair company, some kind of school supply maker, nothing much bigger than that."

"Not exactly the usual suspects," Travis said.

Paige shook her head, then nodded toward the door to the hallway. A moment later they were outside the residence, moving along the corridor toward the elevator.

Nearly every level of Border Town had the same basic layout, its hallways in the shape of a big wagon wheel. One giant ring corridor at the outside, a dozen spokes reaching inward to the central hub that housed the elevator and the stairwell.

"Nellis said he and a few guys at the top asked around," Paige said. "Discreetly, among people they trust, mostly in the intel community. They even talked to some retired guys, on the possibility that *Scalar* is an older reference. Which it seems to be. So far the only people to recognize the word were both from around President Reagan's time. One was a senator who chaired the Intelligence Committee back in the day, and the other was the deputy CIA director for a good chunk of the eighties. Both of them recalled *Scalar* as the name of an investigation from that time, but here's the interesting part: neither one of them was ever cleared to know anything about it, beyond the name. Although there were some things they ended up learning anyway—things that couldn't be hidden from them."

"Like what?"

"Like the investigation's budget. Whatever Scalar was—whoever was running it and whatever they were looking for—it had no spending limit. Any requested resource—I imagine things like satellite access, classified records access—was granted by the White House without delay, no questions asked. Scalar cost hundreds of millions of dollars, and spanned most of the 1980s, yet nobody in Congress, and nobody at the CIA, knew anything about it."

They reached the elevator. Paige pressed the call button. She turned to Travis as they waited. He saw something in her eyes. Some kind of understanding.

"Nellis said he wouldn't have believed that," she said, "except that he heard it independently from each of these guys tonight. Even then, it's pretty hard to swallow. He said he couldn't imagine there was anybody out there with that kind of authority. Anyone powerful enough and secret enough to get that sort of cooperation from the United States government, with apparently zero oversight."

Travis suddenly understood what her expression was about.

"It was us," he said. "Scalar was a Tangent investigation."

"I think it had to be," Paige said. "Nellis made a few more calls, this time to higher-level people who are in power right now. He ended up getting a couple minutes on the phone with, well, I guess it's *President* Holt now. Holt's known about Tangent for some time—vice presidents are usually in the loop. When Nellis described Scalar for him, I'm sure Holt made the same assumption you and I just made."

The elevator *dinged* softly and the doors parted. Travis followed Paige into the car. She pressed the button for level B48. The archives. It made sense. Though the files down there were mostly related to Breach entities and the experiments done on them over the past three decades, there were other kinds of records kept there too. If Tangent had been behind the Scalar investigation, whatever it was, the archives should contain a massive amount of data about it.

"Did the president give the FBI your number?" Travis said. That was hard to believe.

Paige shook her head. "The White House must have set up the call through a blind socket. Nellis didn't even know my name when he introduced himself on the phone. Didn't know anything about Tangent, either."

Travis thought it over, watching the button display as the elevator dropped through the complex. He understood now why Paige had told Nellis it was a dead lead. If she'd told him the truth—that crucial evidence for an FBI investigation might exist here in Border Town—it would've created all kinds of jurisdictional problems. The FBI would've wanted access to this place, and they would've wanted to do a lot more than just look through the archives.

That wouldn't have happened, of course. Not in a million years. The FBI would have been denied without even getting confirmation that Tangent existed. But it would've still been a political mess. And an unnecessary one. The simplest move was for Tangent to review the evidence itself. Then any information worth sending to the FBI could be routed through the White House, credited to a classified source. Nice and neat.

The elevator chimed again and the doors slid open on the archives. Travis followed Paige out.

The place had the look and feel of a library basement, some kind of periodical dungeon not set up for public use. Simple, black metal shelves. Narrow channels between them—just enough room for a person to pass through. The shelves reached the ceiling, ten feet up, and were lined with gray plastic binders. Each binder had a handwritten label fixed to its spine, filled out in a standard format with a given Breach entity's name and number, followed by a string of letters and numbers Travis couldn't make sense of. Some improvised Dewey decimal system created by Tangent's founders back in the early years, before computerized storage had become standard.

As Travis understood it, the most recent fifteen years of data had been created on PDAs and filmed on digital camcorders. All of that information now fit easily onto a few rack-mounted servers, tucked away somewhere on this floor. But all the data older than that—roughly the same amount in terms of information content—had been written out by hand and filmed on analog tape. That data filled essentially the entire floor, ten thousand square feet of densely packed physical storage.

Paige led the way toward a clearing among the shelves, fifty feet out from the elevator. A desk stood centered in the open space.

"I take it you've never heard of Scalar yourself," Travis said.

"Not even as a passing reference. Unless I've forgotten. And I can't imagine I would have— whatever Scalar was, it sounds like it was a very big deal."

"Doesn't that strike you as odd? That nobody ever mentioned it to you? All these years?"

"It strikes me as close to impossible," Paige said. "If Scalar happened in the eighties, my father would've known all about it. So why would he have kept it from me, later on when I came to work here?"

They passed into the open space and crossed to the desk. It was a big, practical thing: four feet by eight, black metal legs and surface, the same as the shelves. Five wooden chairs shoved under it at random. The desktop was bare except for a giant binder lying on its side, gray like those on the shelves, but much thicker. Ten or twelve inches wide at the spine, the thing was essentially a cubic foot of paper encased in hinged plastic. The word *INDEX* adorned the cover in adhesive block letters.

Paige heaved it open to about the midpoint of the post-bound stack. There were little tabs sticking out of the pages' sides at intervals, marking the alphabetical arrangement. The pages were tightly packed with text under headings that were mostly entity names, though some were simply the names of people, or various labs or stations within Border Town.

The entries themselves, beneath the headings, each consisted of just a date and a string of letters and numbers—the same kind that appeared on each of the shelved binders. A locator code, pointing to a specific place in the archives. Each heading had dozens of such entries below it, indicating random places all over level B48. Travis understood the basic logic: for any given entity, each time a new experiment was carried out, the results were filed away in the archives wherever space was available, and the location was recorded in the index. It was much easier to do it that way than to continually rearrange all the shelves to keep related material bunched together.

The index had clearly been updated often over the years—each page bore a mix of typed and handwritten text.

Paige flipped to the *S* section and navigated to where Scalar should've been.

It was there.

And it wasn't.

The heading was certainly there, right at the top of its own page.

SCALAR.

Beneath it, Travis counted seventeen separate entries, with dates ranging from 1981–06–04 to 1987–11–28. The locator codes were there too. The entries looked like all the others in the index, with one exception.

They were all crossed out.

Each had a simple line drawn through it, horizontally, in pen. The same pen, for all of them. It'd been done in one sitting—a single decision to cancel it all out. Yet there'd been no real attempt to conceal what the entries said. Travis was sure he knew why—was sure Paige knew too.

Five minutes later they'd confirmed it. At every

one of the shelf locations listed in the seventeen entries, the Scalar files were gone. In their place the shelves were either empty or else filled with newer, unrelated material—binders labeled with entity names. Paige opened each of them anyway and flipped through their contents, on the chance that the relevant data had simply been disguised within them. It hadn't.

"But it was here," Paige said. "This was a real investigation, and Tangent was behind it. It lasted at least six and a half years, and during that time they filed the paperwork here in the archives. And then they got rid of every trace of it, and as far as I know, they never even talked about it again."

She looked at Travis. Shook her head.

"What the hell was it about?" she said.

CHAPTER FOUR

They were back in their residence on B16, in the living room. Travis was sitting in a chair by the couch. Paige was pacing a few feet away. The LCD screen was on, tuned to CNN. The coverage was the same as when they'd left the conference room upstairs; all that'd changed was that the damage to the Oval Office was now concealed by a giant white tarp, pulled tight and square over a framework of scaffolding. It looked sharp and clean and dignified. Like a flag on a coffin.

For the past few minutes the commentary had focused on Garner's legacy, including measures he'd supported and signed into law. An extension of the tax credit for electric vehicles. An aggressive education reform bill. Additional funding for a much-derided research program at Harvard and MIT called the Methuselah Project, aimed at learning how to counter—and even reverse—human aging by the middle of the century. It'd never sounded all that crazy to Travis; no crazier, at least, than sending a person to the moon or plugging most of the world's computers into one another.

There was no mention of the message the assassin had left behind.

"The top people at the FBI have already called the best sources they can think of," Travis said, "including the new president, and they've turned up almost nothing. Our safest assumption is that they're done making progress—that no one in power knows anything about Scalar. No one who wants to help, anyway."

"Which means Nellis is probably right: whoever did this left the message just for us, no doubt assuming we'd know what the hell it meant."

Travis considered the strangeness of their situation. "Not only don't we know who we're playing against, we don't even know what the game is. We better find out on our terms before we find out on theirs."

Paige sank into the couch. "I don't understand why my father never told me about Scalar."

That would be a tricky question to answer. Paige's father was dead, along with nearly every member of Tangent who'd known him. Paige herself, though only thirty-two years old, was by far the most senior member of the organization, with just over a decade's involvement. There was a reason for that. Three years ago, the chain of events that'd originally brought Travis to Border Town had also, in the end, brought about the deaths of all but a handful of its inhabitants. The cataclysmic violence responsible still visited Travis's dreams. Paige's, too. He woke her from them a few times a month.

In time new members had been recruited, as

quickly as caution afforded. Within a couple years the ranks had been essentially refilled. Then, while Paige and most of the senior personnel were on business in Washington, D.C., they'd come under attack by heavily armed assailants—the opening salvo of a new conflict. Paige alone had survived. From that moment on she'd been the only person in the world capable of leading Tangent. The strongest of the few threads tying its present form to its past.

"I worked here alongside my father for the bulk of the last decade," she said. "Him and a hundred others. And most of them had been here since the beginning, which means Scalar happened on their watch. Why wouldn't a single person have ever spoken of it?"

"Can't have been a trust issue," Travis said.

"Not a chance. We all trusted each other with everything. With our lives."

"What other reason, then?" Travis said. "Embarrassment?"

Paige glanced at him, visibly uncomfortable at the thought. She shook her head, but Travis thought he saw more uncertainty than refutation in the gesture.

For thirty seconds neither of them spoke. The just-audible television took the edge off the silence.

Then Paige's eyes widened a little and she said, "Blue."

The word seemed to surprise her even as it came out. She stood from the couch and crossed to the short hallway leading to the bedroom. Travis stood and followed.

She had the computer's monitor switched on by the time he entered the room. The computer itself had already been running.

"Blue status," Paige said. She clicked open the file manager and navigated through a series of folders. Travis didn't even try to keep track of them. "It's a set of security measures we use for people who retire from Tangent."

"I didn't know anyone ever *had* retired from Tangent," Travis said. "Except me, for the time I was gone."

"It almost never happens," Paige said. Her attention stayed with the computer as she spoke. "Three times, total, in thirty-four years. Not counting you."

She reached the end of a directory tree, and Travis saw a folder icon that looked identical to all the rest, except that it was tinted blue. Paige clicked it. An input field opened, calling for two distinct passwords. Paige typed them quickly; only the second required any thought.

A personnel file opened on the screen. The format was familiar enough to Travis. He'd seen his own file and several others during his time here.

But he'd never seen any of the three names that now appeared on the monitor.

Rika Sengupta.

Carrie Holden.

Bartolo Conti.

"All three were here from the early days," Paige said. "My father probably recruited them himself."

Within seconds Paige clicked open each of their files and arranged them in three separate windows, visible at the same time.

All three had joined Tangent between the summer of 1978—the year the organization was formed—and the end of 1979. Original cast members, so to speak. Travis scanned the retirement dates for each file. Sengupta, Holden, and Conti had resigned in 1989, 1994, and 1997, respectively. All three had been with Tangent for the entire time Scalar was under way.

"Sengupta and Conti left for health reasons," Paige said. "Both were very old when they retired—they wanted to spend time with their families while they could. Neither made it to the new millennium."

"And Carrie Holden?"

"I only know a little about her. She was young when Tangent formed—early thirties. So, mid to late forties when she retired in ninety-four. She'd be into her sixties now."

"Why did she retire?"

"I don't know. I remember my father talking about her, sometimes. She was pretty important around here, in her day. But he never said why she left."

She clicked to expand Holden's file, filling the screen with it. There was a thumbnail photo that probably dated to the late seventies: a young woman with blond hair and green or hazel eyes. The file's text dealt mostly with her pre-Tangent background—she had degrees in chemical and physical engineering from Caltech. There was nothing about her retirement, neither the reason for it nor the identity she'd assumed upon leaving.

"She'd have to know something about Scalar,"

Paige said. "Certainly more than anyone else we're going to find."

"*Can* we find her? If she's hidden as well as I was, her new name won't be in the computer. Only the person who created the identity would know it—someone with Tangent in 1994—and that person has to be dead by now."

Paige nodded. "That person was my father."

"I don't suppose he randomly let the information slip."

"No. Not directly."

Paige swiveled her chair to the side. She traced a path on the carpet with her foot, back and forth.

"I think they had a history," she said. "She and my father. Some connection during the time they both lived here. He never said so, but that was the impression I got. The way he spoke when her name came up. Things other people said, and stopped short of saying." Her foot slowed and came to rest. She looked at the computer but made no move to use it. "There was this strange little moment, one time. One of those things you end up filing away and never really thinking about, because it's awkward. It was probably five years ago. I walked into my father's office in the Primary Lab, and he had two things on his computer screen: a picture of Carrie Holden, and a Google satellite map. When he heard me come in, he flinched and closed them both, the map first and then the picture. It was very out of character for him—hiding something, being jumpy. But a second later when he turned to me, it was like nothing had happened. Totally casual—he ignored the moment entirely. So did I. I pretty much had to. And later on, when I had time to think about it, I was glad I'd done that, because I was pretty sure of what I'd walked in on. I think the map must've been the place Carrie relocated to, and my father was just . . . thinking about her. No special reason. You know what I mean?"

Travis nodded. He thought of the two years he'd worked in a shipping warehouse in Atlanta before coming back to Tangent. On occasion he'd found himself slapping a label onto a box of brake pads bound for Casper, Wyoming, less than eighty miles from Border Town. He'd stare at the box for a few seconds, dwelling on the fact that in a day or two it would be much closer to Paige Campbell than he himself would probably ever be again. Irrational as hell, but he'd done it all the time. It wasn't hard to imagine Peter Campbell, in a private moment, gazing at a map of the place where Carrie Holden had ended up.

"You didn't see the map clearly enough to get the location," Travis said.

Paige shook her head. "There wasn't time to see it, even if I'd wanted to. I was way across the room, and it was gone by the time I'd taken a few steps."

She went quiet again. The only sound was the soft drone of the computer's cooling fan.

Travis met her stare.

He knew what she was about to say.

She said it.

"We've both been thinking the same thing for the last ten minutes: there's a way I can find out exactly what my father knew about Scalar, and failing that, I can certainly learn what location that map was showing. The same approach works for both problems."

Travis nodded. "I've been trying to think of an alternative."

"Me too. But there isn't one. We could rack our brains all day and it'd be for nothing." She looked at him. "You hate that I'm the one who has to do it. If you were the one, I'd hate it too. But I wouldn't try to stop you. Okay?"

Travis exhaled. He thought about it for another five seconds. Finally he nodded again. "Let's go."

CHAPTER FIVE

L evel B42. The Primary Lab. Other than the chamber that held the Breach itself, this was the most important place in Border Town. All entities that were unique or nearly so, sufficiently powerful, and still being studied on a regular basis were stored on this level, behind blast doors as heavy as those at NORAD's Cheyenne Mountain. Travis and Paige passed through them into a long central corridor with extensions branching away left and right. B42 was one of the few levels with a distinct layout—it was more than twice the size of any other floor, its boundaries having been expanded over the years by excavation of the surrounding deep soil.

The place was deserted. Their footsteps echoed strangely in the silence.

They came to the door they needed within a minute. It was standard sized but heavy duty, with a palm scanner beside the lock. Paige put her hand to it and a moment later they were through into the space beyond, a room the size of a walk-in closet with a bank of small vault doors on the opposite wall. One bore a magnetic placard with crisp black lettering:

ENTITY 0728—TAP

Travis felt his jaw tighten at the sight of the name. Paige looked at him and noticed.

"I'm not a fan either," she said. "Let's get it over with."

She crossed to the vault, turned the dial back and forth in sequence, heard the lock disengage, and hauled the door open. Inside was a single tiny object: a rich green translucent cube half an inch across. It might have been a blank die cut from emerald. But it wasn't.

Paige stared at it a moment, then picked it up and turned from the vault. Her movements were casual in a way that seemed deliberate to Travis. A forced calm. He didn't blame her. She crossed the small room, stepped back out through the heavy door, and stopped in the middle of the corridor.

"Right here is as good as anywhere," she said.

Travis joined her in the hallway. For a second her calm facade slipped. Then she discarded it altogether and sat down at the base of the wall. She leaned her back against it and drew her knees close to her body. Travis sat beside her.

"Deep, slow breaths," he said.

"I know."

"Give anything to trade places with you."

"I know."

She had the Tap lying on her open palm, eye level in front of her. Travis watched how the light played over and through it. Strange, silvery shapes in its depths. Tiny swirls and arcs, like scimitar blades.

Then in one fluid move Paige took the cube between two fingertips and put it to her temple. She pressed it against her skin, and Travis saw the thing's edges blur as it vibrated.

Paige's breathing accelerated in spite of her efforts. She reached across her midsection with her other arm and took hold of Travis's hand.

"You're okay," he whispered.

She nodded quickly, probably not even processing the words.

Then it happened. The little cube liquefied in the span of a second, and collapsed to what looked like a thick drop of aloe gel between Paige's fingertips. In almost the same instant the top of the gel rose and formed a point—and then a filament. A wirelike structure maybe a centimeter tall, thin as fine guitar string. It stood there swaying to the tremor of Paige's body. Then it pointed itself inward and plunged through the skin and bone of her temple.

Her hand spasmed and gripped Travis's tightly. Her breaths turned into little cries, betraying the pain but only just. Travis knew how much it hurt. He'd experienced it himself. The Tap had emerged from the Breach during the two years he'd been away, but had still been in frequent testing when he'd returned. Like many others he'd volunteered to have a go at it, and his single use had gone as smoothly as he could've hoped. Despite the pain involved, he'd intended to use it again.

Then a woman named Gina Murphy had taken a turn with it, and everything had changed. In the six months since, not a single person had used the Tap.

Travis watched as the gel drop shrank by the second. The thing was feeding itself into Paige's skull through the tiny hole made by the filament. Though Travis couldn't see what was happening inside, he could easily recall how it felt: like a living thread, ever lengthening, darting and slipping among the deep folds of the brain's surface. Flitting and hunting and finding its way like a snake's tongue. Every second of it agony.

But that was normal for the Tap. So far, everything was going well.

Paige's cries intensified. Her eyes were screwed shut.

"I'm right here," Travis whispered.

Five seconds had passed since the lead end had gone in. The gel mass on her fingertips was half spent. The insertion never took longer than ten or twelve seconds.

Paige got control of her breathing just before the end. She went quiet and let her face relax. The last trace of gel shrank to wire thickness and slipped in, leaving nothing but a tiny drop of blood at the entry point.

Paige opened her eyes.

"Better?" Travis said.

She nodded.

The tendril always stopped moving once it was fully inside; the pain stopped with it, for the most part.

She was still gripping his hand. With his fingertip against her wrist, he could feel her pulse pushing three beats per second, though it was slowing by the moment.

"I'm ready," Paige said. "Catch me if I start to tip over."

"Wait." He repositioned himself so that he was seated facing her. She got the idea and scooted forward from the wall, until their chests were touching and their legs were around each other's hips. He hugged her close to him, and she rested her head on his shoulder.

"No worries about falling over," he said.

She nodded against him and let her body relax, her breathing now almost back to normal.

"See you in three minutes and sixteen seconds," she said.

She felt the effect begin as soon as she closed her eyes. One moment there was a floor beneath her and Travis's arms were around her, and the next she was gone, floating in some neural equivalent of a sensory deprivation chamber. She felt the Tap vibrating softly inside her head, its pathway wandering from her temple across the underside of her skull, to the parietal lobe on the opposite rear side. No sense of her limbs. No sense of anything but her thoughts.

And her memories.

She focused on the one she wanted. Envisioned her father's office—*her* office, now—on that day five years ago. He'd been sitting with his back to her, the map on one half of his monitor and Carrie Holden's face on the other.

The image came to her almost at once—much more easily and vividly than it normally could have. She saw it from her own point of view as it'd been in that moment, just passing through the office doorway, her shoe scuffing the tile and making her father flinch. She froze the image just like that, in the instant before he closed the map.

The Tap was a hell of a thing. The memory image hovered in front of her like a projection, as complete and accurate as a high-res photo of that moment would've been.

But this capability wasn't what made the Tap special. If it *had* been, she would've come up empty: at this range she couldn't read any of the map's labels. Not the street names. Certainly not the town's name, if one was there. She could resolve only a road running north and south, and a modest grid of streets clumped along the middle of its length. A few lesser roads strayed off left and right from the bunch. It could've been any of a hundred thousand small towns in the world. The image told her nothing.

She allowed the memory to slip forward in time. The desk and computer began to grow in her field of view as she advanced into the room.

Then her father's hand moved on the mouse, and the map vanished—its clarity had improved hardly at all.

She froze the image again, then let it begin to run backward. Her viewpoint drifted away toward the door behind her. The map popped onto the screen again. Now came the doorway's edge, sliding into her view from the side. With it came the scuff of her foot, sounding eerie in both reverse and slow motion. She pulled back all the way into the corridor and kept going, retreating to maybe five seconds before she'd entered the room. She knew from experience that if she wanted to, she could play the memory stream forward or backward at just about any speed she could make sense of. It was scarcely different from rewinding or fast-forwarding a video file. She could plunge back through a spastic wash of images at an hour per second, skim through a day in less than half a minute, then slow down and dial in on anything she wanted to see. Every split second of it would be rich with photo-accurate detail. Every moment of her life was there to be revisited and studied. It should've been impossible—with even her passing grasp of neuroscience she knew that. Human memory was good, but not *this* good. However adept the Tap was at pulling information from her brain, this much information shouldn't have been there to begin with. The Tap was a hell of a thing.

Yet this function was still not what made it special—or difficult to accept as possible. Not by a country mile on either score.

Paige let the image freeze again.

Five seconds from the open doorway. Out of sight beyond it, her father was staring at Carrie Holden and the map, unaware of Paige's approach in the corridor.

Perfect.

To use the Tap's real selling point, all she had to do now was wait. The controls were simple and intuitive. A few seconds passed, the memory still frozen, and then she began to feel her feet beneath her. She was hovering in the void, but her feet tin-

gled as if they could sense the ground half an inch
below them.

She willed herself to drop, and felt her shoes connect solidly with the surface.

In that instant the memory came to life. It was
no longer an image in front of her—it was a world
around her: the hallway and the fluorescent lights
and the hum of air exchangers and the trace smell of
cleaning solution on the floor. Her body was there
too, propelled forward by its own momentum—
she'd been mid-stride at this point in the memory.
The movement almost threw her off balance as she
came to a stop. She put out one hand and caught
the wall, and silently halted herself two feet short
of the doorway.

To all of her senses she was really standing here,
in this moment that was five years gone. Her father
was really in the next room, just beyond the edge
of this doorway. The Tap let you relive memories
exactly as they'd been—but that still wasn't what
made it special.

What made it special was that it let you relive
them as they *hadn't* been.

Paige moved forward into the doorway.

She took care not to let her shoe scuff the floor.

She saw her father seated at the desk, staring at
the map and the picture of Carrie. He had no idea
Paige was there.

She took a step into the room. Then another.

He sat there, adrift in his thoughts, eyes fixed on
the screen.

Another step, and another.

She could see the map more clearly now than

before. She was closer to it than she'd gotten in real life.

Another step.

Still not close enough to resolve the words on the screen.

But almost.

When she'd heard the early accounts from those who'd first used the Tap, she hadn't believed them. It just couldn't be true; how could you remember details you hadn't actually seen the first time around? Then she'd tried it herself, and there'd been no more denying it. In fact the Tap's power was far greater than she'd supposed in the beginning. You could do more than just cross a room you hadn't crossed and read words you hadn't been close enough to read. You could pick up a book you hadn't opened at the time—or ever—and flip to page 241. You'd see the words on that page as they existed in real life, and you could verify it for yourself after snapping out of the memory and finding a copy. If she wanted to, Paige knew she could back out of her father's office right now and, in the middle of this memory, go upstairs and schedule a flight to Paris. She could take that flight and walk the Champs-Élysées, and it would be swarming with the very same tourists who'd been there on this day five years ago. The scene would be accurate to the last detail. Every lock of hair brushed from a forehead. Every smile.

As with all entities, there were only guesses as to how it worked. The technician who'd spent the most time testing it, a man named Jhalani who'd once been a colleague of Stephen Hawking's at Cambridge, imagined the Tap to be a kind of antenna. Clearly it did more than just draw information from the user's brain—Jhalani believed it drew from something quite a bit grander: the set of all possible universes. Paige had heard of the many-worlds interpretation of quantum mechanics, but only as an interesting hypothetical notion. She'd been surprised to learn from Jhalani that it was actually a mainstream idea in modern physics. The thrust of it was that every event that could go one way or another actually went *both*. Every time you looked at wheat bread and white bread and chose white, some other version of you, out there in the great who-the-hell-knows, chose wheat. Physicists mainly talked about it happening at the level of subatomic particles, but if it applied down at that scale, then it certainly applied to loaves of bread and flights to Paris and shoe scuffs on tiled floors. In the end, Paige thought Travis had summed the Tap up best: it let you remember not just everything you'd done, but everything you *could have* done. A hell of a thing.

She took another step toward her father's desk. She'd be in his peripheral vision soon—right about at the point where she could read the map. The margin would come down to inches at best.

It was critical that she get this right the first time—the first time would be the only time. The Tap's one limit was that you couldn't revisit the same memory twice. The techs liked to say that a memory was *burned* after you relived it. Not only couldn't you drop into it again, you couldn't even remember it the old-fashioned way afterward. The original would be forever replaced by the revision. Therefore an especially cherished moment—a first kiss, say—was better left alone.

Another step.

If it came down to it, she had options. This was, for all its considerable bells and whistles, only a memory. Nothing she did here would be of consequence in the real world after she woke up. Which meant she could leap at her father, shove him away from the computer, and read the map before he had time to react. At that point she could simply be done with the whole thing—to end this memory she needed only to concentrate hard on her last glimpse of reality: she and Travis sitting in the deserted corridor on B42. A good ten seconds of that image would take her right back to it.

But she hoped to avoid attacking her father. Doing so would preclude the other move she planned to make here. The more obvious move, by far, though she wished she could forgo it.

Another step. And another.

The labels on the map were right at the brink of her discernment now.

Another step.

She could see the number on the big road running north and south. U.S. 550, it looked like. She thought that was somewhere in Colorado. Just above and to the left of the grid of streets was a word—almost certainly the town's name. A short word.

She squinted.

Ouray.

Ouray, Colorado. She'd heard of it. Some friends in college had stayed there when they went skiing at Telluride.

Good enough. If she really wanted to, she could end the memory now.

A big part of her *did* want to. The same part that hated the second move.

Which was simply to talk to her father.

It wasn't that she didn't *want* to talk to him. Quite the opposite. She'd been very close to him, especially in their last years together, and then she'd lost him in the worst imaginable way. When she'd first learned what the Tap could do, she'd considered reliving a moment with him. Something happy and good and warm, to replace the ending life had given them.

But she'd resisted. Always. As real as it would feel, the moment would be fake. And desecratory, somehow. The whole notion had seemed wrong from the beginning.

It still did.

She watched him sitting there, unaware of her. She took a breath and smelled his aftershave. She couldn't remember smelling it on anyone since she'd lost him. All those years, that scent had just been part of the background. A thing to hardly notice, if at all. It could make her cry right now, if she wasn't careful. She let the emotions swim a few seconds longer, then shoved them all down into the deep.

Time to do this.

She backed away from the desk, turned and left the room without a sound. She walked to a spot in the hallway ten feet from the door, pivoted and faced it again.

And cleared her throat loudly.

She heard her father's chair squeak at once, and heard the mouse scrape on his desktop.

She walked to the doorway and leaned in, and

found him staring at a file directory. She knocked on the frame and he looked up at her.

"Hey," he said.

"Hey."

Her throat constricted; she couldn't help it. Jesus, even a random moment like this. *Especially* a random moment like this. The kind they'd had a million of—should've had a million *more* of.

She swallowed the tightness and stepped into the room. "I have a question."

"Shoot."

No reason to drag things out: "What was Scalar?"

He didn't quite flinch. It was more subtle than that—all in the eyes. A flicker of fear and then perfect calm. He tilted his chair back and appeared to search his thoughts.

"Rings a bell," he said. "Where'd you come across it?"

"In the archives. There's an index page for it, but all the entries are crossed out."

"Oh—I remember. Let me guess, the entries went from the early to late eighties."

Paige nodded.

"It was a clerical thing," her father said. "Had to do with videotape formats, way back. We used to shoot everything on standard VHS, and then we switched over to VHS-C—digital was still a ways off. Anyway, when we made the switch we decided to transfer all the old stuff too, for shelf-life. Huge pain in the ass. Couple thousand hours of stock. Probably took us six years or more, on and off."

He shrugged, waiting for her to let it go.

She returned his gaze and wondered if he'd ever lied to her before this. Sure, he'd kept his work with

Tangent secret from her, all through her childhood, but what choice had he had? This was different. And harder to stomach than she'd have guessed.

"That all you wanted to know?" he said.

Only a memory. She held onto that idea like it was a handrail at the edge of a cliff. If she called him on his lie, she wouldn't actually be hurting him. He wasn't real.

"Honey?" he said. "Everything okay?"

"I've already asked some of the others about Scalar," she said. "No one wants to say much, but I'm pretty certain it wasn't about transferring videotapes."

His expression went cold.

"There was government involvement," she said. "And it cost hundreds of millions of dollars. I want to know what it was."

He stared. He seemed to be coming to some careful decision. When he finally spoke, it was in a calming tone, but one full of fear—*for her*. As if she were standing there with a gun to her head.

"Paige, you don't want to get into this."

"I have a right to know. And I don't appreciate being lied to."

"You're right—I lied about the VHS stuff. But you lied too. No one here in Border Town told you a thing about Scalar. There are maybe half a dozen who know the parts you just described, and none of them would've said anything without coming to me first. Which means you talked to someone on the outside. And that scares the hell out of me."

She couldn't think of what to say to that. Almost every word had caught her off guard.

Her father stood from his desk and crossed to

her. He stared at her with that strange, minefield caution still in his eyes.

"Who have you spoken to?" he said.

"First tell me what Scalar is."

"Paige, this is more serious than you can know. If you've talked to the wrong people, you may have already triggered things we can't stop."

"Then tell me. Everything."

He shook his head. "Knowing about Scalar puts a person at risk. I wouldn't tell you a word of it to save my life. Now I need to know exactly who you spoke to. I'm not kidding."

"If others here know about this, then I should know too—"

He grabbed her arm and pulled her toward him—she had to step fast to stay balanced—and shouted into her face. "*Who did you talk to?*"

She pulled her arm away, turned and ran. Through the doorway, along the corridor, the lights sliding by and her father's footsteps coming fast behind her. She shut her eyes as she ran. Pictured the deserted B42, where she and Travis were sitting. It was hard to focus on it now.

"Paige!"

Running. Eyes shut tight. Only a memory.

Travis held on to Paige and waited. Three minutes, sixteen seconds. It always took that long, no matter how much time someone spent inside a memory. During his own use of the Tap, Travis had revisited a random night of his stretch in Atlanta. He'd dropped into the middle of a long shift at the warehouse, then just walked out of the place and got in his Explorer. He drove west all that night and all the next day, stopping only for gas, food, and a couple naps, and reached the Pacific in about thirty-six hours.

Had he wanted to, he could've stayed in the memory for months—probably even years. Techs had remained under for as long as six weeks without encountering trouble. They'd even tried staying under while catching up to the present time and surpassing it; had it worked they would've found themselves *remembering* their own futures, a trick with all kinds of fun potential. But all attempts to do that had failed—even the Tap had its boundaries. Subjects hit the present and saw their vision start flashing green and blue like some system-crash warning, and then they involuntarily emerged from the memory—three minutes and sixteen seconds after going under, as always.

Only one person had ever come back sooner. Gina Murphy. Her eyes had popped open at around two minutes and thirty-five seconds, and she'd screamed and held her head as if it were being pried apart. The screaming had lasted for over a minute, while Travis and others carried her to the medical quarters. Along the way Gina managed to evict the Tap from her head—another intuitive control, you got it out by simply *wanting* it out— but that didn't end the pain. Her death ended it, around the time they set her on a bed in medical. By then she was bleeding from every opening in her face, including her eyes. An Army medical examiner, off-site, did the autopsy the following day. The results, understandably, were unprecedented in medical literature. Gina had died from laceration and hemorrhaging of the brain, confined to a narrow pathway atop the neocortex. In the doctor's words, it looked like someone had taken a radial saw to the contents of her head, but had managed to do it without cutting the skull.

More disturbing than those answers were the questions that didn't have any. Above all, what had gone wrong? Had something about Gina's biochemistry triggered the problem? Had she used the Tap in some incorrect way? What would that even mean? She'd gone under to relive a memory, like everyone else had done—some sibling's birthday party she'd missed years ago. The fact was that the questions weren't just unanswered. They were unanswerable. As with all entities, Tangent was simply out of its depth. There was a way to get yourself killed using the Tap, and no victim would ever live to say what it was.

Travis watched the time on his phone.

Two minutes and thirty-five came and went.

He relaxed only by a degree.

Three minutes.

Three minutes and ten.

Fifteen.

Sixteen.

Paige jerked against him and took a hard breath.

"*Fuck*," she whispered.

She raised her head from his shoulder.

"One for two," she said. She rubbed her forehead, looking badly rattled by something. "I'll explain while we wait for the plane."

CHAPTER SIX

Before they'd even returned to their residence, Paige called Bethany Stewart—one of the youngest people in Tangent, at twenty-five, and very likely the smartest. Bethany answered on the second ring with no edge of sleep in her voice, despite it being four in the morning.

"I need DMV files, with photos, for everyone in Ouray, Colorado," Paige said. She spelled out the town's name. "Narrow the results to females in their sixties, and send them to my computer."

"Take five minutes," Bethany said.

It took three—and less than another two for Travis and Paige to spot Carrie Holden among the candidates. She'd dyed her hair dark brown, but nothing else had changed except her age. Her name in Ouray was Rebecca Hunter.

They were in the air by 4:20. Though Tangent kept no aircraft on-site at Border Town, it had a small fleet stationed at Browning Air National Guard Base in Casper, ten minutes' flight time away.

The jet, a Gulfstream V with seating for eighteen, felt enormous with only the two of them in the cabin. The pilots' voices up front were lost under the drone of the engines. Travis looked out as the aircraft climbed, but there was only unbroken darkness below. The nearest towns were faint pinpricks of light, far out on the plain beyond the limits of the Border Town Exclusion Zone.

For a few minutes neither spoke. The jet's turbofans throttled back an octave as the aircraft reached altitude and leveled off.

"You're thinking about it," Paige said.

She didn't have to frame it as a question any more than she had to specify what *it* was.

It was almost all Travis thought about these days.

He nodded without meeting her eyes.

Fourteen months ago Travis had rejoined Tangent after two years of self-imposed exile. He'd spent the fourteen months doing the same kind of work as everyone else in Border Town—helping to study Breach entities, both new and old—while also cramming for hours a day to give himself the underpinning of scientific literacy that every other Tangent recruit had come prepackaged with. He'd taken to it surprisingly well. At ten months he'd passed the equivalent of MIT's Calculus 4 exam, and had at least a solid undergrad-level hold on physics, chemistry, and biology. The joke was that none of it really mattered where entities were concerned: the smartest people in the world were probably about as qualified as sparrows to study the objects that emerged from the Breach. Still it was nice to speak the same technical language as everyone else, and Travis had found his awe of the

Breach only deepening as his intellect grew. Like staring at the night sky through increasingly sharp eyes.

More to the point, his recent training meant he could do real scientific work at Border Town. He felt like he belonged there now—as a contributor, not just an outsider taking up space.

But that wasn't why he'd come back.

That wasn't *it*.

"Are you wondering if there's a connection?" Paige said. "Between whatever's going on right now and . . . the thing about you?"

"I'm always wondering that," Travis said. "Every time something new comes along, I ask myself if it's all starting. Sooner or later, the answer will be yes."

The issue was complex, but Travis thought of it in simple terms. Like delineated notes in some PowerPoint presentation. Or individual black flies circling his head.

The first piece of it was certain: somewhere down the road, Tangent would learn to use the Breach to send messages to the past—propelling them into the tunnel from this end, against the resistance force at its mouth, in such a way that they would re-emerge *before* they were sent in. The reason Travis was certain of this was that two messages had come back already. Some future Paige, and some future Travis, had given their lives to send them—the physical process of doing so was unavoidably fatal.

There were lots of details, but they all shook out to this: something bad was coming. Something that would end about 20 million lives. Something Travis himself would be responsible for, and might have no choice but to do, because to *not* do it would be worse.

Paige's future self, perhaps acting on limited information, had opposed the action—whatever it was. Her message to the past had been a retroactive order—to herself—to kill Travis, in the hope of preventing this thing from happening at all.

Travis had countered her move by sending his own message—a *messenger*, really: a radically advanced, self-aware handheld computer called *Blackbird*, though almost everyone knew it as the *Whisper*. The Whisper had emerged even further in the past than Paige's message to herself, and had set about manipulating people and rewriting history in order to put Travis in front of the Breach when Paige's message came through.

In doing so, it'd allowed him to intercept it.

In the present, Travis and Paige had only limited clues as to what the hell it all meant. Their future selves had sent perfectly contradicting pleas, each important enough to merit dying in the bargain. All that differentiated the sacrifices was that Travis's had been sent *after* Paige's—it must've, since it'd been a response to hers. Had he known something she didn't?

The details ended there. That far-off Travis had withheld them, no doubt fearing they would turn his present self away completely. All Travis could do was wait for it. Wait for any sign that it'd begun. The first link in the chain that would pull him down into the dark.

Down toward *it*.

"Let's not dwell on it too much," Paige said. "Save tomorrow for tomorrow, right? With any luck we won't live to see it anyway."

The man in the white parka had a name—Dominic—but his employers didn't know it. Maybe they had a nickname for him, or more likely a number, but if so they never addressed him by it. They didn't address him at all. They just called and gave him instructions. They were the only ones who knew the number for the blue cell phone.

That phone had rung last night while Dominic was painting the den in his condo in Santa Fe. A nice rich green that contrasted well with the white trim and the walnut desk. Dominic set the roller in the tray and answered before the ringtone reached the first drumbeat of David Bowie's "Modern Love." Dominic listened as the caller spoke, committing everything to memory, then hung up and went to his closet and opened the cavity behind the back wall. He selected a white parka with battery-powered heating good for twelve hours of lying still in the cold, and a matte-white Remington 700 with a four-power scope. Two minutes later he was in his car en route to the private terminal at Santa Fe County Municipal.

Now he was lying prone in the snow five hundred feet above and half a mile east of Ouray, Colorado. He lay at the pinched, far end of a valley that rose from the town's outskirts. The town looked like a snow globe village, its streetlights casting cones in the big papery flakes that were coming down.

A halo of light-bleed surrounded Ouray itself—a barrier of visual warmth against the dark.

Dominic lay far outside that warmth, out in the deep, empty night.

So did the cabin he was watching.

He put his eye to the scope and panned across the windows. A pale glow rimmed the blinds at one of them—maybe a fluorescent light in a laundry room left on all night. Every other window was dark. There was a mercury lamp on a post in the front yard, though its glow served only to make the cabin appear lonelier. Only two other structures stood in the valley: a low-slung ranch and a mobile home, both tucked in close to town. The cabin was on its own.

Dominic raised his eye from the scope and looked at his watch. Not quite five in the morning. He'd taken position just after midnight. Nothing about the cabin had changed since then. Daylight was two hours away, but it would present no problem when it came. Dominic would remain invisible, and so would the five-man team he knew was lying much closer to the place—probably within forty yards of the front door.

CHAPTER SEVEN

They landed at Telluride Regional and rented a Jeep using the perfect false identities that, in recent years, all Tangent personnel traveled under. Travis drove. They rolled into Ouray from the north at a quarter to six in the morning, the still-dark streets of the town all but empty.

Travis swung left off of Main Street onto the valley road that led to Rebecca Hunter's address. He thought he could see the place already, high in the darkness above town. A cabin in a little pool of light, seeming almost to float in the void. The emptiness around the place disquieted him on some level. His hand went to the shape of the SIG Sauer P226 holstered beneath his jacket. In his peripheral vision he thought he saw Paige do the same.

There were entities they could've brought along to make this trip less dangerous, but Tangent rarely sanctioned taking Breach technology outside Border Town. The risk was obvious: if things went badly, the entities could end up in someone else's hands. It'd happened before, with one of the most dangerous things ever to emerge from the Breach:

a full-body suit that rendered its wearer perfectly transparent in every kind of light. The resulting misery and violence had plagued Tangent for years before they recovered the damned thing—no one wanted to go through it again.

"Wonder if she's an early riser," Paige said.

"She is today, like it or not."

They pulled into the cabin's drive sixty seconds later, the headlights sweeping over a landscape of low evergreen shrubs and scattered pines, all shrouded by a four-inch layer of snow. Travis killed the lights and the engine and they got out. Their feet crunched on gravel beneath the powder.

The cabin was single-story, closer to small than big. Maybe two bedrooms in there, depending on their size. No sign of movement yet. There was a light at one window, but Travis had seen that long before they pulled in. If Rebecca—Carrie—had noticed their arrival, it wasn't evident from out here.

There was an older model Ford F–150 nosed up against the place, matching the description in the DMV registration. Its tire tracks, all but erased by the night's snowfall, led back out to the road.

A layer of rock salt had been scattered around the cabin's entry to a radius of ten or twelve feet, reducing the ground there to moist gravel. Travis and Paige crossed it and went to the door, a heavy construction of knotted pine planks with no window. Its one notable feature was a peephole. Travis pressed the doorbell and heard the chime sound inside.

For five seconds nothing happened. He was reaching for the button again when a light came on at the far end of the house, to their left. Another ten seconds. Then footsteps, drawing close and stopping. Travis imagined Carrie Holden standing right there with her eye to the peephole, a foot and a half away from them. What could they look like to her? What could any two strangers look like at 5:50 in the morning? It occurred to him that she might simply refuse to open the door. He wondered what they would do in that case, but only for a second—the lock disengaged and the door swung inward eight inches, and Carrie Holden stared out at them through the gap, clad in a quilted robe.

She looked older than in the DMV picture, as Travis had expected; the license had been updated three years ago. Maybe sick with something, too— her features seemed drawn and pale—though she was perfectly alert. Her eyes went back and forth between the two of them.

"We're with Tangent," Paige said. "We need to speak to you—Ms. Holden."

If any of that startled the woman, she didn't show it. Her eyes stayed fixed on Paige's. Then she exhaled softly and nodded, not upset but nowhere near happy, either. She pulled open the door and stepped back to admit them.

Inside, the cabin was close to what Travis had pictured: the cozy side of rustic. Timber walls, rough-hewn beams supporting the vaulted ceiling, potbellied woodstove on the hearth. The huge living room window was a living postcard of Ouray. Travis could think of worse places to hide out from the world.

Carrie didn't offer them anything to drink. Just

led them across the entryway into the living room, sat in a chair facing the couch and left them to conclude that they should sit too. They did.

"This is Travis Chase," Paige said. "And my name is Paige Campbell."

Carrie nodded, politely if not quite kindly.

"I'm not coming back to Border Town," she said. "So if that's what you came to ask about—"

Paige cut her off, shaking her head. "We're just looking for information. We need to know about an old Tangent investigation called Scalar. Do you remember it?"

As before, the woman showed no trace of surprise.

"I remember it to the extent I knew about it," she said.

"Can you tell us what you know?"

"Why would you need me to? You're with Tangent, you should have better sources than me."

"We don't," Paige said. "The reasons would take a while to go into, and they wouldn't brighten your day. Can you just tell us? I'm sorry to be this blunt, but it's important. Something's happening, and it relates to Scalar, and we need to know as much as we can."

Carrie nodded, but only vaguely. Her hands, as fragile looking as the rest of her, moved nervously on her knees.

Travis studied her face. The stretched skin. The withdrawn eyes.

The voice alone was strong. Surprisingly so, for someone apparently ill.

He glanced at the end table next to the couch. Its

base had shelves for magazines, all of them cluttered with old issues of *Newsweek*, *National Geo-
graphic*, and some local paper.

There was also a notepad with a pen clipped to
it, its front page covered with phone numbers and
random pieces of scribbled info. No doubt the pad
had been there for as long as the cordless phone
cradled atop the end table.

Travis indicated the pad and met Carrie's eyes.

"Mind if I take notes?" he said.

She nodded again.

Travis took the pad, unclipped the pen, and
turned to a fresh page. He began writing something
immediately, though Carrie hadn't spoken yet.

"Please start with the basics if you can," Paige
said. "What was the investigation about? What
were we looking for?"

For a long time the older woman said nothing.
Then her hands went still and she looked up at
Paige.

"I'm sorry," Carrie said. "Before I say anything,
I need to hear whatever *you* know about Scalar."

"I just told you," Paige said. "We *don't* know
anything. Just the name."

"Here's the problem," Carrie said. "There are
at least a few people outside of Tangent who
know that investigation by name only. People in
the government—people in *several* governments.
Those people were *kept* from knowing more than
just the name, and for good reason. It's not unthinkable that such parties, should they manage to
find me here, would pretend to be with Tangent
and ask me for information."

Paige was already shaking her head. "Ma'am, I can assure you—"

"There has to be *something* else you know about Scalar," Carrie said. "Some detail to prove you're not an outsider."

Travis turned the page he'd written on and began writing on the next. After only a few seconds he turned that one too, and continued on a third.

For a moment, pondering Carrie's demand, Paige appeared lost. She pulled her bangs back from her forehead and stared into empty space in front of herself. Then she looked at Carrie.

"In the archives index in Border Town," Paige said, "on Level B48, there are seventeen entries devoted to Scalar. The first is dated June 4, 1981. The last is dated November 28, 1987. All seventeen of them are lined out in blue ink. Is that good enough?"

Carrie looked impressed. But still undecided. She took a breath to speak, but before she could, Travis finished writing and set the pen aside. He turned the pages back until his first was on top, then calmly handed the pad across to Carrie. The move surprised her, but she took it and read the few lines Travis had written:

Nod if the real Carrie Holden is still in this cabin.
  If you make a sound I will kill you.

By the time the woman looked up from the pad, Travis had drawn his SIG Sauer and leveled it at her face.

CHAPTER EIGHT

She didn't make a sound.

Her hands began to shake again, and she lowered the notepad to her lap.

Travis was too focused on the woman to see Paige's expression, but whatever her reaction was, it didn't freeze her. Or lead her to a different conclusion from his. She drew her own weapon and aimed it at the woman.

Travis raised his eyebrows and pointed at the pad with his free hand, prompting her for an answer.

The woman swallowed and seemed to consider her options. She didn't have any.

She nodded forcefully. Yes, the real Carrie Holden was still here.

Paige began speaking, her tone as casual as Travis had ever heard it. Anyone listening to an audio feed of this room—as someone undoubtedly was—would've heard no hint of tension. "If you need me to, I can put you in touch with other Tangent personnel to confirm we're who we say we are. We need your information, Ms. Holden."

Travis gestured for the woman to turn the page. She did.

How many are watching this place?
Nod if they are inside.

She thought about it. Raised a hand and extended all four fingers and her thumb. Then she shrugged and added the index finger of the other hand. Five, maybe six.

She also shook her head, slowly and deliberately. No, the watchers were not inside the cabin.

"Maybe you've guessed," Paige said, "but the thing that's going on right now is tied to Garner's assassination last night. Which in turn is linked to Scalar. How, we don't know."

Nothing she was saying was especially sensitive— the people listening in almost certainly had that information already.

Travis gestured again: turn the page.

The woman complied.

Say you need to use the restroom.
Make no other sound.

Another swallow. A final moment of decision behind her eyes.

"I'm sorry, I need to use the powder room," the woman said, and before the last word was out, Travis set his gun aside and lunged across the space between couch and chair. He got one hand over the woman's mouth and nose before she could change her mind and scream, and looped the other arm around her neck, sliding right down onto the cushion beside her as he did it.

He left plenty of space between the crook of his

elbow and her throat—he had no intention of strangling her. Instead he pressed his bicep to one side of her neck and his forearm to the other, in a sleeper hold—a blood choke, as they'd called it on the force in Minneapolis. Full compression of the carotid arteries on each side. You could kill someone if you weren't careful with this move, though admittedly Travis wasn't all that concerned for this subject.

She lasted seven seconds, then went limp against him.

On the possibility she was faking it, he took hold of her left index finger and pried it radically backward toward the top of her wrist, far beyond the ninety-degree limit it was built with.

She didn't react.

She wasn't faking.

He lowered her to the chair and stood. Paige, already on her feet, handed him back his gun. He holstered it, then crossed the room to the hallway and the half bath there, wide open and empty. He closed the door loudly for effect, then turned back to find Paige right beside him.

She leaned close and whispered against his ear. "They won't buy this for long. We've got a couple minutes, tops."

He nodded.

She drew back, then pressed in again. "I suspected, but I wasn't sure. How'd you know?"

"She didn't react to your last name. She should've, if she was close with your dad."

"I thought the rock salt out front was overdone. Should've just been a path to the truck. Now we know why there was so much."

Travis nodded again. Sometime last night a group of people had descended on this place. Maybe they'd parked on the road and come around behind the house to hide their footprints. Maybe the woman—the decoy—had rung the doorbell alone and gotten Carrie Holden to open up. Whatever had followed had been fast and brutal, and left lots of tracks going in. All of which had been erased by the salt.

Travis indicated the woman on the chair. "Find something to bind her with. I'll find Carrie."

Paige headed for an open closet near the entry. Even from here Travis could see random articles of clothing inside. Long-sleeved shirts whose arms would do fine as makeshift ropes.

He turned his attention farther down the back hall, past the bathroom. There were two doorways at the end, facing each other, both open. One room dark, one lit.

He hadn't bothered to ask, in writing, whether Carrie Holden was still alive. Partly that was because he'd been in a hurry, but mostly it was because he'd assumed she was. Anyone who'd gone to this much trouble to set a trap for him and Paige must have a good reason to take them alive—it would've been far easier to open fire on the Jeep the moment they pulled in. Certainly that approach wouldn't have required finding a passable lookalike. It followed that the aggressors would keep Carrie alive, too—the more Tangent prisoners, the merrier.

He advanced along the hall.

Dark room, lit room.

The decoy had been waiting in the lit one. She'd

turned on the light when he rang the doorbell. It seemed likely that Carrie was in that same room: the impostor would want to keep an eye on her.

It occurred to Travis that the woman could've lied about the people watching this place: they could well be inside right now. They could be in either or both of the rooms ahead. In any such scenario he was outgunned. It almost wasn't worth drawing his SIG. He drew it anyway. If someone was about to take him out, he might as well return the favor as best he could.

Behind him he heard Paige tying the woman's wrists and ankles. The sound was vague, indistinct. To a listener it might have been someone shifting awkwardly in a seat.

Travis covered the last ten feet of the hallway at a fast walk, reached into the dark room to where the light switch had to be, and flipped it.

Home office. Big oak desk with a laptop and a green glass-shaded lamp and a scattering of papers. No closet. Nowhere for anyone to hide.

Travis spun in the hall and faced the other room. Carrie's bedroom. Bigger than the office. Walk-in closet on the far wall, full of clothes and random boxes. No one hiding there, either. No one hiding anywhere, here. There was only Carrie Holden herself, bound and gagged with duct tape on the floor beside the bed, staring up at him with wide and alert eyes.

He holstered the gun and crossed to her, kneeling and putting a finger to his lips as he met her stare.

He removed the tape from her face first; it was triple wrapped but the overlap was sloppy, leaving the lowest layer exposed at the edge. Travis tore through it easily and pulled all three pieces aside. Carrie took a deeper breath than she'd probably taken in hours.

"Do you have a gun here?" Travis whispered.

Carrie nodded.

"Are you good with it?"

Another nod, accompanied by a look—mild annoyance at the question. Which boded well.

Travis considered what he'd seen of the cabin's layout so far. One fact stood out: there was no back door. No easy way in or out but the entry he and Paige had used.

That was good.

He met Carrie's stare again as he turned his attention to the rest of her binds.

"We can make it out of here alive," he whispered, "but you have to do exactly what I say."

As he freed her wrists he began to explain the plan.

CHAPTER NINE

Every instinct told Dominic something was wrong. The decoy's decision to use the bathroom was entirely out of line. Granted, she wasn't a professional at this kind of work—Dominic had no idea where his employers had found her, though without a doubt she'd come from somewhere within their own ranks. Probably *high* in the ranks. She was someone. Or someone's sister or mother. They would've only chosen somebody whose loyalty was beyond question.

What wasn't beyond question was her capability. Clearly she had no experience at being a stand-in. Who the hell did, aside from undercover cops and a few deep-cover intel people? It was pressure work of the worst kind. Contrary to what some believed, deception did not come naturally to most people. Even telling a small lie triggered all kinds of stress reactions, and this woman was telling a big one.

For all that, she'd done well at first. Right on script, as far as Dominic could tell. Her job was to get the visitors talking. Get them to disclose what they knew about Scalar—whatever the hell that was—in a setting where they felt comfortable enough to speak freely. Later on, after the team had taken them, there would be time to interrogate them at length, but that sort of questioning was chancy at best; Dominic knew that from long experience. You could torture someone for a computer password or a vault lock combination—information that could be confirmed on the spot—but you could rarely get at their deeper secrets. Broad, general information was hard to extract by brutal means. You couldn't force the answers when you didn't even have the questions.

Hence the decoy.

And she'd done fine until the bathroom thing.

Maybe her nerves had gotten to her. Maybe she'd needed a break to rein in the jitters and refocus. Splash some water on her face.

Maybe.

Offhand, Dominic could think of no other reason. If there was another reason, it was something bad. Something very fucking bad.

He spoke into the microphone that extended from his earpiece. "What are you seeing?"

The team leader near the cabin responded softly. "Nothing you're not seeing."

"I don't like this," Dominic said.

"Same. Standing by—for now."

Travis finished whispering the plan as he got Carrie to her feet. She winced at the stiffness in her joints but looked steady enough.

Paige was standing in the doorway—Travis realized she'd been there for some time.

"Need me to repeat it?" he said.

She shook her head. "I heard."

Travis guided Carrie into the hallway and the three of them returned to the living room.

Paige had done a thorough job on the decoy. She lay on the floor at the base of her chair, her wrists tied behind her with one arm of a cardigan, her ankles with the other. The sleeve of a wool sweater had been wedged between her teeth and tied around her head. There was some risk of her waking up and making noise—banging against the furniture if nothing else—but Travis wasn't worried. One way or another, this would all be over in the next minute or two.

He wondered where the listening device was, but didn't look for it. It could be anywhere. Under the couch. Tacked beneath the top of the end table.

He spoke at room volume: "She seems nervous, doesn't she?"

"Probably just caught off guard," Paige said. "It's not every morning she gets a visit from Tangent."

Travis moved silently across to the bathroom. He eased the door open, slipped inside and closed it gently behind him. Then he flushed the toilet, banged the lid down, and turned on the faucet.

Dominic relaxed a notch.

"You hearing this?" he said. The running water was just audible over the feed.

"Got it. Guess she just had to go. Jesus."

A moment later the faucet shut off and the door clicked open.

"Sorry about that," he heard the decoy say. Her

tone sounded different—probably because of her distance from the microphone. "Please continue."

The young female visitor spoke. "As I said before, Garner's death has some connection to Scalar—"

The young woman stopped speaking. Dominic cupped his hand over the earpiece and listened carefully, but couldn't hear anything happening— any reason for her to have cut herself off.

"What's going on?" the team leader said.

"Quiet," Dominic said.

For three more seconds the silence held.

Then the older woman spoke. "Is there a problem?"

Dominic's stomach tightened. He thought he knew what was coming.

It came.

The young woman said, "You're not Carrie Holden."

Fuck.

The team leader spoke up, fast and tense: "Ready to move on my mark."

"I beg your pardon?" the decoy said.

There was no reply from either the young woman or her male friend. Instead there came a burst of commotion. Furniture sliding. Bodies interacting. Voices raised and jumbled over one another. The male visitor said, "Get her legs!"

"*Move now!*" the team leader said. "*Now, now, now!*"

Two seconds after that Dominic saw the team sprinting into the pool of light in front of the cabin. All five of them, Heckler & Koch automatics in hand, rushing the front door in a tight group. Like a sledgehammer coming down on a knuckle.

* * *

Travis gave the end table a kick to create the last of the commotion, then turned and ran for the firing position he'd picked out moments earlier. Paige and Carrie had each already settled into theirs—Paige behind the corner at the hallway's mouth, Carrie behind the iron woodstove. Carrie had retrieved her own pistol—a Beretta 92FS—during the long silence in the living room.

Travis reached his cover: an island in the kitchen. He dropped to a knee behind it, drew his SIG and leveled it on the door.

Already he could hear the footsteps outside, crunching hard on the exposed gravel. Seconds away.

Three protected shooting angles on a solitary chokepoint, against aggressors who didn't even expect to come under fire—who expected to burst in on a scuffle among unprepared subjects.

Travis took a breath and steadied his hand on the granite.

The footsteps outside covered the last stretch to the door. Whoever was leading the pack didn't stutter-step. He hit the lock at full speed and the latch-plate splintered from the frame and the door exploded inward.

Dominic didn't really expect to hear shooting. The team would seek only to control the situation. At most they'd trigger a few three-round bursts into the ceiling for intimidation, though even that was unlikely. These men were professionals. They knew how to assert themselves without theatrics. And their orders were explicit: take the subjects alive. Gunfire of any kind would be an unnecessary risk.

Dominic's own orders were in the same vein. His role was to disable the visitors' vehicle if necessary—one shot to the engine block would do—but otherwise to withhold fire.

Only under the most implausible scenario, in which the visitors eluded the team and seemed likely to escape, was Dominic to engage them with lethal force.

It wouldn't come to that. The decoy plan had failed pretty miserably—almost comically—but the rest would be warm butter on toast.

He was thinking that very thing when he heard the front door crash in—and right on top of that sound came the first gunshots. He flinched and tore out his earpiece, but not before recognizing what he was hearing: not the 9mm bursts the team would fire, but single shots of something heavier. Forty-caliber Smith and Wesson, it sounded like. And maybe a few 9mm shots among them, but not in three-round bursts. All the shots were sporadic but one at a time.

Then it was over.

Three seconds, start to finish.

In the silence he heard his pulse in his ears. And the wind sighing over the ridge into the valley, pushing the big snowflakes almost sideways.

He felt for his earpiece and put it back in place, but for the longest time he heard nothing.

Travis stood and surveyed the aftermath. His eyes picked out the relevant points in order of importance.

Paige and Carrie were unhurt.

All the bodies in the entry were down and still.

There was no one else coming in. No footsteps outside. No voices. Just empty darkness and blowing snow.

The decoy was still lying bound in front of the chair. Still unconscious. And unharmed.

The women stood from their cover. They met each other's eyes, and Travis's.

Travis crossed from the kitchen to the front door, his gun still trained on the bodies. He scrutinized them, saw that each had taken at least one headshot, and felt his tension step down a degree.

A second later it stepped back up.

Five bodies.

In his mind he saw the decoy extending five digits of one hand, then adding another finger with a shrug.

Five, maybe six.

If there was a sixth man, where was he? Why wasn't he with the group?

Travis thought of the terrain surrounding the cabin, and the answer suggested itself. And made his skin prickle.

A lookout, up high. Almost certainly armed.

He saw earpieces on each of the corpses. He stooped and took the nearest one, and fixed it to his own ear.

"Are you listening?" he said. "Do you hear that? That's the sound of none of your friends breathing."

He waited.

No reply.

He hoped he was talking to dead air. But doubted it.

Dominic had already swiveled the mouthpiece behind his head so the man wouldn't hear his breath. He kept the earpiece in place. He listened. Time drew out. It felt like the audio equivalent of a stare-down.

"Correction," the man in the cabin said. "One of your friends *is* breathing. The nice old lady who lied to us. I guess it's possible she's not really *your* friend—but she's somebody's friend, isn't she? I bet she matters to the people who hired you."

Dominic felt his adrenaline begin to climb. He could see exactly where this was going.

"She has to be someone personally close to them," the man said. "Who else would they trust to do this? I don't think they found her on Craigslist."

Fuck. *Fuck.*

"So here's how this happens," the man continued. "The three of us, plus your decoy, are leaving right now. In a tight group. You won't have a shot that doesn't risk hitting her. We're going to stay tight all the way to the Jeep, and we're going to sit tight *inside* the Jeep, and we're going to keep it that way until we're long gone. And if you try to kill the vehicle and strand us here, my first move is to put her brains in the snow. Try me if you think I'm bluffing."

A hard plastic clatter ended the speech: the man had dropped the earpiece on the floor.

He wasn't bluffing. Dominic was clear on that.

Even if he'd thought it *was* a bluff, he couldn't have taken the chance. He had no idea who the decoy really was—therefore risking her life wasn't his decision.

It was someone else's.

He reached into his parka and withdrew the blue cell phone. He double-pressed the send button and saw the display light up, the phone already dialing the man who'd called him last night.

First ring. No answer.

Far below, a broad shape emerged from the cabin. Four bodies clumped together. Three walking, one being carried. Even without looking through the Remington's scope Dominic could see there was no shot. No single head was distinct—they were all shoved together in a silhouetted mass.

Second ring. No answer.

The group reached the Jeep and piled in and the engine roared. The headlights came on.

Third ring. No answer.

The vehicle backed around in a tight arc until it faced the road, then lunged forward, taking the turn fast and racing away down the valley toward town.

Fourth ring. No answer.

Dominic put his eye to the scope and centered the reticle on the Jeep. He did the math, the variables stacking up automatically in his head: range, velocity, elevation, time.

He could kill the vehicle easily right now. Once that was done he could put shot after shot into the passenger compartment, then sprint down to it and make a thorough finish.

That would hold true for maybe twenty seconds, given the Jeep's speed. After that it would be more luck than skill.

Twenty seconds, if the call connected right now.

Twenty seconds to explain the situation and get a decision.

Nineteen seconds.

Fifth ring. A click on the line. A man's voice: "Talk to me."

Travis hated having the headlights on, making an easier target of the vehicle, but he had no choice. Under this cloudcover the valley would be ink black, and he couldn't afford to lose the road. Burying the Jeep in snow would be fatal if there really was a sixth man back there.

A memory from childhood came to him: Ichabod Crane and the Headless Horseman. Some point along this road represented the fabled bridge, the margin beyond which they would be safe.

He was certain they hadn't reached it yet.

Paige was next to him in the passenger seat. Carrie sat centered behind them, leaning forward over the console. She had the decoy slumped across her lap, still bound, the Beretta pressed to her head in case she woke. Which she seemed to be doing—she was making noises.

How long since they'd pulled onto this road? Ten seconds? Fifteen?

Ahead lay the town, bright and welcoming beyond the darkness that engulfed the Jeep. They were ten seconds shy of the light when the first bullet hit. It struck the left edge of the hood with a sound like a baseball bat's impact, but deflected without penetrating the metal. Travis felt the others flinch, and his hands jerked on the wheel, and for a terrible second the vehicle began to fishtail on the snowy road. The back end went left, the wheels spinning without purchase. A second shot skipped off the hard top three inches above Travis's head. He felt cold air seethe down through the resulting rupture in the material. Then the Jeep straightened and surged forward again, and for the next three seconds nothing happened except that the town got closer and the darkness ahead of them got shorter. Three seconds for them to think they might make it.

Then the rear window shattered and a spring *twanged* inside a seatback, and blood splattered all over the windshield.

CHAPTER TEN

*N*ot Paige.

Later, that would be the only thing Travis remembered thinking as the next seconds played out. Not the calculation of how far they had to go to reach safety, or how long that would take. Not the awareness that he needed to keep the Jeep under control. Not even the fear of another shot.

Not Paige. That was it. He could handle anyone else in the vehicle dying, himself included. Just not Paige.

If anybody was screaming, he couldn't tell. His ears were ringing with increased bloodflow and the wind was keening through the hole above him, drawn by the pressure differential from the missing back window.

They passed into light on the east edge of town and the first available cross street came up fast. Travis braked and hauled right on the wheel, and halfway through the turn he saw a newspaper box on the streetcorner buffeted by a shot. The papers inside fluttered as if they'd caught a moment's breeze. Then the Jeep was fully onto the side street and accelerating, with two-story brick buildings shielding it from the shooter.

The blood on the windshield was running down, each thick drop now a vertical line.

Travis turned to Paige.

Her left coat sleeve and the left side of her face were bloodier than the windshield.

But no more damaged than the windshield, either. It wasn't her blood—a fact she seemed to be just verifying for herself. She turned in her seat and looked back at Carrie Holden.

Carrie wasn't leaning forward over the console now. She was pressed against her own seatback, one hand to the lower left side of her abdomen.

Her fingers were soaked with blood.

"Jesus Christ," Paige said. She repositioned herself so she was kneeling, facing Carrie; she switched on the dome light and bent down to study the wound.

Her first discovery was notable: the rifle bullet had clipped Carrie's side—and fragmented in the decoy's head. Most of which was now gone. As Travis looked more carefully at the blood on the windshield he saw that not all of it *was* blood. There was gray matter there. And a few chips of bone. He wondered if a death had ever mattered less to him.

He glanced back again and saw that Carrie had pulled up the bottom of her shirt to examine her own injury. It was all but superficial. The bullet had hit her so far to the side that it had almost missed—a quarter inch would've made the difference. The result was like a shallow knife slash to her side. Some bleeding, but no serious trauma. She let the shirt fall back over it and shoved the decoy's body to the floor.

Travis glanced at Paige as she faced forward again. He saw her working out the pieces of what'd just happened.

"I guess it's possible that whoever killed Garner could've found this place," she said, "if they had the right connections. The government would've had no record of where you relocated to, Carrie, but they would've seen your name drop off Tangent's personnel list in 1994. They'd know you were out there somewhere. In the past few years, facial geometry software could've probably narrowed DMV records to ten thousand or fewer. Narrow further by age and then look for a real-estate purchase or lease agreement in ninety-four, and they'd be in the ballpark. Wouldn't take much legwork beyond that point. They might've found you five years ago and filed it away under *useful*."

Carrie nodded. She looked emotionally drained, but still alert. "I used to be so careful about everything. Paranoid, even. After a while, it felt nice to think I didn't have to be."

Paige looked at Travis. "I think I was wrong earlier. The note they left for us—I don't think they *did* expect us to understand it. Not in full, anyway. If they anticipated our showing up here, they must have known we'd be hard up for information about Scalar. They knew we'd come here to ask Carrie about it."

"That makes the trap contradict itself," Travis said. "Why set up a decoy to get information out of us, if we were only coming because we were clueless?"

He considered it for two seconds and then answered his own question.

"Confirmation. They *believed* we didn't know anything, but they wanted to be certain. Like whatever it is they're doing, they had to rule us out as a threat."

Paige looked at him. "There's no way they killed a president just to set all that up."

"Not a chance. They'd need a bigger reason for that. This feels more like an afterthought."

"Could the real reason involve putting Stuart Holt in power?" Paige said. "Maybe he's involved. He's the one who pointed the FBI toward us, ultimately leading us here."

"It's something to keep in mind," Travis said.

They reached the end of the street and Travis took a left. Three blocks ahead lay Main Street, which was also Highway 550 running north out of town.

"I heard your introductions from the other room," Carrie said. "Travis Chase. Paige Campbell." A pause. "You're Peter's daughter."

Paige looked back at her and nodded.

"I watched you grow up in photographs on his desk," Carrie said. "You were fourteen when I left." Again she paused. Then she said, "He's dead, isn't he? If he were alive, he wouldn't have let you come here to ask me about Scalar."

Paige nodded again.

Travis made the right onto 550. He could see the road extending ahead beyond the edge of Ouray, north into the darkness.

Then Carrie drew a hard breath with a shudder in it, and both Travis and Paige looked back at her. Travis had guessed the pain was getting worse, but she wasn't wincing, and her hands were nowhere near the wound; they were relaxed on her knee.

The only thing tense was her face—with fear.

She looked at them both. "Is it really starting again? Everything Scalar was about?"

"Yes," Travis said. "How much do you know about it?"

"Some. I know all about how it started. What led to it. Not much detail of the investigation itself. Peter was . . . hesitant to talk about it."

"So I learned," Paige said.

"Please tell us as much as you can," Travis said. "Right now all we've got are questions."

Carrie nodded. She sat there a moment putting her thoughts in order. When she spoke again, Travis could still hear the fear, though contained, subdued.

"The Scalar investigation was a cold case. It was cold even when Peter and the others started working on it in 1981. In a way, it was a manhunt, though they knew the man in question was already dead. Their goal was to learn about something he'd done just *before* he died—something that might have long-term consequences. The man's name was Ruben Ward. I'm sure you've both heard of him."

The name was instantly familiar to Travis, but he couldn't place it. It was like trying to match an obscure actor's name to a face or a role. He looked at Paige and saw no such struggle in her expression— she knew exactly who Ruben Ward was.

She glanced at him. "You read about him your first day in Border Town, in the journal down on Level 51."

It came back to him before she'd even finished speaking. In the first *hour* Travis had spent in Border Town, more than three years earlier, Paige had given him a tour of the essentials. Which was to say she'd shown him the Breach. But first she'd taken him into a fortified bunker down the hall from it, and let him read a bloodstained notebook that dated to the Breach's creation—March 1978.

That journal had been written by a man named David Bryce, a physicist and a founder of the Very Large Ion Collider project, which had once—very briefly after its completion—resided on the premises. Bryce had decided to keep an informal account of events at the VLIC: a journal that he and others could write in whenever they felt like it. The first entry had been jotted a few hours before the collider's maiden test shot; Bryce's tone had been lighthearted and hopeful. The same couldn't be said for the rest of the entries.

The remainder of the journal chronicled not only the hellish first days after the Breach's formation, but Bryce's own descent into something like an animal mind-set, his cognitive functions and his inhibitions stripped away by exposure to the Breach—specifically the sounds that issued from it. Breach Voices, as they were now known.

The journal had also mentioned Ruben Ward, the man who had actually thrown the switch to initiate the VLIC's first shot. The man who, in the strictest sense, had opened the Breach.

Ward had paid instantly for the privilege. According to the journal, he'd collapsed at the moment of the shot—possibly jolted by the switch or its metal housing—and never woke during the days that followed. Travis had heard a bit more about him afterward: Ward had been transferred to some hospital out east, still unresponsive, and ended up in a coma unit. That was as much as Travis knew. In all the time since he'd first heard the story, he'd never brought it up again. Neither had anyone else.

"I was under the impression he died at Johns Hopkins," Paige said, "a couple months after the VLIC accident. April or May of 1978."

"That's what we told people," Carrie said. "People who joined Tangent later on, after Scalar had come and gone. Kept them from asking unwanted questions."

"So where did he really die?" Paige said.

"In a hotel room in Los Angeles, late that summer. August 12. He walked out of the coma unit at Johns Hopkins by himself in the first week of May, vanished off the grid for three months, then checked into a room on Sunset and put a .38 in his mouth. At the time we all thought we understood, more or less. Whatever the VLIC accident did to him must have left him scrambled. Maybe deep depression, maybe anxiety. He struggled with it that summer and then called it good, we figured. It wasn't until a few years later that we found out we were wrong. Very wrong. At which point Peter launched the Scalar investigation to try to piece together those missing three months. He was desperate to find out where Ward had gone during that time, and what he'd done—desperate to learn *anything* about him, really."

"Why desperate?" Travis said.

Carrie met his eyes in the mirror. "Because Ruben Ward knew what's on the other side of the Breach."

CHAPTER ELEVEN

Travis felt a chill crawl over his scalp. It had nothing to do with the air pouring through the bullet hole in the roof.

"How is that possible?" Paige said. "How could anyone know that?"

"I'll tell you the parts I know," Carrie said, "in the order they happened." She went quiet again, thinking. "They took Ward to Johns Hopkins right after they got him out of the VLIC. He was unconscious for something like two weeks after that, and then he was in and out, never fully awake, but maybe halfway at times. He started talking a little, almost all of it incoherent. His wife was there with him—Nora, his only living relative. In one of his more lucid moments Ward asked her to write down everything he said, no matter how strange it sounded. So she did. She bought a notebook and jotted every word she heard him say. Later—a lot later—she would tell Peter that it seemed like science fiction. She thought Ward was drawing it from the books he'd read all his life. Crazy ramblings about a wormhole, alien technology, and something about a war. It was all absurd—but also consistent. Like a story."

She paused for a few seconds and then went on. "At the same time, in those weeks at the hospital, there were guards outside Ward's room at all hours. Federal officers of one kind or another. The accident at the VLIC was so sensitive, everything connected to it was under protective watch, including Ward. But whoever made that decision must've relaxed after enough time went by; the guards left on May 7, and late that night, after Nora went back to her hotel room, Ward extracted his own feeding tube and made his exit. Took the notebook with him, stole some orderly's street clothes from a locker down the hall, and eventually found his way out."

"Nobody tried to stop him?" Paige said. "After two months on his back he'd have been staggering like a drunk."

"Once he was out of the coma unit, all he encountered were strangers," Carrie said. "To them he probably looked like a physical-therapy patient. I know there were camera feeds the cops studied the next morning; they pieced it all together. From what I recall, it took Ward something like twenty minutes to get out of the building. He went out a north exit onto Monument Street and that was it. No one who knew him saw him alive again."

They were two miles up 550 now. The last outposts of the town—a few motels and a campground strung out along the canyon—slid by, and then the terrain opened to flat emptiness bound by pasture fencing.

"Three months later, the suicide. I think the LAPD identified him by his prints; he'd been arrested at a couple war protests in college. Everything about the scene was straightforward. He checked in alone, killed himself, no sign of foul play. No sign of the notebook, either—not that anyone was even thinking about it by then. And my understanding of the story goes blank at that point, until June of 1981, when Nora remarried. Some of the wedding guests were old friends who'd known both her and Ruben, including former VLIC people who now belonged to Tangent. Peter Campbell was there too. He and Nora talked about Ruben—about how it wasn't his fault what'd happened to him. He just wasn't himself at the end. Nora reinforced that point by mentioning the notebook—all the sci-fi things he'd said in his stupor. Peter asked her to elaborate. What kind of sci-fi things, specifically? Nora rattled off what little she remembered, and as I'm told, Peter had to set down his drink to keep from spilling it. I suppose, technically, the investigation began at that moment, right there in that reception hall. Peter asked Nora if she could set aside a few hours the next morning, before leaving for her honeymoon, and speak to him at length about the notebook. I doubt she was thrilled at that idea, but she did it, and in those hours she managed to recall a little more, including a visual description of the notebook, for what it was worth: black cover, with the word *Scalar* in the bottom corner. The company that made it, I'm sure. Nora remembered that easily enough. It was the stuff *inside* the book she had trouble with. All she could summon by then were bits and pieces, which I'm sure were maddening for Peter to try to make sense of. In the end, though, those scraps were enough to give him a rough sketch of what had happened. Enough to scare the hell out of him."

Far out across the open ground on either side of the highway, the yard lights of ranch houses glided past. Steep foothills rose beyond them, just discernible against the near-black sky.

"It all reduces to something like this," Carrie said. "In the days after the accident at VLIC, when Ward was still in the bunker, he wasn't entirely unconscious. He was aware of conversations around him—the fear and the tension down there. But there was something else he was aware of. Something he referred to as 'tunnel voices.'"

"Breach Voices?" Paige said.

Carrie nodded. "Ward could hear them from inside the bunker, just like everyone else. But *unlike* everyone else, he could understand them."

Paige had been staring forward at the snowfall in the headlights. Now she turned in her seat. Her eyes went back and forth between Carrie and Travis.

"*Understand* them?" Paige said.

Carrie nodded again. "They really are voices. And they're saying something. A message that repeats every few minutes, endlessly."

Paige shook her head. "We've analyzed the Breach Voices to death. Not with human ears, obviously, but microphones and every kind of pattern-recognition software. From the very beginning there were people who hoped those sounds contained a message, but the computers never turned up a thing."

"Computers can't decipher whale song either," Carrie said, "but biologists are convinced it has meaning. In principle that meaning could be expressed in a human language if we had a translator."

"You're saying Ward was our translator for the Breach Voices?" Travis said. "That whatever knocked him unconscious gave him that ability? Wouldn't that imply that someone on the other side *wanted* him to understand?"

"Peter believed that very thing after talking to Nora."

Travis considered the idea. At a glance it seemed impossible: the Breach had been created by an accident of human origin, the VLIC's first shot. A prepared message from the other side—bundled with some effect to grant a witness the means to understand it—didn't fit that scenario at all. *Had* it been an accident? Or had the Breach always been intended to open? Had it been waiting for the human race—or any race out there in the great black yonder—to build the right kind of ion collider and switch it on? Why would someone on the other side have set things up that way? There would have to be a purpose for it—but what?

"How do we know Ward wasn't just crazy?" Paige said. "Like everyone originally assumed?"

"There were things he said that craziness couldn't account for. Rough descriptions of entities that didn't even emerge until months after he was dead. He couldn't have known about those things unless someone told him. Someone—or something—over there."

"Christ," Travis said.

"But that's only a small part of the picture. There

were bigger issues, though they were less clear, at least given what Peter could get from Nora."

"Like what?" Paige said.

"There was a sense that the message contained general information about the place on the other side, though Nora had forgotten essentially all of it. Understandably, I guess—that stuff would've made the least sense in the first place. Like if I asked you to transcribe a few pages from a legal brief, and then quizzed you on them three years later."

"You said there was something about a war," Travis said. "Did she remember anything else about it?"

Carrie shook her head. "No details. Ward had *spoken* in detail about it, and Nora had written it all down, but none of it was still in her head in 1981." She went quiet a moment. Then: "There was something else. Probably the most compelling part of the message. A step process of some kind—a set of instructions. But again, Nora had lost the specifics."

The chill returned to Travis. It arced like electricity down his neck and along the skin of his arms.

"The Breach gave Ruben Ward instructions?" he said.

Carrie nodded. "He walked out of Johns Hopkins in May of 1978 with a set of orders literally in hand. Presumably he spent the next three months following them, and when he was done he put a bullet in his brain."

CHAPTER TWELVE

Nobody spoke for a long time. Travis watched the highway roll out of the darkness ahead. Snow and tire ruts and wind-scoured pavement.

"What could the instructions have been?" Paige said.

"That's what Scalar was about," Carrie said. "That question. Where did Ward go that summer? What did he do? What had he been *told* to do?"

"Did they make any headway on it?" Travis said.

"I really don't know. I learned about the run-up like everyone else in Border Town, but once the investigation started Peter kept it tightly contained. Even the files in the archives were stored in secure cases. He and five or six others handled it all. Worked with the government to use their resources when necessary—probably things like law-enforcement databases, or even command of federal agents to follow up on leads. Once in a while we'd get a sense that there'd been some progress, but we never got the specifics. The only concrete thing I ever heard about the investigation was how

it ended. Peter and the others flew somewhere—
maybe D.C., but it could've been anywhere—to
meet with a small group of very powerful people.
From what little I heard they seemed to be a mixed
bag: people way up in politics, intel, maybe even
finance. The one detail I know is that Peter and the
rest of his team prepared a report for these people
before leaving Border Town. Some kind of sum-
mary of what Scalar had turned up, as well as a
response plan. Like, *Here's what Ruben Ward did
in 1978, and here's what needs to be done about
it.* The rest of us called it the cheat sheet, because
even though we never read it, we saw that it comprised just a single page."

"Pretty concise plan, whatever it was," Travis
said.

"Important ones often are," Carrie said. "And I
had the feeling that whoever they met with agreed
to it. Peter seemed relieved when he got back. He
called us all together and said the investigation
was over—Tangent's role in it was, anyway. He
said what mattered most now was simply forgetting about it. Said the subject was taboo." She
shrugged. "That was it. As far as we knew, the
whole thing was settled for good."

Travis thought of Paige's encounter with Peter in
her memory. The man's fear that she'd mentioned
Scalar to someone outside Border Town. That
she might have triggered some unthinkable chain
of events simply by doing so. Peter had harbored
those fears just five years ago—two decades after
shutting down the investigation. Whatever Scalar
had uncovered, Travis was pretty certain it wasn't
settled for good.

"What exactly are we saying?" Paige said. "The moment the Breach opened it gave Ruben Ward instructions to do something, right? Something on behalf of whoever's on the other side. They *wanted* him to do it. And he did. Then years later, my father learned about it—learned enough anyway, by the end of Scalar, to know Ward's actions had to be countered." She paused, thinking. "It's like Ward set something in motion, and my father stopped it. Halted it, at least, got a lid on it—and spent the rest of his life terrified that the lid would come off. That means whatever this thing was, whatever Ward did, there's no question it was something bad. Something *very* bad, with long-term consequences."

"That's about the only way to read it," Carrie said. The fear had risen in her voice again.

Paige looked at her, then at Travis. "So whoever they are on the other side of the Breach," she said, "they're . . . malignant. They're flat-out bad. That's what we're saying."

Travis glanced at her. Saw her expression drawn tight, her own fear unmistakable. And something else—almost a sense of betrayal. He understood why. For as long as he'd known her, Paige had been the closest thing Tangent had to an optimist. She harbored no illusions that those on the other side of the Breach were especially *good*—there was no basis for believing that—but she'd long held onto the idea that they were at least ambivalent. That they'd never meant for their dangerous technology to come spilling into human hands. That they probably didn't even *know* about the accident that'd tapped into one of their transit tunnels. The

Breach was dangerous, but only in the way that earthquakes and hurricanes were dangerous. There was no intent behind any of it. Whoever they were over there, they weren't *trying* to do us harm. That belief had shored up Paige's world for a long time. Probably since the first day she'd set foot in Border Town.

The betrayed look flickered through her eyes for maybe a second, and then it was gone, vastly eclipsed by the fear that came with it. Her breathing accelerated and shallowed. For a moment she seemed overwhelmed, unsure how to respond.

Travis felt it too. No doubt Peter had felt the same, by the time he'd finished speaking to Nora. By the time he'd grasped even the basics:

Ward had done something for *them*.

Something he'd needed to keep secret.

Something he'd killed himself over, after the fact.

Maybe Ward had followed the instructions against his will, his mind as fried by the Breach Voices as David Bryce's had been.

Travis tried to imagine Peter's mind-set on that first day, in the summer of 1981—knowing that Ruben Ward's work from three years before must still be playing out. That somewhere out there, at that moment, the dominoes were falling. Scalar had been a mad scramble to understand. To find the dominoes and stop them before the last one tipped.

Peter *had* stopped them.

So why was someone trying to set them falling again? One way or another, the people who'd killed Garner and laid the trap in Ouray were working against the end result of Scalar. Someone behind it all, pulling the strings, wanted to overturn the outcome. In all likelihood they'd already begun to do so.

"Whatever Peter did was in all of our best interests," Travis said. "Who could possibly have the motive to undo it?"

The words hung in the air. No one had an answer. Snowflakes swirled in the headlights like stars broken free of the sky.

"We need details," Paige said. "We need to know who my father met with in 1987. We need to find one of them, preferably one who still has a copy of the cheat sheet locked away somewhere."

"It'd be a tall order getting your eyes on that document," Carrie said. "It's right up there with finding the original Scalar notebook, which Ward probably burned in a vacant lot before he killed himself."

At the edge of his vision Travis saw Paige turn to him. He looked at her and didn't have to ask what she was thinking.

"The Tap," she said.

"Nora," Travis said.

CHAPTER THIRTEEN

E ven as hope flared in Paige's eyes it guttered. On the one hand it'd be trivially easy for Nora to revisit the notebook in her memory— she'd written the damn thing; she could drop in and reread it at some point just before Ward disappeared. On the other hand, the Tap could kill her before it was even fully into her head. Forget whatever had happened to Gina Murphy; the pain and stress and increased pulse rate would be bad enough.

"If it worked, we'd know everything," Paige said. "I just don't have any confidence that it would."

"Are you talking about an entity?" Carrie said.

Paige nodded, and explained the basics of the Tap in less than a minute—including the part about Gina. By the time Paige had finished, Carrie looked skeptical. Just like everyone who'd ever heard of the thing, before using it themselves.

"You can forget about Nora, in any case," Carrie said at last. "She died of breast cancer in 1989." A silence. Then: "What if I gave it a try? I was thirty years old in 1978, and living in New York. If this thing works the way you describe it, I could go back, take a drive to Baltimore, and get my hands on the notebook without much trouble."

"The guards outside the room might be a problem," Travis said. "Not to mention Nora herself."

"I'm not talking about sneaking in. I could walk up and introduce myself as a colleague of Ruben's. I wasn't, but I was close enough. I'd certainly followed his work. I only ended up with Tangent because I swam in the same academic circles as people like him and Peter Campbell. I could wing it with Nora, easily. Go in and sit at the bedside, wait for some distraction and grab the book."

Travis glanced at Carrie in the mirror.

"How's your heart?" he said.

She shrugged with her eyebrows. "It's not great. I've had a systolic murmur all my life. It's louder in recent years, but that's expected."

"Sorry to be blunt," Travis said, "but your age alone is an issue. I'm forty-four and I thought it was going to kill me when I used it."

He didn't add the rest of his thought—the part that was even more blunt: Carrie would have to *think* the Tap back out of her head once it was inside, a task she might not have the focus for in the middle of a fatal heart attack. What would happen if she died with it still inserted? Would the thing extract itself and revert to its cube shape, or would it just be stuck in there, useless forever? Carrie's life was a lot to risk, but so was the Tap. As much as Travis hated the thing, there was no denying its usefulness.

"It's an unnecessary risk anyway," Travis said.

"I have an idea. Let me think about it for a few minutes."

For a while no one said anything more. The bullet hole whistled and the wind moaned at the open back window.

Paige looked at Carrie. "You can still come back to Border Town with us. Probably the safest place for you."

Carrie thought about it, then shook her head. "If you don't need me, I'd rather stay as far from Tangent as possible. I can take care of myself. In my less trusting days I hid stashes of money, and made a few useful contacts. Leave me the Jeep and I'll be fine." She was quiet a long moment, staring out the side window into the darkness. "I need to tell you one last thing, for what it's worth. Something I overheard about a year after Scalar ended. I was heading toward the conference room, and I heard Peter inside, speaking to one of the others. They were alone. Something in their tone made me stop before going in, and before I could leave to give them privacy, I heard the end of the conversation. Peter said something like, 'It's clumsy as hell, the way we wrapped it up. If it goes bad now, it'll happen fast. We won't have much time to stop it.' 'How much time?' the other man asked, and Peter said, 'The first sign of trouble would be something big, and from that moment we'd have just about exactly twenty-four hours.' I remember he paused for about ten seconds then, and when he spoke again he sounded more scared than I'd ever heard him. He said, 'Yeah, twenty-four hours to the end of the road.'"

Travis glanced at Paige and then, in unison with her, looked at the Jeep's console clock.

6:05 A.M.

Garner had been killed at a quarter to ten the night before, in the eastern time zone—7:45 here in mountain time. Therefore the end of the road—whatever that implied—would be 7:45 tonight. Thirteen hours and forty minutes from right now.

Paige called Border Town and arranged for a jet to meet them at a regional airstrip near Cimarron. No flight plan; the pilots radioed for clearance five minutes before arrival, on the likelihood that unfriendly elements were monitoring air traffic.

Carrie was gone with the Jeep by the time the plane landed. The aircraft was on the ground less than three minutes, and as it climbed above the clouds and the first hard beams of sunlight shone through the cabin, Paige said, "Tell me."

Travis squinted in the glare. "In May of 1978 I was ten years old. Pretty big for my age. Stocky, probably four-nine."

"You can't be serious."

"We know Ruben Ward leaves the hospital the night of May 7 by a north exit, carrying the notebook. We know the time to within a few hours. And we know he's so weakened right then he can barely walk. Physically, between me and him it's no contest. Snatch and run."

"You lived in Minneapolis. How are you going to get halfway across the country by yourself at that age?"

"Steal my dad's car and put the seat all the way

forward. Minneapolis to Baltimore's probably fifteen or sixteen hours if I obey the speed limit. Which I'd better, I guess."

He watched her warm to the idea in spite of herself. But only to a point.

"You'll have to make stops for gas," she said, "and any station attendant is going to dial nine-one-one the minute you step out of the driver's seat. That's not to mention interference from other customers at the pumps. All of whom will be a lot older than ten, and not just emerging from a coma unit."

"I won't need gas stations at all. Five feet of plastic hose will do the trick."

The biggest problem, Travis knew, would simply be other drivers on the road. Even at night he'd be visible at the wheel, at least in brightly lit areas like cities and busy stretches of the freeway. Though no one in 1978 would have a cell phone with which to call the cops, there was no question that people would take action at the sight of a kid driving a car. But after only a few seconds, Travis thought he had the answer to that problem too. He considered it a moment longer, felt certain of it, then pushed it away and turned to Paige.

"I've been trying to think of someone better suited to taking a shot at it," Travis said, "but no one comes to mind. Outside Tangent, we might've trusted Carrie if we weren't likely to kill her in the process. Or Garner, if he were alive—though I'd have worried about his age too. And inside Tangent there are—what—four people older than me?"

Paige nodded, her eyes suddenly far away as she

consulted a mental roster of Border Town. Travis had already covered that ground in his own head. Tangent's population was skewed pretty young these days, given the near total replacement of personnel three years earlier. The new recruits hadn't come straight out of grad school, but nearly all of them were under forty. Academics with solid track records and sufficiently few ties to politics or industry, drawn from all the nations that'd jointly founded Tangent. Of the four people older than Travis, none were American. Two were just a year older and had grown up in France. Another was maybe three years older and Russian. The oldest, at fifty-one, would've been seventeen the night Ruben Ward made his escape from Johns Hopkins. Seventeen and living in a remote village in northern China.

Whatever resistance Paige had harbored for the idea was slipping fast. She looked at the time on her phone; she'd been doing that every few minutes since Carrie had spoken of the deadline. Travis had done the same. Even this flight back to Border Town, dead straight at five hundred fifty miles per hour, felt like a colossal hemorrhage of time.

"I can get to Baltimore," Travis said. "I can get the book. It only costs us three minutes and sixteen seconds to try."

"I guess your odds are better than mine," Paige said. "I was negative two in 1978."

They called Bethany and brought her up to speed, and by the time they'd landed, taken the Tap from the Primary Lab and returned to their residence on

B16—at 8:25 in the morning—Bethany was waiting for them with all the useful information she'd unearthed. Which wasn't a lot.

"Couldn't nail down the exact timing of Ward's exit," she said. She adjusted her glasses, the same oversized pair she'd been wearing when Travis first met her last year in Atlanta. She looked young even for her age—could've passed for twenty without a hitch. When she really *was* twenty, she'd already been out of college and working for information-security firms, engineering the software that guarded the world's secrets. In that field, the set of people on Earth with her skill level could've squeezed together into a good-sized elevator.

"I assume the Baltimore PD got involved," Bethany said, "once the hospital realized Ward was missing, but any dispatch info from that time is long gone. The computerized records only go back to the late eighties. If there was more detailed paperwork filed, like a missing-persons report with witness statements, and maybe a description of the hospital's camera feeds, I couldn't find it. There might be a hard copy on a shelf somewhere, but there's nothing I can read over broadband."

"How about dated schematics of the hospital?" Paige said.

Bethany frowned. "I scored a hit on that one, but you're not going to like it."

She took a tablet computer from a big pocket on the side of her pants, switched it on and opened an image file. It was a huge high-resolution scan of a blueprint: an overhead view of part of the Johns Hopkins campus. She dragged it down so that only the top edge was visible: Monument Street running from Broadway to Wolfe—a distance of more than eight hundred feet.

"You're going to stand outside the place on the north side and watch the exits there, right?" Bethany said. "Wait for Ruben Ward to come out?"

Travis nodded.

"The good news," Bethany said, "is that you should be able to see them all at once. The north stretch was pretty much the same in 1978 as it is now: four separate exits onto Monument, all of them roughly visible from any point on the other side of the street. Given the coma unit's location within the building, Ward could've used any one of the four just as easily as another."

"Especially if he wandered at random for a while before he found one," Travis said. "I won't make any assumptions about where he might come out."

"Well, see, that's the bad news," Bethany said. "You're going to have to."

She zoomed in until the middle third of the north stretch filled the screen. At that resolution, something became visible that hadn't been before: a broad zone of Monument Street crossed out with diagonal lines. They extended right up onto the sidewalk to the building's edge. All told, about fifty feet of the street's length were marked out.

"What the hell is that?" Paige said.

"Construction. A service tunnel for the Baltimore Metro. The system didn't go live until 1983, but they spent years building it before then. In the spring of seventy-eight they hadn't yet started on the rail tunnel itself, the one that terminates at Broadway and Monument. Instead they were putting in a conduit for power and maintenance access four hundred feet east of that intersection, dead-centered on the hospital's north side." She dragged the image left and right and pointed out the exits Ward might use. "Two doors are west of the dig site, two are east. Whichever side you choose to wait on, you're stuck with. I don't think you're going to get across the construction zone."

"I might," Travis said. "If it's late at night, the work crew may have already gone home."

"Can't count on that," Bethany said, "but even if they have, the dig itself is a major obstacle. This isn't just some torn-up blacktop with plastic fencing stretched around it. I found an old *Baltimore Sun* article about the whole thing. The project ran from March to September of that year, and they installed the conduit thirty feet below street level. If they started in March, then the excavating would've been done by early May for sure. It'd be the Grand Canyon, cutting off the whole width of the street."

"So if you guess wrong about which side he comes out on," Paige said, "you'll have to run around the block. How big is the one north of Monument? Is it square like the main hospital's block, or is it shallower?"

"Normally, shallower," Bethany said. "Madison Street is just a couple hundred feet north. But that's dug up, too, so you'd have to go up to the next street, Ashland Avenue. I already did the math. No matter where you stand to watch for Ward, if you're on the wrong side, you'll have to run at least half a mile around. During which time he could wander off down a dozen possible alleys or even flag a cab—so what if he'd have to stiff the driver? He was desperate to get away from that place."

Paige looked up from the computer at Travis. "I hope you were a fast ten-year-old."

"Me too, because there's no second shot at this. The memory's burned whether I get the notebook or not."

CHAPTER FOURTEEN

They planned what they could, as quickly as they could, devoting just under twenty minutes to it. They mapped the route—eleven hundred miles, about sixteen hours' drive time with present speed limits.

"But not 1978 limits," Travis said. "Fifty-five everywhere back then."

"Even on the freeways?" Bethany said. She looked doubtful.

Travis nodded. "Sammy Hagar wasn't kidding."

He did the math in his head: at fifty-five the trip would take twenty hours.

Which was a problem.

Realistically, he'd have to steal the car late at night when both his parents were asleep. That would be well past midnight, probably closer to one or two. Twenty hours after two in the morning was ten the next night—in the central time zone. In Baltimore it would be an hour later. Factoring in stops for gas—which might take a while the way Travis was going to do it—could easily add another full hour. He'd be lucky to reach Johns Hopkins by midnight.

"Ward could already be gone by then," Paige said. "All we know about the timing is that he leaves at some point after Nora does, and we don't know when *she* leaves either. Could be nine o'clock the night of May 7—Sunday—or it could be three in the morning Monday. Getting there at midnight's risky."

"And I could be a lot later than that," Travis said. "My dad might stay up until four instead of two. I might hit traffic jams." He stared at Bethany's computer, the highlighted route winding through seven states. "I'll go a day earlier. Steal the car Friday night, get into town Saturday night."

"You'll have a lot of downtime in Baltimore," Bethany said.

"Maybe I'll head over to Camden Yards. Jesus, Ripken wasn't even there yet."

A minute later Travis was thinking about a different baseball player—one who'd done something newsworthy two days before Ruben Ward disappeared. Travis hadn't remembered the event himself; it was just one of a dozen stories Bethany had pulled from a news archive to help him dial in on the date he needed. On his own he couldn't recall a thing from within months of that day. Just random flashes of fifth grade, impossible to place in a timeline.

"The game happened on the Friday you're shooting for," Bethany said. "That's May 5. The story would've been in Saturday's paper, probably somewhere on the front page—even in Minneapolis. So you want to pinpoint Saturday and then rewind to Friday night before you drop fully into the memory."

Travis nodded. He tried to focus on the news about the game. He'd been into baseball as much as any kid in the neighborhood, and would've definitely heard about this story when it happened. Almost certainly would've glanced at the headline sometime Saturday.

"If you had any real awareness of it at the time," Paige said, "you'll remember it when you've got the Tap in. Just picture the name in headline print. And that number."

The Tap was sitting on the table in front of him. Staring at him, in its way.

No reason to wait any longer.

He snatched it up, pressed it against his temple and screwed his eyes shut. Already his pulse was accelerating, before the pain had even begun.

Ten seconds. Agony overwhelming all other feeling. The tendril snaking and darting across the top of his brain. Coiling, advancing, pressing.

Then it was fully in, and still. As the pain ebbed Travis became aware of Paige draped over his shoulders from behind, her cheek against his own.

He went to the couch and lay down. Paige and Bethany sank into chairs and watched him. Win or lose, the outcome was minutes away for them.

Travis closed his eyes. He heard Paige's cell phone begin to ring just as the world dropped out from under him.

* * *

Formless dark. No body. No limbs. Thoughts and memories suspended in the void.

The name.

The number.

He'd barely begun to picture them when the image came up, clear and brilliant as a photo held in front of his face. It was a view of the dining-room table in his parents' house. Yellow afternoon sunlight slanted in, swimming with dust motes. He saw it all from an oddly low angle, his eyes only a couple feet above the scattered mail at the table's edge.

On top of the mail, like it'd been set there a minute before, lay a newspaper. Travis's eyes went to a headline at the lower right corner, just peeking above the fold.

Rose hits 3,000.

The paper was dated Saturday, May 6, 1978.

Travis let the moment begin to slide backward in time. He watched the viewpoint drift away from the table, reversing along the path he must have just walked.

Out of the dining room. Down the hall toward his bedroom. The details were as strange as they were familiar—this was the *old* house. The little one they'd lived in before his parents' illicit income sources began to blossom. The one place, at least in his childhood, that had really felt like a home to him. All at once he didn't want to see its specifics.

He sped up the reverse until it was a blur, his viewpoint surging backward through a firehose stream of imagery he could hardly follow. Crazy bursts of walking movement that felt disturbingly like falling down a well. Jittery spells of holding still with his face over a magazine, or watching TV—he caught shutter-quick glimpses of Elmer Fudd and Bugs Bunny and Road Runner and Wile E. Coyote. There came a sudden rush of shower spray and soap and shampoo and then a split-second view of his own small face in a mirror, a toothbrush humming in and out of his mouth like a jigsaw blade. A glimpse of his pillow followed and then there was darkness, and the spooky tumble of dream visuals running backward through the night. These sights he could make no sense of at all—trees and fields and hallways and classrooms—and then he was awake again, propped up on his elbows in bed, staring at a book in the glow of his nightstand lamp. His hand flickered up and reverse-turned a page. Then again.

He slowed the memory stream down. All the way down. Froze it.

His field of view took in the book, the nightstand, and the alarm clock at the base of the lamp.

11:57 P.M.

Good enough.

Travis left the image still and waited. Two seconds passed. Three. Then, sensation. Not the soles of his feet but the entire front of his body: his legs and chest and elbows, all seeming to hover at static-spark distance above the bed.

He let himself drop.

The change was so jarring he flinched. On his previous use of the Tap he'd gone back only two years; his body had been indistinguishable from its forty-four-year-old state.

Ten was different—startlingly different—and his size and shape were the least of reasons.

The reasons were everything else.

His senses. The richness of the world came through them like a high. Had he really *felt* this way all through his childhood? This alive and feral? Had he lost it so gradually he'd never noticed it going away? He took a breath of the humidity coming in through the screen. He tasted cut grass and damp pavement and the pulp stock pages of the book lying open beneath him. A blue hardcover with no dust jacket. He flipped it shut. *The Hardy Boys Number 2: The House on the Cliff.* He set it beside the lamp and listened to the night. Crickets, katydids, distant tires hissing on asphalt. His hearing had to be half again better than what he was used to. His vision, too, though not in its clarity—at forty-four he still didn't need glasses. It was more about the depth of colors. The saturation, maybe. Whatever it was, plastic lenses wouldn't give it back to you once you'd outgrown it.

Beneath all the sensations lay something else, harder to name but more powerful. Some mix of hormones and oxygen-rich blood and uncluttered emotion. The simple, wild energy of being a child. It made him want to swing from the trees. If there'd been a drug to make a grown-up feel this way, it would've put to shame all the shit his parents were probably already selling in 1978.

He looked through his doorway into the room across the hall, and saw his brother Jeff asleep in the blue-white glow of his Captain Kirk night-light. Jeff was seven and already a certified Trekkie. Travis resisted the urge to wake him and tell him the movie version was coming out next year.

Further away was the sound of the TV in the living room, cranked down almost to silence for a commercial break. His father had done that all his life, even before he had a remote control. Now the floor creaked and the volume rose. Trumpets swelled and cut out, and then Johnny Carson was talking.

Travis killed the light, rolled onto his back, and lay waiting.

His father went to bed at 1:07.

Started snoring at 1:12.

Travis waited five more minutes, then got up and dressed.

He'd expected walking to feel strange in this body, but it was fine—the same unconscious act it'd always been.

He took his dad's keys from their hook in the kitchen, pocketing them so they wouldn't jingle. He opened the silverware drawer, slid aside the compartmentalized tray and found the envelope that'd lain beneath it all through his childhood. Inside was a quarter-inch stack of tens and twenties. He took them all, then returned to his bedroom and eased the window screen from its frame.

The car was a 1971 Impala, shit brown and already rusting around the wheel wells. Travis had actually driven it lots of times—as late as 1984 it'd been pretty reliable. It was parked on the street; there was no garage. He slipped in and racked the seat forward and got his foot on the gas without a problem.

He hit Kmart and bought everything he needed. Bread, chips, cookies, crackers, peanut butter, a twelve-pack of Pepsi. It all looked absurd in its ancient packaging. He got a coil of clear plastic tubing from the hardware department, and a five-gallon drum with a pouring spout. The last two things he bought were a wire coat hanger and a slotted-head screwdriver.

The checkout girl gave him a look when he walked up alone.

He nodded toward the parking lot. "Mom's feet are killing her."

The girl shrugged and started keying the prices by hand.

He found what he wanted in the fourth nightclub parking lot he searched: a Chevelle, maybe five years old, lime green with a white racing stripe down the middle.

And heavily tinted windows—including the windshield.

It took thirty seconds to defeat the door lock with the coat hanger, and another thirty with the screwdriver to break open the ignition and hotwire it. Ten minutes later he was heading east on I–94, the needle dead on 55 and the night air rushing in through the windows.

CHAPTER FIFTEEN

The Grand Canyon, cutting off the whole width of the street, just like Bethany had said. The hole was three stories deep and stretched from one foundation wall to the other: the hospital on the south side, a seamless row of academic and research buildings on the north. There were sectional concrete barriers along each side of the chasm, plastered with orange warning signs for those who didn't grasp the concept of gravity.

Traffic on Monument had been blocked at the cross streets—Broadway to the west and Wolfe to the east. There was a sporadic stream of pedestrians going in and out of the hospital and the academic buildings, but otherwise the street was bare.

Which was going to make it hard to stand around without drawing attention, especially for a ten-year-old. Especially as the night drew on.

It was six o'clock Sunday evening. The air was chilly and the long sunlight filtered through trees on the sidewalk. Travis was sitting on a bench near Monument and Broadway, far west of the construction zone. He could see the hospital's nearer two exits, but not the other pair. He'd have to be two hundred feet closer to the gap for that, and standing—there were no benches farther along than this one.

As it was he'd already begun drawing looks, just sitting with a comic book in his lap, though he'd only been here for ten minutes.

Drawing looks had been the story of his weekend. Within the first hour of daylight on Saturday he'd realized the Chevelle's tinted windows weren't giving him perfect cover. For one thing, they naturally drew the focus of passengers in other cars. People saw tinting and instinctively wanted to see past it. And in glaring sunlight, maybe they could. They were seeing *something*, it seemed, if only his silhouette. Whatever the case, in the span of ten minutes two different cars going by in the passing lane had braked and run parallel to him for over a mile, then dropped back and veered hard for the first available exit, each no doubt bound for a pay phone to dial 911. Travis responded by ditching the freeway and taking to the back roads, crawling east on county two-lanes from Chicago to Cleveland before deciding he'd had enough. He hit another Kmart, bought a blanket to conceal himself in the backseat, and slept until nightfall.

Everything was easier in the dark. Even siphoning gas. All you needed was a big parking lot with a few cars clustered out near the edge. Duck out of sight among them, and the rest was simple.

He'd rolled into Baltimore this morning, half an hour past dawn, left the car at a meter three blocks west of the hospital—the closest space he could find—and set out on foot.

For much of the day he'd avoided attention easily

enough. The trick was to move with purpose. If he stood still anywhere for even a minute, people stared. They saw him, looked around for a nearby parent, and failing to spot one approached him to ask if he was lost. But moving around had been easy, early on. Upon arriving he headed for Monument Street and checked out the dig site, then went into the hospital by the entry just west of the excavation. Though Bethany's schematics had suggested otherwise, he'd held on to some hope that the building itself might provide a shortcut. A way to dart in on one side of the canyon and back out on the other, on the precise half chance that Ward would emerge where Travis didn't want him to.

He saw right away that it was no good. All the north entrances opened at the ends of long, separate wings running up from central areas of the complex, and though there was a main east-west corridor tying them together deep inside the old building, the whole idea of cutting through this place in pursuit of Ward felt risky. It was understandable that Ward himself, shuffling along in street clothes, could make it past the staff without being stopped. A ten-year-old sprinting hell-bent through the corridors would be a different story.

For good measure Travis went up to the coma unit, on the fourth floor and dead centered in the hospital's footprint. It was easy to see how Ward would get away unseen by the nurses: the nearest station was down the hall and around a corner from his room, and in the opposite direction was a bank of elevators. Travis spotted Ward's room easily; it was the one with two guys in crew cuts and black suits flanking the door.

He walked by and tried to look casual while stealing a glance inside. Ward was right there, occupying the room's only bed. His head was shaved smooth as Travis had expected, given the likelihood of EEG testing.

Nora was seated beside him. A beautiful woman with haunted features. She'd look worse by this time tomorrow, and stay that way for at least the next three months. Probably a lot longer.

The last thing Travis's eyes picked out was the notebook. It lay on the deep windowsill behind Nora's chair, a pen stuck into its spiral binding. Its black card-stock cover was already worn by weeks of use, and the word *Scalar* was just visible at the lower right corner. Travis had all of half a second to stare at it, and then he was past the door frame and moving on.

Now, some twelve hours later, he sat on the bench on the west end of Monument, trying to avoid the increasingly frequent stares. He turned a page of the comic book, for appearances. *Star Wars #10: The Behemoth from Below.* On the cover, Han and Chewie were blasting away at a giant green lizard. Travis wondered what a mint copy would be worth thirty-four years from now. Probably about five bucks. Not that he could bring it back with him anyway.

Neither could he bring back Ward's notebook if he got his hands on it. The plan was simply to hole up somewhere and read the damn thing a hundred times. Read it until he could shut his eyes and recite it word for word. Then he'd snap out of the memory and transcribe the whole thing. Paige had already set up a laptop on the dining room table, the cursor ready and blinking in Microsoft Word.

Travis looked up at the hospital again. He watched people come and go from the two exits he could see.

The lack of a shortcut was trouble, but not disaster.

The lack of a stakeout position was.

It was the one problem he and Paige and Bethany hadn't been able to plan around. No way to know exactly what he'd find on the north side of Monument Street, in terms of hiding places. In his most optimistic scenario there'd been a Dumpster sticking out of an alley, full to the brim with trash he could hide in and stare out through. No luck there—no Dumpsters *or* alleys along the north side of the street. Nothing but the unbroken row of buildings.

Travis had seen all of that this morning, then spent the day wandering the city trying to think his way through the problem. As an adult he could've solved it any number of ways. Buy a cheap harmonica and a little wooden box and stand there on the sidewalk busking. Wouldn't matter that he sucked at playing harmonica—it would help push attention away from him, in fact. People would consciously *not* look.

But even the busking would've been unnecessary. A grown man could just walk up and down Monument, from the dig site to either intersection, back and forth all night long. Hours and hours, the same circuit, four hundred feet east and four hundred feet west. If anyone noticed the repetition and found it strange, would they even consider asking him about it? Not likely. People tended to see strangeness as trouble, which in turn they tended to avoid.

But none of those options existed for a ten-year-old.

Shit.

He turned another page of the comic book. Let his eyes drift over the images and words without processing them.

A shadow fell across his lap.

"Excuse me."

Travis looked up and saw a woman in her thirties, a five-year-old girl in tow. The girl stared at Travis with big eyes and tried to hide behind her mother's leg.

"Do you need help?" the woman said.

Travis offered a quick smile and shook his head. "I'm good. Thanks."

Another trick—when you weren't moving with purpose—was to be direct and certain. Let no ambiguity into your words or your tone.

He turned his eyes back to the comic book and ignored the woman.

The shadow stayed put.

"You've been alone here the whole time I've been waiting for the bus," the woman said. "If you need to call someone, I have change. And we can wait here with you if you like—"

"Really, I'm fine," Travis said, looking up at her again. "My dad always meets me here at six-fifteen sharp. He says it's a safe spot 'cause it's busy. I'm just early, that's all."

The woman frowned. Looked like she wanted to wait anyway, if only to have a word with his father about this arrangement.

"Seriously," Travis said, "don't miss your bus. I'd feel terrible."

Another frown. The woman started to say something else, but didn't. The little girl tugged on her hand, gesturing with her whole body back toward Broadway.

The woman exhaled deeply. "I don't like it," she said, and then she was gone, back to the knot of people at the intersection.

Her bus came two minutes later, and when it'd left, Travis stood and stuffed the comic book into his pocket. He stood there thinking, getting the mental equivalent of a test pattern. It could be nine hours before Ward staggered out of the hospital, and Travis couldn't imagine how to stand watch for even thirty minutes.

He wandered toward the construction zone. The crew was still at it. From beyond the waist-high barrier and far below came the shouting of men and the rattle of air-driven tools. There was a stereo blasting Bob Seger's "Hollywood Nights." The glow of halogen worklamps shone upward onto the inside face of the far barrier, just beginning to compete with the dying sunlight.

Absent a Dumpster, the closest Travis had come to a plan had been a vague thought of hiding within the site itself. Slip over the barrier and stand on the edge of the chasm, and hope to find some kind of material scraps with which to conceal himself. Three or four wooden planks might've done—

stand against a foundation wall on the north side of the street and lean the wood around himself in a jumble. In darkness it would've been hard for anyone to see him among the boards, and maybe he could've arranged them to create viewing angles on all four exits.

But there were no scraps of wood or anything else, and with the workers still on the job it was a moot point.

Travis stopped fifty feet shy of the concrete blockade. "Hollywood Nights" finished and "Still the Same" kicked in.

Travis ran his hands through his hair. How much longer could he loiter out here before somebody waved down a cop?

That thought had hardly formed when another shadow slid into view, paralleling his own as it stretched away down the pavement. Footsteps scuffed to a stop behind him, and a man softly cleared his throat.

Travis turned, half expecting a cop already.

Instead it was a guy in a dress shirt and khakis, fortyish and visibly awkward.

"Hey there," the man said. The voice was gentle. He might have been addressing a stray kitten. Behind him there was nothing but wide-open street all the way back to the intersection. This guy had come a long way to say hello.

When Travis didn't answer, the man stepped closer. Ten feet away now. "You look a bit lost. I couldn't help noticing. I live right back there." He nodded absently behind him, toward the block immediately beyond Broadway.

Travis shook his head and looked down at the roadbed, suddenly unable to stand the guy's nervous expression.

"Just waiting for my dad," Travis said. "I'm fine."

The man advanced again. "You don't look like you're waiting. I saw you on the bench, and now you're standing around down here. How would your dad find you if you're all over the place?"

The voice was still soft, but under the awkwardness there was an edge of excitement.

"You need a place to sleep tonight?"

Jesus Christ. So there were *two* problems he and Paige and Bethany hadn't planned around. He pictured them laughing their asses off when he told them about this one.

Another step. The man was close enough to touch him now, and when he spoke again he was almost whispering. "Nothing has to happen. Nothing you don't want. I promise."

Travis was still looking down. He fixed his eyes in the deadest glare prison had taught him, and raised them.

The man stepped back as if shoved.

"You better get the fuck out of here," Travis said.

The guy nodded quickly and didn't say another word. A second later he was gone, walking away down Monument at just less than a jog. He'd gone thirty yards when a fragment of his pick-up spiel came back to Travis.

I couldn't help noticing. I live right back there.

Travis looked past the intersection of Monument and Broadway. The next stretch of Monument, west of Johns Hopkins, had a parking garage filling most of the south side and a row of town houses on the north. No doubt most of them had been converted to multiple units.

Any one of which would offer a perfect viewing angle on all four of the hospital's north exits.

"Mister!" Travis yelled.

CHAPTER SIXTEEN

He introduced himself as Garret and led Travis up to his place on the third floor, four units west of Broadway. Garret's every move was nervous and excited. He had a high, quick laugh with which he interrupted himself in almost every sentence.

He opened the door to his apartment and ushered Travis directly into the living room. The air smelled like a mix of candlewax and macaroni. Travis hardly noticed. His full attention had gone at once to the bay window overlooking Monument. Through the 45-degree pane on the left, facing Johns Hopkins, he would have a better vantage point than he could've dreamed of.

There would be a delay issue, of course. He'd be fifteen seconds getting down to the sidewalk from this place, and another ten or more sprinting to the intersection. But that was fine. He'd have plenty of time to catch Ward if he emerged from one of the nearer two exits, and if he came out beyond the Grand Canyon, well, that was always going to be a pain in the ass. Even starting at a Dumpster right across from the hospital, Travis would've been forced to backtrack a couple hundred feet before heading north on Broadway to circle the block. Garret's bay window was as good a starting point as he could've hoped for.

Travis took in the living room's details. The coffee table was littered with magazines and beer cans and used paper plates and three heavy ceramic mugs. Travis crossed to the room's midpoint and came to a stop with his shin at the coffee table's edge. He heard Garret stop a foot behind him. Felt him standing there, holding his breath.

Travis turned around and looked up into his eyes. Garret returned the stare, then glanced at the top of his head. Travis knew his hair was matted from sleeping in the car yesterday—he hadn't been able to fix it since then.

"You can take a shower if you like," Garret said. "Or I've got bubble-bath soap, if that's better. It's an oversized tub, if . . . you know . . ."

He left the sentence unfinished.

Travis didn't respond. He waited until Garret was looking him in the eyes again, and then darted his own gaze just past the man's shoulder and flinched hard.

It never failed. Few people could help but react to the sudden, primal belief that something dangerous was right behind them. Garret pivoted, and in the same instant Travis scooped one of the mugs from the coffee table and swung it as hard as he could into the back of the man's head. It would've been bad enough for Garret even if the mug had broken, but it didn't. All of the force of the impact went into his skull instead. He made a grunting sound—"*Uhnn!*"—and crumpled and then sprawled. Travis dropped onto him and arced the mug down on his head three more times, putting all his weight into each swing, then scrambled backward away from him. He held the mug ready and watched the man.

Garret didn't move.

After a moment Travis heard him breathing, slow and ragged. Travis stood and circled wide around him. He went to the closet by the entry door and found a roll of duct tape, came back and used a third of it binding Garret's limbs and covering his mouth.

It was 10:30. Monument Street lay in pools of sodium light and the apartment was pitch black away from the windows. Travis had stood watch for over four hours. Realistically it would be hours more before Ward would likely appear, but there was no reason to look away. Garret had stirred and moaned a few times in the darkness, but had mostly remained unconscious. In the minutes after binding him, Travis had made a quick survey of the apartment. Mainly he'd hoped to find a pair of binoculars. No luck. He found a stack of photos showing Garret rock climbing with a woman, presumably his girlfriend. She was taller than Garret and built like a pretty serious weight lifter. Travis thought a psychologist could make a whole career out of the guy's libido.

He also found a loaded snub .38 in the nightstand drawer. He left it there. Couldn't imagine having a use for it in the coming hours.

Foot traffic on Monument north of Johns Hopkins had dropped to practically nothing at nightfall. No one was coming or going from the academic buildings on the north side of the street, and only a few left or entered the hospital—at least from these four exits.

Binoculars would've helped with the more distant pair of doors. They were between seven and eight hundred feet away, about the limit of Travis's ability to tell bald from blond. He hoped Ward's posture and movement would simply make it obvious. Hoped he'd see him and have not the slightest doubt who it was. The nightmare possibility—clawing at Travis all these dark hours like some animal inside his chest—was someone emerging beyond the construction zone who only *might* be Ruben Ward. Anyone bald and stooped would fit the bill, and there had to be all kinds of men like that inside the place. If one stepped out, there'd be no time at all to make a decision. Travis would just have to run. Half a mile around the block, as fast as he could move. And if he got there and found some arthritic sixty-year-old, he'd have to make the same sprint right back here, hoping like hell he hadn't missed Ward in all the lost minutes.

He tried not to think about it.

He watched the street.

He waited.

Ruben Ward stepped out of the nearest of the four exits at seven minutes past midnight. So close Travis could see the black notebook under his arm. Travis watched the man just long enough—maybe three seconds—to be alarmed at how quickly he was moving. Ward staggered, but not slowly. More like a drunk perpetually chasing his balance. He made three lurching steps along the sidewalk, braced a hand against the building, then withdrew it and lurched forward again. Fast. Way the hell too fast. Between lurches and pauses he probably matched the speed of a healthy person walking.

Travis turned and sprinted for the apartment's entry, vaulting over Garret as he went.

He was almost to the door when he heard a key plunge into the lock from the other side.

CHAPTER SEVENTEEN

It didn't happen like it would've in a movie. There was no drawn-out moment in which the lock disengaged and the knob made a hellishly slow turn.

It happened in half a second, start to finish: click-turn-shove.

Travis checked his momentum just in time to keep from catching the door with his nose, and just like that he was face to face with the woman from the pictures. The rock climber. Taller and stronger than Garret.

She startled and fell back a step, dropping a bag of groceries she'd been holding. Something shattered. Something rolled.

The woman was wearing a uniform of some sort. In the split-second he had to think about it, Travis guessed she was a stewardess. Or a car rental clerk. Or one of a thousand other things.

Her panic disappeared in the next second—probably the time it took to realize she was staring at a ten-year-old—and anger took its place. She came forward, kicking aside the fallen groceries, and swatted the light switch upward.

Travis squinted, not quite blinded but sure as hell stung by the sudden brightness.

"What the fuck is this?" the woman said. Her volume suggested she wasn't just talking to Travis. She wanted an answer from Garret, wherever he was.

Travis drew back from her advance, realizing even as he did so that he was clearing the way for her to *see* Garret.

She saw.

For the second time in as many breaths she flinched and recoiled. Her eyes registered the purest bafflement, and then regardless of the conclusion she'd drawn—if any—she simply reacted. She lunged at Travis, shoving the door fully aside as she came on.

There was no chance of getting past her and onto the landing. Even if he did, he wouldn't get away. She'd be faster than him. Much faster.

Travis staggered back and hit the coffee table with his calves. He lost his balance and went down hard in front of the couch, the woman already descending on him, getting a fistful of his shirt. Half of Travis's attention was on her, and the other half, like a mental split screen, was on Ruben Ward. Lurching and bracing. Lurching and bracing. Probably halfway to the intersection by now. Once he reached it, there was no telling which direction he'd go, but in any direction there were places he could duck into within the next hundred feet. Which he might well do, out of fear that hospital staffers were right behind him—he'd have no way to know they weren't.

Ward could reach concealment in the next thirty or forty seconds. Could be *gone* in the next thirty or forty seconds.

Travis became aware of the woman screaming at him. Asking who he was. Grabbing for both of his arms and trying to pin them. She got one. Went for the other. Travis yanked it away and did the only thing he could think of: put his index and middle finger together into a fused, rigid spike, and stabbed her in the eye with it.

She cried out and let go of his other arm, both of her hands flying to her face to feel for damage.

Travis twisted beneath her, got hold of one of the couch's legs and pulled himself free. He heard her cursing and shouting and felt a rush of air as her hand just missed his back.

Then he was on his feet, bounding over the coffee table and toward the doorway.

The bedroom doorway.

Behind him he heard the woman's tone change from anger to fear. Maybe she understood what he had in mind. The table clattered as she shoved it away and came after him.

The doorway was just ahead now. He hooked the frame with one hand as he went through, swinging his body like a sideways pendulum toward the nightstand. He got his free hand on the drawer pull just as the woman crashed into him from behind.

The drawer came fully free of its seat. Its contents flew. Reading glasses. A little box of tissue. The snub .38. Travis's hand closed around its grip as he went down, and then he tumbled, knees and elbows hitting the floor in random sequence.

He came to rest with his shoulder blades against the far wall, the pistol in his hand and leveled back toward the direction he'd come from. Toward the woman.

She pulled up short six feet away, frozen on all fours like a cat in the last instant before pouncing.

Her eyes were locked onto the pistol's barrel.

"Take it easy," she said.

"It's only a memory," Travis said, and pulled the trigger.

The bullet shattered her collarbone and she collapsed, screaming and holding the wound. Travis was already up and sprinting, ignoring her, going right over her and through the doorway.

Across the living room. Through the still-open entry door and onto the landing. He was two flights down before he realized he still had the gun. He stuffed it into his front pocket coming off the final step, hit the exterior door's latch bar and burst out into the cool night.

He faced the intersection, and the north stretch of Johns Hopkins beyond it.

No sign of Ward at either one.

The man was already out of sight. He'd reached the crossroads and made a turn, one direction or another.

Travis broke into a sprint toward Broadway. He dissected the situation as he ran. Ward couldn't have crossed Broadway and continued along Monument—Travis would've seen him already in that case. He also couldn't have gone into the parking structure; there was no entry to it anywhere near this street corner. That left north or south on

Broadway, and south would keep Ward right next to the hospital for another eight hundred feet. The place he was desperate to get away from.

North, then. Had to be.

Travis was already looking in that direction as he passed the last townhouse. The whole width of Broadway slid into his view.

Ward was nowhere on it.

Travis spun to look south. No Ward there, either.

He faced north again. Looked for places the man could've ducked into. Only two were close enough to be plausible options: an alley behind the row of academic buildings to the east, and another behind the row of town houses to the west.

Something metal crashed onto concrete. Maybe a trash-can lid. Definitely in one of the alleys—but which? The acoustics were tricky.

Travis sprinted again, covering the hundred feet north to the midpoint of the shallow block. Faced the left-side alley—behind the town houses—as he stopped hard.

The lid lay thirty feet away in the spill of amber light from the street. Five feet beyond it there was only darkness: a channel of fractured and cluttered space that separated the town houses on the south half of the block from those on the north. It stretched all the way to the west end, almost three hundred yards.

But there were lots of ways out of it, north and south. Mini-alleys that divided parallel homes here and there. Travis could see these only by the gaps in the rooflines three stories up. Down in the dark at ground level there was no detail at all. Ward could be slipping into one of these passageways right in front of him, right now, and he wouldn't know. Travis threw himself forward into the channel.

Deep shadow. Random shit strewn everywhere. Hazy light from the occasional back room.

Travis found his eyes adjusting after the first ten seconds. Saw a child's wagon and stepped over it quietly.

Something moved in the dimness fifty feet away. A clatter of wood and concrete and—what else? Human hands striking the ground, Travis thought.

A man cursed softly.

Travis advanced. One careful step at a time.

Faint sounds of movement ahead. Junk being shoved aside. Plastic bags rustling. Ward was struggling to get back on his feet.

Travis tried to fix his eyes on the sound source. No good. At any distance the darkness was still nearly perfect.

He took another slow step—and crushed an aluminum can that'd been lying on its side. In the stillness the sound might as well have been a car alarm.

A man's voice called out, raspy and sore and full of fear: "*Who's there?*"

Travis didn't answer. He waited. Took soundless breaths with his mouth wide open.

Five seconds passed, and then the rustling noise came again. Ward was still trying to get up.

Was it really that difficult for him to do? That was hard to believe, given the agility he'd shown so far.

Bags slid on the alley floor. Something made of plastic flipped over and skittered.

Suddenly Travis understood.

These weren't the sounds of a man laboring to right himself.

They were the sounds of a man searching for something.

Ward had lost the notebook when he'd fallen.

Travis advanced again, still trying for silence but not as carefully as before. His right hand went to his pocket and settled on the .38.

He was forty feet from the sifting sounds now, still trying to peg the location. The brick walls on either side played hell with his directional hearing.

Travis was keenly aware of the situation's risk: Ward knew now that someone was here hunting him. The instant the man recovered the notebook, he'd go silent again, and the advantage would be all his. He could pick any narrow alley at random and disappear.

Travis continued forward. Thirty feet away.

The rustling stopped.

So did Travis.

He froze and held his breath and listened for movement.

Instead there came a shout: *"Leave me alone!"*

It echoed crazily along the rift between the townhouses, in staggered and distinct reverberations.

But Travis's ears picked up something else. Some other sound, barely audible beneath the panicked words. He thought he knew what it was, though it made no sense: a zipper being undone.

What zipper could Ward have except the fly on

his jeans? Had his pants snagged on something when he'd sprawled? Was he sliding out of them so he could get away?

The echoes of the shout faded and the alley dropped to absolute silence.

Five seconds.

Ten.

Travis felt panic begin to stir. Ward was leaving, and there was no way to stop him.

Fifteen seconds.

Not a sound anywhere.

Travis let go of the gun in his pocket, cupped his hands to his mouth and shouted.

"Ruben! I know about the VLIC! I know about the instructions!"

A foot scraped on concrete, maybe stopping fast and turning, far away in the dark. Fifty or sixty feet.

Silence.

"I'm supposed to help you!" Travis said.

For a moment nothing happened. Then Ward called out: *"Who the hell are you?"*

Travis thought about his reply. Saw no reason to be inventive.

"Travis Chase! Let me help!"

He heard a fast exhalation. It sounded like confusion, though it was hard to tell. More likely it was just a physical response to the past minute's stress.

"You're only a kid!" Ward yelled.

Travis started moving again. Homing in on the voice's location: not just far ahead but all the way against the alley's left side.

"I'm old enough to be useful," Travis said, letting his own voice relax.

"The instructions didn't say anything about this," Ward said. Still unnerved. Still on the brink of fleeing.

"What, there's a rule against someone giving you a hand?"

The points of the conversation didn't matter. Keeping Ward talking mattered. And closing in on his voice.

But the seconds drew out, and Ward didn't reply.

Travis continued moving forward. Slowly. Silently.

Then the man said, "Is it already happening?"

Travis started to ask what he meant, but stopped. Asking for clarification might clash with what he'd told Ward a moment earlier: that he knew what was going on. While Travis didn't need to make sense, he did need to avoid scaring the guy away.

"The filter," Ward said. "Is it starting now?"

The filter?

Travis hesitated, still advancing, then decided to wing it. "It's possible," he said.

Ward breathed out audibly again. Same location: ahead and to the left.

"It's not supposed to happen yet," Ward said. "Not for years and years."

Travis kept moving. Forty feet to go. He'd have to speak more softly now to hide the fact that he was getting closer.

"Whoever it affects," Ward said, "it's not their fault. Not really. Under the wrong conditions, anyone could end up the worst person on Earth."

Travis's leading foot touched down and froze. So did the rest of his body.

Are you wondering if there's a connection? Paige had said. *Between whatever's going on right now and . . . the thing about you?*

Travis stared at the blackness where Ward had just spoken, and found his thoughts suddenly vacant. The question came out before he realized he was asking it: "What are you talking about?"

He noticed only halfway through—too late for it to matter—that he hadn't tempered his voice at all.

There was another quick scuff of shoes on asphalt—Ward flinching, maybe—and then a sustained burst of movement as the man took off running through the cluttered dark. Crashing past whatever lay in his path. Stumbling and staggering, but moving fast.

Travis pushed away the confusion and sprinted after him. Following the sound. Gaining now.

All at once he caught a glimpse of Ward, in the vague pool of light below a curtained window. Bald head and T-shirt and jeans—he was still wearing them.

The man had almost passed beyond the light when he sprawled. Caught his foot on something and went all the way down. The notebook flew free again.

Travis doubled his speed and yanked the .38 from his pocket—enough fucking around.

He leveled it as Ward pushed up to a crouch.

But he didn't fire.

He didn't need to.

Ward made one desperate grab for the notebook,

almost collapsing again as he did, then heard Travis's running footsteps and threw himself sideways out of the light. The book stayed right where it'd fallen.

Travis pulled up short beneath the window. Stood there catching his breath and listening. He heard Ward staggering in the dark twenty feet off, and then silence again. Had he stopped? Was he weighing his chances of fighting for the notebook?

Travis kept the pistol leveled, aimed toward the last place he'd heard movement. He kept his eyes in that direction too, as he knelt and scooped up the book.

He stared another five seconds, the gun shaking in his small hand.

Then he tucked the notebook against himself like a football, turned back the way he'd come from, and ran.

Travis emerged into the light on Broadway. He heard sirens nearby in the night, coming from several directions and getting louder by the second. He remembered the gunshot inside Garret's place. There'd be a dozen police cars on this block within minutes.

He sprinted across both wide sections of Broadway and went north toward Ashland, the first street free of construction.

He went east and north for two blocks, then turned west and made a wide swing around the hospital and the crime scene, coming at last to where he'd left the Chevelle. There was a serious-looking ticket stuck under the wiper. He discarded it, set the notebook on the passenger seat, started the car, and got the hell out of Baltimore.

Twenty miles south on I–95, he took an exit to a huge shopping mall. The parking lot was a ten-acre tundra of neat yellow lines and stark white cones of light. There wasn't a single car in it but his own. He parked out in the center so he could see trouble coming a long way off. He turned on the dome light and opened the notebook.

The first page was blank.

So was the second.

And every other page in the book.

He flipped back to the beginning and saw what he'd missed at first glance: four or five ragged strips trapped inside the spiral binding, where pages had been torn out.

He understood what the zipper-like sound had been, and why Ward had shouted to obscure it.

He got out and stood beside the car and screamed loud enough to hurt his throat. An animal shriek that rolled away across the dark fields and half-built developments at the edge of suburbia.

He paced for a long time, wandering between the car and the nearest light post. Its base was bolted into a concrete cylinder covered with flaking yellow paint. He found himself kicking it every time he reached that end of his track, and wondered how much of his ten-year-old self he was experiencing, emotionally.

He realized he was putting off snapping out of the memory. Stalling. Had no idea how to break the news to Paige and Bethany. He could lie and put his performance in a better light—it wasn't as if they could check—but had no intention of doing so. He'd tell them the whole thing. He just didn't want to do it yet.

Reaching the car again, he leaned in and took the notebook off the seat. He stood with his back against the door and stared at the cover in the pale mercury light.

He flipped it open. An entirely idle move.

But he drew a quick breath at what he saw.

The angled light revealed indentations in the page. The ghosts of whatever had been written on the sheet above it, pressed deep by the tip of the pen.

He straightened and moved closer to the light post. Tilted the book and swiveled his body, seeking just the right glare.

The instant he found it his optimism faded. There were indentations, for sure, but they'd come from *several* pages above this one. A stacked mess of handwriting, so jumbled that he could make no sense of it.

Except for two lines.

Two places where, as it'd happened, there'd been no overlap.

He put his eyes three inches from the paper and scrutinized the words, feeling his skin prickle even before he'd begun to read. It struck him that this was an alien message. Spoken by a human and transcribed by a human, but an alien message all the same.

He let his eyes track over the two lines.

The first was impossible to draw meaning from—it was the end of one sentence and the beginning of another.

a passageway beneath the third notch.
Look for

He considered it for a moment anyway. It seemed to be part of a detailed set of directions. A route to take and something to search for at some given location—a place with notches, whatever that meant in this context. A castle wall? A rock formation somewhere? There had to be a million places that fit the bill, and there was nothing in the line to narrow the field. Travis stared at it a second longer and then let it go.

The second line was farther down and more softly impressed—it must've come from an even earlier page. It was a perfect sentence. Travis read it and felt the blood retreat from his face.

Some of us are already among you.

PART II

THE STARGAZER

CHAPTER EIGHTEEN

Paige and Bethany stared at the two lines Travis had typed on the laptop. For a long time they neither spoke nor blinked.

The Tap sat nearby on the table, cooling. Travis stepped to the kitchen counter, grabbed a napkin and wiped a thin trail of blood from his temple.

Already he could feel the strange effect of the burned memory: while the past two days in Baltimore were as fresh in his mind as if he'd just experienced them—as he had—they were *also* stitched into his distant past, foggy as a recollection of a school field trip he might have taken way back then, that spring when he was in fifth grade. The Baltimore memory had simply replaced whatever real memory he might've had of those two days, like an exotic film clip recorded over a section of home video. He let the sensation fade and tossed the bloody napkin into the trash. As he did, his eyes went to the microwave clock.

8:50 A.M.

Ten hours and fifty-five minutes to the end of the road.

He heard a group of people go by in the corridor outside the residence, talking. They sounded animated about something.

"This second line," Paige said. "You're certain the first letter was capitalized?"

Travis nodded, seeing where she was going. He'd gone there himself while still holding the notepad under the light post, exhausting every possible way the sentence could mean less than it appeared to. If the first letter were lowercase, then the unseen earlier portion of the sentence might change the meaning. Might contain a negative that reversed it entirely.

But all such possibilities could be discarded.

"The *S* filled the line, top to bottom," Travis said. "Every other letter without an ascender was exactly half that height. Nora's handwriting was perfect."

Travis saw Bethany's shoulders twitch as a shudder climbed her neck. She read the line again and exhaled softly. "Already among us. That makes it sound like they blended in."

Paige seemed to react to that idea. She looked up at Travis. "Remember what you asked in Ouray? Who has the motive to undo what my father did?"

Travis's mind called up images of full-floor penthouses eighty stories above Manhattan or Hong Kong, from which a few encrypted phone calls could launch private armies or sway governments—could direct arterial flows of cash to influential interests that didn't care where the money came from, or why. The notion that such places existed was unnerving enough, even if their occupants were *human*.

"It doesn't make sense," Paige said. "If some of them were already here before the Breach opened, why bother sending instructions through it to make a pawn of one of us? Why would they need a pawn at all? They're millions of years more advanced than we are. Maybe billions. Anything they wanted to do here, they could've done it themselves like you or I would get a glass of water. They wouldn't need to sneak around and pull strings from behind the scenes." A silence. "So why did they?"

Travis found only about half his attention going to the question. The other half kept going back to what Ruben Ward had said in the alley—the disconnected talk about the *filter*, whatever it was. Something that wasn't supposed to become an issue for years and years—from the vantage point of 1978. Travis had said nothing of the filter since waking from the memory. Though it obviously tied into what was happening now—might simply *be* what was happening now—it just as obviously had a connection to Travis's own future, and whatever was waiting for him there. *It.*

Which he'd never spoken about in front of Bethany, as much as he trusted her. He'd never told anyone but Paige.

"It doesn't make sense," Paige said again.

Travis could only shake his head. He stared at the laptop screen, the two short lines surrounded by vacant space. He thought of the blade-thin margin by which he'd lost the notebook—lost all the answers and come back with only these impossible questions.

* * *

"Does the first line give us anything actionable?" Paige said. "Is there more to it than we're seeing?"

She leaned close and studied it.

" 'A passageway beneath the third notch,' " she said. " 'Look for . . .' "

For a long time no one spoke. Then Bethany shrugged. "It tells us Ruben Ward went somewhere that had notches and a passageway. I'm sure we'd hit some kind of jackpot if we could find the passageway now. But we can't. Not with only this to go on."

Paige straightened and paced away from the table, hands on her head.

More footsteps sounded in the hallway. More lively—if not quite happy—speech. Like something was going on. The moment triggered a memory for Travis—one that was minutes old for Paige and Bethany but more than two days old for him.

"Who was on the phone?" he said. "You got a call right before I went under."

Paige looked at him. "One of President Holt's aides. *Air Force One* is landing here within the next fifteen minutes."

CHAPTER NINETEEN

Ostensibly, he's only coming to tour the place," Paige said. "Every new president does that, early on."

"You believe him?" Travis said.

"Not for a second. You?"

Travis shook his head. He looked at the microwave clock again. 8:52.

"What are you thinking?" Paige said.

"It's three hours since the trap in Ouray failed," Travis said. "Which is about how long it takes a 747 to fly here from D.C. The timing just about works out—Holt learns it all went to hell down there, and he hops in his plane to pay us a visit. Like some kind of Plan B."

Paige considered it. "It's plausible. But whatever the case, he's not coming in here with any kind of armed presence. Not even Secret Service; that's been policy here forever. If he doesn't accept that, we won't even open the elevator."

"Then Plan B is something more subtle than Plan A was," Travis said. "Some spoken threat, thinly veiled, or maybe not veiled at all. Or else just a lie to throw us off track entirely. Remember, Holt doesn't know we suspect his involvement."

"And we want to keep it that way," Paige said. "So we'll give him the tour and not share anything we've learned, and assume every word he says is bullshit."

Travis indicated the Tap, still sitting on the table.

"There's one more place where I can intercept Ruben Ward," he said. "That motel on Sunset Boulevard, August 12."

"Probably fifteen minutes before he blows his brains out," Paige said. "I doubt he'll be in a talkative mood. And by then the notebook's already gone."

Travis recalled Ward's fear in the alley behind the townhouses. He tried to imagine getting information out of him, in the last hour of his life. As a ten-year-old. He considered it for five seconds and dropped it.

"All right, we concentrate on the cheat sheet," he said. "It's everything we need to know, on a single piece of paper. We work the information we have, starting with your father's meeting in 1987, right before he closed down Scalar. We find out who he met with—who he gave copies of that report to—and where they lived, and then I'll use the Tap to drop into their lives again and again, in the months right after that. That part won't be hard; I was nineteen years old by then. I'll do whatever it takes to get that document. Break into houses—anything."

"If we get Holt in and out of here fast enough,"

Paige said, "say forty-five minutes, then we'll have ten hours left to work with. In the first hour alone you could use the Tap a dozen times, if need be." She winced at the thought of his actually making that many trips with it, but the power of the idea shone clearly in her eyes. "If we find out what's actually going on, what's happening right now, today, we'll still have hours left to go on offense against it."

"No kid gloves," Travis said. "If it's a matter of just finding certain people and killing them, we do it. We use any Breach technology necessary. We do it. Simple as that."

Paige was nodding. So was Bethany. Both looked a little unnerved, but neither looked uncertain.

"So who did my father meet with?" Paige said. "Carrie called them a mixed bag of powerful people. Politics, intel, finance. How do we find them?"

"We need a starting point," Bethany said. "Any little piece of information about your father's meeting with them—location, date, someone's flight number, anything at all. Just something I can get my nails into."

"What *about* flights?" Travis said. "We know the meeting happened at the end of the Scalar investigation, which should be sometime near the final entry in the index downstairs—November 28, 1987. Assuming Peter flew there from here, could we find a record of his departure and destination? Does the airbase in Browning have traffic logs?"

Paige shook her head. "Not for us. We've never allowed any of our comings or goings to be documented. Anonymity's a good line of defense."

Bethany looked thoughtful. "There might be other records from that time, though." She turned to Paige. "Do you have your father's social security number somewhere?"

"It should be in the system," Paige said. She minimized Word on the laptop and opened the personnel records. Ten seconds later she read the number to Bethany, who entered it into her tablet computer and got to work.

Paige's cell rang. It was someone from Defense Control on level B4, which served as Border Town's air traffic control center. *Air Force One* was five minutes out.

A minute later Bethany said, "Might have something." She continued navigating on her computer as she spoke. "Do either of you remember the rough dates of the two index entries before the last one, on November 28? I can run down to the archives and check, if you don't."

Paige closed her eyes and concentrated. She opened them a few seconds later and said, "The second-to-last one was about a month earlier, at the end of October, and the one before that was six weeks earlier still—mid-September."

"Definitely have something then," Bethany said. "Take a look."

Travis and Paige pressed in behind her and stared at her screen. Travis realized he was looking at a financial record of some kind, with credits and debits listed in columns, along with transaction labels.

"These are Peter Campbell's credit-card statements beginning in September of 1987," Bethany said.

If the invasion of privacy bothered Paige, she didn't show it.

"He didn't use the card a lot," Bethany said. "Understandably. Living here, why would he? But in mid-September we've got four charges clustered over three days. A gas station and three restaurants, all located in a place called Rum Lake, California." She looked at Paige. "Ever hear him mention it?"

"Never heard of it at all until just now."

"Well he went there a few more times," Bethany said. "Late October and late November, a couple days each trip, corresponding with the final two entries downstairs in the archives, and then one last trip that *doesn't* match an entry. That was in mid-December. I've looked back through these statements to the beginning of 1984—that's as far back as it goes—and there are no other Rum Lake charges. No more of them *after* these four trips either. So it wasn't just some getaway he went to all the time, with the dates of his trips just happening to match the Scalar entries. This place was directly tied to Scalar, right at the end."

"Carrie said he flew somewhere for the meeting," Paige said. "But it was just one meeting—not four of them separated by weeks."

"I'm thinking the meeting is just the final trip," Bethany said, "in mid-December. It makes sense that there's no index entry for that one downstairs, if he purged the files right when he got back from it. Why create a new file just before you get rid of them all?"

Paige nodded, following the logic.

Bethany minimized the window and opened another. "So for starters I'll focus on the last trip, and see if I can identify anyone else who showed up in Rum Lake at the same time. I'll get into the merchant accounts of these places where Peter ran his card, and pull up the rest of the transactions over those days. Maybe some other customer's info will send up a flag—like if it's someone who lives in D.C. or works in the intelligence business. Power players, right?"

"That sounds like a lot of digging," Travis said. He thought of all the card charges that would've happened at those businesses during the days in question. Once she had that information, Bethany would need to access personal information on every one of those customers to see who stood out.

"It'll take time," Bethany said. "There's not exactly an app for that. Not until I script one, at least. Give me a few minutes."

Sixty seconds later the three of them were in the elevator, rising toward B4. Bethany held the tablet computer in one hand while the fingertips of the other flew over its touch-screen. She kept her focus on it even as the doors parted and the three of them stepped out. The open doorway to Defense Control was twenty feet ahead and to the left. Light from its numerous LCD screens bled into the corridor, along with the voices of half a dozen people inside. Paige led the way in.

Defense Control was about the same size as the conference room, though more spacious because its ceiling was twice as high. The flat wall that paralleled the corridor was lined with small equipment cabinets and much larger, semi-portable mainframe computers the size of industrial refrigerators. The far wall was a sweeping half circle, covered floor to ceiling with giant high-definition monitors. Each one carried a live video feed from one of nearly a hundred cameras embedded in the desert above.

Evelyn Rossi, Defense's ranking officer, paced near the room's central workstation and spoke into a wireless headset. "*Air Force One*, I have you at one-seven-zero knots, heading zero-eight-five. Maintain course and descent."

Evelyn caught Paige's eye and nodded hello.

"Pilot provided the verification code?" Paige said.

"Yeah."

Travis let his eyes track over the room's other workstations, set up to handle less-friendly situations. Technicians sat at or stood near these desks, idle but ready to engage in a hurry. Along with the network of cameras, the desert around Border Town hid one of the world's most formidable defensive systems, designed to counter both ground and air-based attacks. The most critical ingredient, though, was simply the policy of not allowing unauthorized aircraft anywhere near the place. Even *Air Force One* had to forgo its usual complement of escort fighters when it visited.

Several of the screens on the curved wall had a visual of the giant aircraft, less than a mile out now, though its details were still vague. Every camera up top was either snug with the ground or raised above it by no more than a foot, which meant that when focused on a distant, nearly ground-level subject, they all looked through curtains of heat-ripples rising off the baked landscape. The effect was present now on every screen in the room, reducing the distant 747 to no more than a shimmering blob with wings.

Evelyn turned to Paige again as if to say something, but stopped herself. She'd noticed something on her desk display. She keyed her headset.

"*Air Force One*, I have you changing to heading zero-eight-seven. You are outside the glide path. Please acknowledge."

Her eyes narrowed as she waited for a reply. She didn't appear to get one.

"*Air Force One*, acknowledge change of heading. You are *not on course* for the runway."

"He's climbing," one of the techs said. "And increasing airspeed. One-eight-zero knots. One-eight-five."

"*Air Force One*," Evelyn said, "if you are aborting approach please acknowledge. Say again, please acknowledge this transmission." She looked around at the others. "Why the hell can't he hear me?"

"One-nine-five knots," the tech said. "Still climbing. If he's aborting for a retry he should've turned by now. Still tracking dead straight on heading zero-eight-seven."

Travis picked out the wall screen with the best image of the aircraft, and stepped closer to it. As it climbed and drew nearer, its shape began to resolve. So did its color.

Which was uniform gray, not blue and white.

Someone behind him said, "What the hell?"

At that moment the ripples diminished by a fraction, and the plane's outline, even head-on, became clear. Not the massive bulk of a 747's body with its wings tying in at the bottom. This was a narrower, sleeker form, and its wings met near the top of the fuselage.

Travis understood that he'd been wrong about Holt's intentions: they weren't subtle. They were as far from subtle as they could get.

"That's not *Air Force One*," Travis said. "That's a B–52."

CHAPTER TWENTY

Colonel Dennis Pike hadn't slept much during the night. Along with his wife and older daughter, he'd been up past midnight watching CNN's coverage from D.C. Then he'd gotten a phone call—one he'd expected—and five minutes later he'd logged in at the front gate of his post: Minot Air Force Base in North Dakota. In response to the attack on the White House, all branches of the armed forces were stepping up their levels of readiness. Pike had to oversee the status change for his own command, the 83rd Bomb Wing. It took about six hours, after which he'd gone home and caught ninety minutes' sleep before another call came in. This one he hadn't expected.

The man on the other end was the Air Force chief of staff, with orders coming directly from the new president. Strange orders. A wargame of some kind, to be conducted immediately by Pike himself. It would take place at a target range in eastern Wyoming—a location Pike had seen on maps throughout his career, though it had never been labeled as a practice area. It hadn't been labeled as military property at all, but simply as *Restricted*

Airspace—Undesignated. The president wanted Pike, without a copilot or navigator aboard, to fly a B–52 to the center of that place and test his ability to deploy a very unorthodox weapon, only two of which were even stored at Minot. Stranger still, Pike would relinquish control of his comm system for the entirety of the flight, setting it to a remote-access channel which would allow the Air Force chief and the president—or anyone they selected—to use his radio and do his talking for him.

"Don't ask," the chief of staff had said. "All that matters is that we'll be evaluating your performance. Do this right and we've got something very special in mind for you."

The target was in sight now, less than half a mile ahead: a seemingly arbitrary GPS point ten yards south of what looked like a pole barn, the only structure for miles around. The weapon was to impact that spot of empty ground precisely. Which it would, of course. Given the perfect visibility, low altitude and near-stalling speed, a trained chimp could've hit this target. It occurred to Pike, though only briefly, to wonder what the hell his superiors were evaluating. He'd performed the strange set of approach maneuvers exactly as ordered, but he could've done it drunk. So could every pilot in his command. There was no logic to it. Now, climbing and accelerating in the final seconds of the run, he realized this wouldn't even make for a good story at the Officers Club. Whatever it was, no doubt it would be classified forever.

Well, strange was better than boring.

He reached for the weapons system panel.

* * *

Paige was already running, even as Travis got the last word out. Others in the room were scrambling for their desks, pulling up the defensive controls in seconds, as their training had taught them to do. But Paige's solution would be faster. And simpler.

She all but crashed into the rack-mounted instrument cabinet she'd been aiming for, bolted to the wall near the entry. She pressed her palm to the scanner above the cabinet's door, and with every tense muscle in her body she willed it to respond quickly.

A quarter-second later the cabinet clicked open.

Paige yanked the door aside to reveal a single, coaster-sized red button. It looked exactly like the kind Travis remembered from electrical shop in high school. There'd been one every six feet along the classroom wall, rigged to kill the power in case some freshman touched the wrong wire and started cooking.

The red button in Border Town had a different purpose.

Paige slammed it as hard as she could.

Pike felt a *thud* reverberate through the airframe as the bomb-bay doors locked open. Felt the sudden increase in drag as the slipstream passing under the plane churned and whirled through the complex interior geometry of the bay. He knew that in another second he'd feel the most dramatic change of all: the instant loss of nearly five thousand pounds of weight. The GBU–28 was a heavy son of a bitch, though only a small fraction of its mass was explosive. Well over four thousand of its pounds were just dumb, solid steel. For good reason.

Pike's hand was already on the bomb release

when everything changed. One instant the desert floor was bare and lifeless. The next, it burst open at half a dozen places, long, rectangular sections of ground being heaved aside from below. Pike had the crazed impression of casket lids coming up through the topsoil of a cemetery.

Half a second later he understood what he was seeing—a reality many times worse than a grave-yard come to life.

Kill everything.

That was what the red button did. It deployed every weapon concealed in the desert and gave the system a universal, exceptionless command: target and engage any moving object within range.

Travis had already turned his eyes from Paige back to the wall screens. The bomber had come so much closer in the past five seconds it seemed surreal. Its apparent distance before must've been a trick of camera perspectives and shimmer.

Now, as the aircraft continued to swell on screen, Travis saw that its bomb doors were wide open. Even as he noticed, he felt the building shud-der, and on every television in the room, multiple rocket-exhaust trails raced up out of the ground toward the plane.

Pike spent the last second of his life numb. He didn't feel what his hand was doing on the bomb release, if anything. Didn't bother to reach for the electronic countermeasures switch either—it prob-ably wouldn't have saved him even if there'd been time to use it.

He found his brain doing exactly two things at

once—each half acting on its own, he imagined. The left half recognized the flight profile and outlines of the Patriot missiles that had come up out of the desert to meet him. His eyes went to the one that would reach him first, its RF seeker head having apparently locked onto the B–52's nose. He tried to remember the trigger distance for a Patriot's proximity fuze. Five meters? Ten? Did it matter? The thing was closing toward him at more than twice the speed of sound, and its warhead was a two-hundred-pound frag bomb. Like a hand grenade the size of a keg.

The right half of his brain was looking elsewhere, and more frantically. It was struggling to grab the last image he'd had of his daughter, as he'd left the house the night before. She'd been sitting in the leather recliner beside the couch, in a big purple T-shirt. Bangs in her eyes. She'd looked at him and said what she always said when he left for the base.

Careful.

It meant *good-bye*, but it meant a lot more the way she said it—high and soft, her eyebrows arched. It meant *I love you*. It also meant *If anything happens to you, I'm* always *going to love you*. He knew it meant all those things. He wasn't imagining any of it.

Careful.

That word, in his daughter's voice, was Dennis Pike's last thought.

Travis saw the first distinct explosion maybe a fourth of a second before the next. The leading

Patriot detonated almost nose-to-nose with the bomber, reducing everything forward of the wings to a particle cloud—which the plane instantly outran. The second Patriot, coming from the aircraft's left, exploded just beneath the port-side wing, which at once became a sheet of flame. An instant later the starboard wing, the only intact lifting surface, pitched upward, hauling the entire plane high and left in a roll.

And revealing, like a curtain drawn aside with a flourish, a bomb that'd been freed from the bay less than a second earlier.

Travis heard sharp breaths sucked in around him.

The loosed weapon, so close now that it was visible from multiple camera angles, was long and sleek like a missile, but it didn't fly like one. It had no propulsion of its own. It simply arced forward in a smooth line, gently falling away from the climbing trajectory the plane had held. The bomb's tip dropped to level and then gradually angled downward. Travis could see that by the time it hit the surface, its nose would be pointing straight down, and though he'd never seen one before, he knew exactly what kind of bomb it was.

A bunker buster.

The majority of the thing's weight, mostly up front, would just be dead metal, shaped to penetrate soil and concrete. The explosive portion would be rigged to blow only *after* the weapon had traveled some distance beneath the impact point. What that distance might be, Travis couldn't guess, but without question the bomb would explode inside the complex, not above it. Whether anyone in the place survived was a dice roll now.

He turned and found Paige beside him, Bethany just beyond her, both of them thinking the same things he was. Their eyes were wide—they weren't even trying to hide the fear. None of them said anything. They just waited. Whatever was coming was only seconds away.

In his peripheral vision Travis saw orange light flare across the wall of screens; the last Patriots had converged on the crippled bomber and brought it tumbling downward in a cartwheel of fire. Now the floor of the room began to vibrate with a high-frequency hum—the 30mm chain guns in the desert had opened up, though in all likelihood they were just shooting at the falling aircraft. Travis didn't look to see if any of them were firing on the bunker buster. Even if they were, they probably couldn't stop it.

An absurd thought struck Travis in the moment before impact: an image of the little vault built into their closet wall down on B16.

Where they'd left the Tap for safekeeping.

CHAPTER TWENTY-ONE

The sound the bomb made when it punched through into the building was nothing like what Travis had expected, whatever he'd expected. It sounded like a machine gun. He realized immediately what he was hearing: the successive impacts as the thing slammed down through one concrete floor after another. It seemed to pass very close to Defense Control, maybe just a few feet beyond one of the walls, before thudding onward, deeper into the complex. Travis could no more count the floors it passed through than he could count autofire shots, but he guessed it'd gone at least as far down as B20.

Then it blew.

Every sensation came at once. The air pressure wave, like someone had clapped a pair of hands violently over Travis's ears, nearly rupturing the drums. The ungodly jolt to the building's structure, killing the power and dumping the room into pitch blackness. And then the kinetic shock of the explosion itself, heaving upward, certainly powdering the dozen floors above and below it, and pressing hard against those farther away. Travis felt the concrete beneath his feet arch up impossibly. Heard the reinforcing steel within it groan and crack, and knew without any doubt that when it sagged back a second later it would simply break. He and Paige and Bethany and everyone in the room would plunge with it, pressed to nothing as the interior of Border Town pancaked to a few stories of rubble down at B51.

The floor reached the top of its upward heave. It seemed to linger there for longer than should've been possible—time itself was hard to gauge just now—and then it fell back toward level, and right past it. The rebar crackled and strained again at the lowest extent.

But held.

The floor was rising once more—not quite to even, but close—when Travis heard the screams. They came from directly below: Security Control on level B5. With the screams came the sound Travis had expected to hear all around him—the avalanche roar of concrete falling apart. The floor on B5 *had* given.

A second later the screams were gone, washed out by the maelstrom noise of one story after another collapsing in sequence. A steel-and-concrete waterfall rushing down and away. It sucked the air out of Defense Control and Travis heard a high, surging whine somewhere close by. He realized it was an airstream being drawn down through the line of holes the bunker buster had made.

And then it was over. No more sound. No more air movement. Just the building's remaining framework shuddering with latent energy from the blast and the collapse.

Emergency lighting kicked on within fifteen seconds. Wall-mounted bulbs that normally ran off the grid switched to batteries.

The air was choked with concrete dust. Everyone stood in a daze, looking for one another or for the exits, or doing nothing at all. Travis saw a tech stoop and straighten a keyboard that'd slid partway off a desk.

Bethany was crying. Paige's eyes were red but nothing was spilling from them. Travis had no idea what his own eyes were doing.

He took a step and realized the floor was tilted to a greater degree than he'd first believed. He imagined the entire level, or at least a portion of it, sagging toward some lowest, weakest point.

He indicated the door they'd come in through earlier. "Come on."

As soon as they stepped into the corridor they saw where the bomb had passed. Dead centered in the hall, halfway to the elevator, was a ragged hole two feet wide. There was another in the ceiling straight above it.

Travis turned the other way and studied the stretch of corridor leading out to this level's perimeter. On a normal day he could've seen the hallway's far end, some ninety feet away, where a T-junction led left and right at the outer rim of Border Town. He couldn't see it now; the corridor dipped in a long, severe bow that cut off the sightline. The lowest point seemed to be perfectly centered between the elevator and the building's south exterior wall.

Travis stared for another second, then turned away and moved toward the two-foot hole in the floor. He stopped just shy, knelt, and studied the edge. It looked strong enough. He eased forward on all fours and then lay flat on his chest, his head extended down into the opening.

What he saw, he would remember forever. Beneath him yawned nearly fifty stories of empty space, churning with concrete fog. Border Town, if it'd stood above ground like a regular building, would've been a cylindrical skyscraper with the rough proportions of a soda can. Through the dust, Travis saw that only the southern half of the structure had collapsed—as if the soda can had been cleaved vertically down the middle, and one of its sides had then been crushed flat while the other remained standing.

For all that, the collapse zone looked as big as the world. Stubs of broken floors lined its curved southern sweep like massive, fractured ribs. On the opposite side, the guillotined edges of the north half's intact levels met the open space in a rough, upright plane. It looked strangely like a stack of balconies facing inward onto the atrium of a high-rise hotel, seen from the top floor looking down. Only there were no balconies—just vivisected rooms and corridors and airducts and gushing pipes and sparking electrical conduits, all of it lit up from deep within by more backup lighting. Clothing from torn-open closets spiraled down into the heavy dust, out of sight. Travis saw a bed lying right along the cutoff,

ten stories below, its topsheet held on by one corner
and the rest fluttering like a streamer in the eddy-
ing air.

Two things came to him, so obvious they barely
registered as isolated thoughts. First, his and Paige's
residence lay right along the cutoff. Through the
dust he thought he could resolve which one was
theirs, though it was hard to tell. Second, the
Breach and its protective dome were probably unharmed. Level B51 was not a full floor, but simply
a tunnel that extended straight north from the central elevator hub, before opening to the vast cavern
housing the Breach and its fortifications.

Travis thought of the falling bomb—clear of the
plane before the first Patriot hit. Not just clear.
Dropped. The bomb had arced and landed precisely as the pilot wanted it to. Not straight into
the elevator shaft—the logical bull's-eye if the goal
was to level the entire building—because dropping
it there would've damaged the Breach's chamber,
or at least buried it.

Holt had deliberately avoided doing that. He'd
settled for taking out half the complex and hoping
the shockwave would kill everyone inside.

But he wouldn't rest on that hope. Not for a
minute. Which meant there was more trouble
coming, and probably soon.

Travis considered that as he strained for the
sound he knew he'd hear—would probably already hear if his ears weren't ringing. He turned
his head and held his breath, and finally picked it
up: the crying and calling of survivors among the
intact north-side floors. The sounds all came from

the top five or six residence levels. It made sense: much deeper and the shockwave would've been unsurvivable. Even the backup lighting was sparser below that point—the air compression of the blast had destroyed most of the bulbs. Travis tried to gauge the number of voices he was hearing. Maybe a dozen. That too made sense, given that most of Border Town's population would've been down in the labs at this hour. Only a few would've been up in the living quarters.

He twisted and looked at Paige, crouched just behind him. She could see past his head well enough to understand the situation. She could hear the cries too. So could Bethany and the half dozen others in the hall behind her—the whole crowd from Defense Control.

"Is the stairwell still there?" Paige said.

Travis nodded. He kept his eyes on hers and saw them narrow.

"There'll be kill squads on their way here," she said. "Won't there?"

"Staged and ready to chopper in as soon as the bomb hit," Travis said. "From just outside our radar field. Which is what—forty-five miles?"

"About that."

"Figure Black Hawks. What's their top speed?"

"About a hundred eighty miles per hour," Paige said. "Three miles a minute. So fifteen minutes' flight time. And the defenses up top are all dead—they run on building power."

Travis withdrew from the hole and stood. He faced the small crowd.

Evelyn pawed tear-soaked concrete dust from beneath her eyes, her gaze sliding back and forth between Travis and Paige, the question too obvious to need voicing: *Why the fuck is this happening?*

Travis didn't answer. His mind was running the crucial math. There were six electric Jeeps up in the pole barn, fully charged. Straight-line over the desert, they could reach Casper, and they could do sixty with no trouble. The Jeeps were sandy brown, the same color as the ground, and Travis had never seen them kick up dust on the hardpan around this place. They didn't even leave tire tracks. All of which meant they could avoid being spotted by the arriving choppers—but only with a serious head start. Travis's gut said ten miles was the minimum safe distance; his head could do no better.

Evelyn was still waiting for an answer. So were all the others.

Travis looked at Bethany and indicated the tablet computer she was still holding. He could see its connection icon in the lower corner, red with a diagonal slash through it—Border Town's wireless system had died with the power grid.

"From up on the surface," Travis said, "you can get a signal from cell towers on I–25, right?"

Bethany nodded.

"Can you find out if there are spy satellites in visual range of this place?"

She nodded. "It's not likely. One in four chance, any given hour or so."

"Can you go up right now and find out?" Travis said. "And while you're there, move the Jeeps outside, then scatter random clutter over where they were parked."

She nodded again and didn't say another word. She stepped past the hole and ran for the stairwell.

Travis turned to the others. "Look at your watches or your phones. Fix on a point in time exactly five minutes from right now." He continued speaking as they did it. "You're going to save who you can downstairs, but at the five-minute mark, you're going to be sitting in the Jeeps up top, ready to go. All six Jeeps are leaving at that moment, together. Even one straggler a few minutes behind would get everyone else killed. Be there or you're staying here."

He didn't wait to see what they thought of that plan. It didn't matter what they thought. It was simply the only plan that didn't end with everyone in the building dead. He turned and ran for the stairwell, and heard their footsteps following right behind him.

When they were two levels down Travis slowed and pulled Paige aside on a landing. He let the crowd pass.

"I have to go back up to B4 and do something," he said. "We can't leave that level intact for Holt's people to find. They'll see Defense Control and realize that's where we would've watched the plane coming in. With that room still in place—and empty—they'll know there were survivors who made it out."

Paige's eyes narrowed as she took his point. "If Defense Control were destroyed . . . they'd think they got us all."

"They'd be sure of it. It wouldn't occur to them

that we left in Jeeps—that we even *had* Jeeps, forty miles from the nearest road. The charging station in the pole barn, all by itself, won't tip them off; it could be used for a hundred different kinds of equipment."

Paige nodded. Then fear crept into her expression. She looked upward, as if through the wall of the stairwell, toward B4.

"What are you planning to do?" she said.

"Nothing just yet. I'll need a few minutes to get it ready. Come up with the last of the crowd, and call out into B4 when everyone's above that level."

"Travis, what are you—"

"No time. I'll be fine. I'll be up top right behind you." Before she could say more, he continued. "I need you to do something too."

"I'm already on it," she said. "I'll do it and then help with the survivors."

"I know what you're planning," he said. "What I need is for you to *not* do it, if it looks too risky."

"I have to try—"

"No you don't. Not if it jeopardizes your life. If it's too dangerous, just skip it and go right to the wounded."

She started to protest, but he spoke over her again. "Promise."

A second passed. She looked frustrated—but understanding.

"I promise."

Then she was gone, down the stairs after the others.

Travis turned and sprinted up the flight they'd just come down.

* * *

He passed the hole the bunker buster had punched in the floor, and entered Defense Control, its workstations and its wall of screens dark and dead. He turned to the flat wall, with its row of giant, semiportable mainframe computers—eight in all.

They were on wheels. Big industrial swivel casters the diameter of salad plates, with brake levers that could be locked or unlocked by stepping on them. Travis saw to his relief that only the front casters of each mainframe had been locked. He ran along the row, slamming his heel down on each lever and freeing each wheel. When he'd finished he ran back to the first mainframe in the line, the one nearest the door. He got a hand on its back corner, braced the other against the wall, and pulled.

For a second the thing didn't budge. It had to weigh five hundred pounds. Then one of its casters pivoted and the whole unit lurched outward, exposing its power cord and data cable. Travis ripped both from their sockets, got hold of the mainframe once more and heaved it farther out. It protested again, clinging to its inertia even on the room's slanted floor, but once it'd traveled even a few inches, all four casters fell in line with its direction of travel. It rolled smoothly, gaining momentum as Travis pushed it toward the wide-open door.

He eased it into the hallway and slipped past it, positioning himself on its downhill side. For the moment the huge machine, its wheels still cocked sideways, held still where it'd come to rest. Travis, facing it, turned and looked over his shoulder at the hallway dipping sickeningly behind him. Forty feet away, the low point. The weak point.

How weak, exactly?

Travis doubted the sudden addition of five hundred pounds would make a difference.

Maybe four thousand would.

If it didn't, he and all the others would probably be dead within a few hours, hunted down and captured after Holt's people connected the dots here.

Travis stepped backward—down the slope—and pulled the mainframe gently toward him. The moment its wheels realigned, the thing came at him like a brawler. He dropped his shoulder against it and dug his shoes into the carpet and stopped it, then carefully walked it down the slope, one foot at a time. When he'd gone what he judged to be fifteen feet he stopped again, and keeping one heel braced on the floor, used the other to step on both caster brakes on the unit's lower end.

He let go of it.

It stayed put.

He looked at his phone. Three and a half minutes left before the deadline he'd imposed.

He stepped around the mainframe and sprinted back to the door into Defense Control.

Paige's first glance at the residence twisted her stomach. It'd been her home for over a decade. She'd shared it with Travis for more than a year now. The best year of her life, by an absurd margin, and almost everything that'd made it good had happened here on B16 in this little sanctuary.

Which had now been sliced in two.

She stood in the doorway for a moment, rocked by what lay beyond it. To her left was half of the living room. To her right was nothing at all. Just darkness and churning dust. The wall that'd held the LCD screen was gone, along with ten feet of floor space that'd extended from it. The couch was right on the brink, facing out into the void like some image out of a surreal magazine ad. Behind and to the couch's left was the short hall that led to the bedroom, just out of sight from where she stood.

She stepped out of the doorway, crossed the room to the hall, and stopped at the bedroom's threshold. The same ten feet had been lopped off here as in the living room. The bed was gone. The doorway to the closet was half gone—it'd perfectly straddled the cutoff. The closet itself lay mostly to one side, beyond the door, and had largely remained intact. Even from where she stood, Paige could see its back wall, and the built-in safe that now held the Tap.

She looked at the closet's doorway again, and focused on the floor that passed through it—what little was left. While half the doorway itself remained, there was hardly anything to stand on beneath it. A two-inch ledge at one side. To get beyond, to the intact closet floor, would require holding onto the trim at the doorway's remaining edge and swinging her body past it. Her center of gravity would be out over the emptiness during the bulk of that maneuver.

She moved forward across the room, slowing as she neared the closet's doorway and the edge. There was no telling how strong the floor might be along the drop-off—or here where she was standing, for that matter. The carpet hid any cracks that might've been visible in the concrete beneath her, but she assumed they were there; the wall was spiderwebbed with them, surrounding the closet doorway and leading away from it in all directions.

The doorway's trim was three feet from her outstretched hand now. She took another step. Leaned forward. Put her fingertips to the fluted wood and tested its strength by pushing outward on it, toward the chasm.

The cracked wall around the doorway disintegrated almost at a touch. The trim and three inches of concrete around it simply broke free and pitched out into the darkness and fell away.

Paige flinched and stumbled back, sprawling on her ass on the carpet. She stared at the ragged opening where the doorway had been.

She might still make it through into the closet. Where she'd planned to hold onto the trim, she could press the fractured wall between both hands and swing her body over the drop as planned.

Promise, Travis had said.

She stared at the opening and the wall safe ten feet beyond. Stared at the dust-filled abyss below.

From the levels above she heard the voices of the others, calling out and locating the injured.

She got to her feet, turned, crossed out of the bedroom, and sprinted for the corridor.

Travis pushed the last of the eight mainframes into the hallway and eased it into position with the others: they formed a single line extending down the slope, each butted up against the next, the whole mass held back by the first unit Travis had put in place. That one alone had its brakes on.

He watched the formation shudder and slip downward an inch as number eight settled into line.

Footsteps pounded past up the stairwell. Not the first he'd heard in the last minute. He looked at his phone again: thirty seconds left.

More footsteps, some running, some struggling. He turned toward the door and saw it draw open. Paige leaned through.

"Eleven survivors," she said. "All but two can walk." She frowned, her forehead creasing. "I couldn't get it."

"We'll be okay," Travis said.

Paige took in the mainframes for the first time. She saw the idea. Her eyes widened a little.

"Everyone's above us?" Travis said.

Paige nodded slowly, most of her attention on the computers.

Travis ran to the low end of the line. He studied the two brakes, then stepped forward and jammed his foot hard onto the pedal nearest the wall. As it released the wheel, the entire formation groaned and moved six inches, then halted again.

Travis looked up at Paige in the doorway.

"Do I need to say it?" she said.

"Run your ass off?" He managed a smile. "No."

Paige's own smile was very weak, no match for the fear beneath it.

Travis stomped on the last brake lever and yanked his foot away, coming within a tenth of a second of having it crushed by the caster. He turned and sprinted up the slope, while the array of mainframes bumped and skittered and picked up momentum going the other way. He'd expected them to gather speed quickly, but he saw within the first second that he'd underestimated *how* quickly. Before he'd covered half the distance to the Defense Control doorway, and maybe a quarter of the distance to Paige at the stairwell door, all of the huge units had lumbered past him, thundering down toward the low point faster than a person could run. The whole corridor vibrated with their passage. It seemed to shudder and, though Travis hoped he was imagining it, to tilt even more steeply toward the low point far behind him.

He passed the Defense Control doorway, covered the short distance to the hole in the floor and vaulted right over it. Ten feet from Paige now. Maybe three steps to go. He'd taken only one of them when her body went rigid and her eyes widened all the way, looking past him now instead of at him.

Two steps remained, but in that instant Travis knew there was no time for them. His leading foot touched down. He let the leg bend more than usual, let his weight drop squarely onto it. Then he launched upward and forward, his momentum carrying him airborne toward the doorway.

He was five feet from it when the floor dropped out from beneath him. It ruptured along a line six inches shy of the stairwell, the concrete giving way like it was piecrust. Travis felt air rushing backward around him, pulled down through the stair shaft by the collapsing mass of B4. Paige threw herself aside, out of his way, and he passed across the threshold and crashed down on the landing.

He stopped just short of toppling down the flight directly in front of him.

They missed the deadline by twenty seconds, but the Jeeps hadn't left without them. There were still a few survivors making their way up the last ten feet to the pole barn: the hardest ten feet, since the stairwell didn't go all the way to the surface. The final transit required a climb up the elevator shaft's inset ladder. Travis and another man helped the two who couldn't stand—they were at least able to grip the rungs.

"No satellites," Bethany said. She was standing in the barn when Travis emerged with the last survivor. "We're free and clear for the next hour and then some."

Travis nodded and passed the victim off to a man standing near Bethany, then stepped back onto the ladder and descended again to B2. He closed the shaft doors there, returned to the surface, swung out and closed those doors as well. The barn was empty now; the others had all gone to the Jeeps. Travis looked at the random equipment Bethany had piled and leaned around the charging station. The stuff looked like it'd been there for years. Perfect. He turned and ran out after the others.

They were twelve miles out when they saw the choppers: tiny black dots coming in low over the desert far to the east. They made straight for Border Town, which Travis could still see by the black smoke from the wrecked bomber. A minute later the choppers reached it, formed a stationary cluster, and descended.

Paige, Travis, and Bethany had a Jeep to themselves. The other Jeeps held three or four occupants each, the groupings based on country of origin. Bethany was already contacting the proper authorities within each government, sending them cell phone numbers for the survivors. Their respective intelligence agencies would need to get involved, and help them stay hidden until they could be extracted. Certainly no authorities here—local, state or federal—would be of help. Holt ultimately held sway over all of those.

The Jeeps would split up once they reached Casper. None would have the power to continue on to a different town, but within Casper itself the survivors would be safe enough, even on their own. No one would be looking for them, after all.

Travis already knew where he and Paige and Bethany would go, within the city. What they would do at that point was still undetermined, though he had a solid guess about it.

He looked at his phone.

9:20 A.M.

Ten hours and twenty-five minutes to the end of the road. Without the Tap in their arsenal, that span of time seemed agonizingly shortened, like the moment required for a guillotine to drop.

CHAPTER TWENTY-TWO

Five minutes after breaking formation with the other vehicles, Travis and Paige and Bethany were parked outside a bowling alley three hundred yards from Casper/Natrona County International Airport. While all Tangent personnel carried backup identities, Bethany's alter egos tended to be unusually wealthy. In the past, that'd come in handy for booking charter flights on short notice. It would work here too, once they knew where they were flying.

"I have three hits," Bethany said.

She leaned forward from the backseat. "Three people from outside California who made card charges in the town of Rum Lake while Peter was there—those few days in mid-December 1987."

"Only three out-of-state visitors in the whole town, those days?" Paige said.

"There were others. Most didn't fit Carrie's definition—powerful people. These three did: each at the time had a net worth of over twenty million."

Paige's eyebrows went up a little.

"That's nothing compared to what they ended

up with," Bethany said. "In time all three of them made it into the nine figures. Well into them. They were appropriately paranoid about their data security, too—those card charges they made in Rum Lake were on dummy accounts detached from their real names. I only saw through them because the encryption is so old; at the time no one would've pegged them. Very careful guys."

She ran through their bios quickly. The three men were Simon Parks, Keith Greene, and Allen Raines. All Americans, and all in their late thirties in 1987, when they'd presumably met with Peter in Rum Lake. Parks and Greene had both started their careers as corporate lawyers, one in New York and one in Houston. Then, in the late 1970s, each had begun to dabble in finance, making investments in tech firms and quickly working up to fronting serious venture capital. Each man had possessed an especially keen instinct for spotting winners, and spotting them early. By 1987 both were serious players who had ties not only to the tech sector but politics as well. The third man, Raines, had started out as a physicist with a promising academic career, but sometime around 1980 he'd changed course toward D.C. and become a respected scientific advisor to the powerful. Raines, like the other two, had made very smart investments in the eighties, compounding his sizable political income. But *unlike* the other two, he'd done more than just visit Rum Lake in December 1987.

He'd moved there.

Immediately.

The cash transfer with which he'd purchased

his home there was dated December 23 of that year, not even two weeks after the meeting that effectively ended the Scalar investigation. As far as Bethany could tell, that home had been his only residence from that point forward, even as his investments continued to snowball over the following years.

"Where in California *is* Rum Lake?" Paige said. "Is it a resort? The kind of place you might fall for at first sight and decide to move to?"

By her tone she didn't seem to have much faith in that theory; she was just exhausting a hypothetical.

"It's in the mountains off the Coast Highway," Bethany said, "about an hour north of San Francisco. I don't think it's any kind of resort. Definitely no skiing. Just a little town, about four thousand people, up in the redwoods."

"And Allen Raines still lives there?" Travis said.

"Until recently," Bethany said.

Travis turned in his seat and looked at her.

"All three of these names generated hits from news sites when I ran them," she said. "Parks in D.C., Greene in Boston, and Raines in Rum Lake—each in the past twelve hours. All three men died last night, at more or less the same time as President Garner."

The silence that followed felt like a physical thing. Like the oven wind that scoured the desert and the parking lot.

"There aren't a lot of details yet," Bethany said. "Just little capsule articles online. Parks was stabbed in the restroom of an upscale restaurant in Chicago, sometime just before nine, central time. With Greene it was some kind of carjacking near his home in Boston; his wife was killed too. Article says it happened shortly before ten, eastern time. Raines was a hit and run, right on Main Street in Rum Lake, at a quarter to seven in the evening, Pacific time. No one got a license-plate number off the vehicle." She glanced up from the computer. "All three of those times are within minutes of one another, and of the attack on the White House."

Another silence. Travis felt them all trying to line up the threads.

"These are just the three people we know about," Paige said. "There were probably more who met with my father in that town, but didn't use their credit cards while they were there. It's likely those people died last night too."

Travis shut his eyes and interlaced his fingers on top of his head. "From what Carrie told us," he said, "it sounds like when Peter met with these guys in 1987, he handed them the responsibility for Scalar. He must've known by then that it would take people that powerful to oversee the problem. Maybe he even knew what *we* know: that whoever's on the other side of the Breach has a presence established on this side already. A powerful presence, if they can control people like Holt. It makes sense that Peter recruited power players of his own. The meeting in Rum Lake was a changing of the guard." He was quiet a few seconds. "But I don't think that's *all* it was. I think there's a reason they met there, of all places. Maybe there was something there Peter needed to show them. I think Rum Lake is at the heart of everything. I think whatever Ruben Ward did in those three months before he killed himself, he did it there."

"It fits with the rest of it," Paige said. "The investigation sure as hell dialed in on that place at the end. My father was there three times before the meeting."

"We also know that whatever the solution was, it wasn't permanent," Bethany said. "Peter was afraid it could be undone in a single day, even years later. That would explain why Allen Raines stayed in town for good. Because someone had to—to keep an eye on whatever's there. To babysit it."

Paige gazed away toward the airport. The runways and the white sides of the terminal gleamed in the hard light.

"Without the Tap we're not going to get the cheat sheet," she said. "Not in Rum Lake or any of these places. If we could've gone back a year, or a week, or even a full day, sure. But in the present, forget about it. Holt's people will have raided the homes of everyone who died last night, looking for that document. They wouldn't even need to sneak around; they could go in with authority. He's the president."

Her expression darkened and she shook her head. Travis knew her anger was aimed inward. Knew she was replaying her failure to recover the Tap.

"There was nothing you could do," he said.

If it helped her to hear that, she didn't show it.

"Look at the bright side," Bethany said. "They tried to kill us."

Both Travis and Paige turned to her.

"Think about it," Bethany said. "They took out all these guys last night because they needed them out of the way—because if they'd lived, they might've stopped whatever's unrolling right now. Holt's decision to bomb Border Town is no different: he or whoever's calling the shots had some reason to fear us. They set the trap at Carrie's place to verify that Tangent didn't know anything, but when you got away and took her with you, it was their worst-case scenario. They knew Tangent *would* know something after that. At least as much as Carrie knew. Which wasn't everything, but apparently it was enough to spook them." She paused. "They knew we didn't have the cheat sheet, but they came after us anyway. That implies we're a genuine threat to them. That there's some Achilles' heel we could find, even without the help of that report." She looked back and forth from Travis to Paige. "We should be encouraged by that. If they consider us a threat, then we are one."

"If there's an Achilles' heel, it's at Rum Lake," Travis said.

"And they'll be protecting it with everything they've got," Paige said, "even if they've eliminated all the threats they're aware of. Today of all days, they'd err on the side of caution." She looked at Bethany. "Can you try to get satellite coverage of that town?"

Bethany nodded and got working on it, but didn't look hopeful. Travis recalled something she'd told him once about the likelihood of a place being visually covered. Spy satellites orbited pretty low, and their paths were set up to maximize the time they spent over places of interest. War zones, terrorist-friendly areas, sites of possible weapons programs. Other places in the world *might* end up having consistent coverage, but only if they happened to line up with one of those chosen regions. In most places and at most times, like Border Town in the past hour, it was more miss than hit. The globe was very big, and satellite tracks were very narrow.

A minute and a half later Bethany frowned. "One pass over Rum Lake, just under ninety minutes from now. I should be able to tap into it. We'll get about sixty seconds of visual. That's the only one to go over between now and the deadline tonight."

"Ninety minutes isn't bad," Paige said. "Flight time to Northern California's two hours anyway." She nodded at the airport. "Let's go."

CHAPTER TWENTY-THREE

Travis and Paige sat at a wall of windows overlooking the desert while Bethany spoke to a lone ticket clerk thirty feet away. Except for the four of them, the private terminal was empty.

Travis spoke quietly: "There's something about the Baltimore memory I didn't tell you."

He relayed what Ruben Ward had said in the alley, word for word. When he'd finished, he watched Paige process it. Her eyes tracked over the desert, or maybe just the glass three feet in front of her.

"Filter," she said. "What could it be? Something the Breach itself does? Something that triggers a change in a person, like the Breach Voices?"

"I wondered the same thing," Travis said. "It's all I can come up with, based on what little he said."

Paige repeated Ward's last line in a whisper: "*Whoever it affects, it's not their fault. Not really. Under the wrong conditions, anyone could end up the worst person on Earth.*" She looked at Travis. "You think it's going to be you. You think the filter is . . . *it.*"

Travis stared at a dry weed growing against the base of the window. The breeze batted it endlessly into the glass.

"I can't imagine it's not," Travis said.

Paige was quiet a long time. Then she said, "Maybe it won't happen at all now. The timeline we're in is so different from the other one—the one you and I sent our messages back from. Everything's changed. Tangent doesn't even exist anymore, in this version of events. Maybe whatever was coming has already been cancelled out."

"The Whisper gave me the impression it was inevitable—and the Whisper tended to be right about things."

For a moment neither said anything more. They stared at the empty horizon. Behind them, Bethany was reciting a string of numbers: some kind of financial information related to her alternate identity.

"The instruction that came back from your future self," Travis said. He looked at Paige before continuing. "Do you ever wonder if you should've followed it?"

She turned to face him, and when she replied her tone left no ambiguity. "Never."

Travis saw hurt in her expression. She hated that he'd asked the question—probably hated that he'd even had it rattling around in his head.

"That part we *do* know something about," she said. "We know the disagreement between us—in that future—comes from a misunderstanding. Whatever it is that you do, I interpret it the wrong way. I react on limited information—*withheld* information, from the sound of it. Something you're not able to tell me, at the time."

"That's the part I understand least," Travis said. "Something that important, you're the first person I'd talk to. You might be the *only* person I'd talk to."

He'd kept only one thing from her before: the note from her future self. Its arrival had caught him like a sucker punch, and he'd had only seconds to decide whether to show it to her or not. In that moment he'd simply panicked, but in time he'd told her everything; there wasn't a single secret between them now.

"I really can't get there," he said. "Keeping you in the dark about anything at all—I can't imagine it."

He left his next thought unspoken: that unimaginable wasn't the same thing as impossible.

They chartered a flight to Petaluma, California. Half an hour after wheels-up Travis felt himself begin to nod off. He realized he hadn't slept all night—the sleep he'd gotten in 1978 didn't count, as far as his body was concerned. He reclined his seat and shut his eyes and slipped almost at once into a dream. A strange one: Richard Garner was there with him, tied upright to a dolly—like Hannibal Lecter but without the face mask. President Holt was there, too, standing near an old man who looked like Wilford Brimley. Maybe it *was* Wilford Brimley. The room was small and had no windows. It spun and undulated, calling to mind acid trips Travis had taken in high school. George Washington, in a portrait on the wall, kept pursing his lips and narrowing his eyes, as if he were right on the fence between sharing and keeping some critical secret. The Wilford stand-in was repeating a line from a golden oldie, asking Travis what was behind the green door. But there was no green door in the dream. Just that drug-warped little room, beneath which Travis could hear the drone of jet engines. "We already know the combo," the lookalike said. "Four-eight-eight-five-four. Save a world of trouble and tell us now. What's behind it?" There was pain then. Serious pain. Throbbing in Travis's left forearm. He noticed an empty syringe on a little tray along the wall. He also noticed, now that he was looking around, that he himself was tied upright to a dolly. The pain in his arm surged upward toward his heart, and when it reached it, it bloomed to every part of his body. It felt the worst in his head. He shut his eyes tight. "Now listen to me carefully," the old man said in his ear, and his voice at that range made the headache step up tenfold.

Travis startled awake. Paige and Bethany glanced at him. He shook off the remnants of the dream, though he could still hear the steady droning—the business jet's turbines, running smooth in the high desert air.

Bethany had the tablet computer on her lap. "It's almost time," she said. She held the computer out so that all three of them could see it. At the moment it showed only a dark blue field of view. Travis realized after a few seconds that it was the ocean, slowly drifting through the frame.

"The satellite's camera covers an area much

wider than Rum Lake, obviously," Bethany said, "but this program lets you designate a specific patch of land, and it automatically enlarges that part of the image and tracks it for the whole time it's in range. Should happen pretty soon."

For another five seconds there was only blue water on the screen. Then, at the right edge, the coastline of Northern California appeared. It crept in at a few pixels per second. Travis guessed he was seeing ten or fifteen miles of shoreline from the top of the screen to the bottom. It was hard to make out much detail. Roads were impossible to resolve. Mostly what he could see were forests and mountains and lakes. And clouds—lots of clouds. He wondered if they'd block the view of the town.

"Don't worry about the weather," Bethany said. "The satellite can see in both visual and thermal— it'll look right through the cloud cover. I also set up a roadmap overlay to help us make sense of the imagery."

For a while longer the picture on her screen remained in its wide-angle perspective. The land continued pressing in from the right, the coast now a couple miles into the frame.

Then a little white box drew itself at the edge, defining a square maybe two miles by two, and an instant later it expanded, the land within it filling the entire program window. The view was almost entirely obscured by cloud. For a second that was it: just gray haze and a few inches of forest visible at the top of the screen. Then the thermal and roadmap layers appeared, and the image took on meaning at once.

At the westernmost edge was a major road, probably the Coast Highway. A narrower lane extended from it and wandered along what Travis guessed was a mountain valley: it skipped back and forth through switchbacks and then straightened in the last quarter mile before the town. It was the only road in and out of Rum Lake.

The town itself was more or less an elongated grid. It had a half-mile main drag running west to east, with six or seven cross streets branching off. At their southern ends the cross streets bent and arced around what must've been hills or depressions. At their northern ends they tied into a long, curved lane that hugged the lake—Rum Lake, cool blue in the thermal image and about twice the size of the town that shared its name.

Running vehicles stood out clearly: bright white rectangles against the gray background. A few moved along the streets here and there, but Travis ignored them—his attention went immediately to two places where multiple vehicles were clumped together, stationary. The first was along the valley road, just shy of town. Four were parked there, glowing not from engine heat but from bodies seated inside them. Two vehicles on each side of the road, angled at forty-five degrees. Big, boxy shapes, unusually wide.

"Humvees," Travis said.

Paige nodded.

The second cluster was on the opposite side of town, near a house all by itself on the outskirts. Six more Humvees, these ones neither running nor occupied. They stood out only because of the greenhouse heating of their closed cabs, the effect minimized by the haze that filtered the sunlight.

The vehicles' former occupants were moving like busy ants in and out of the residence.

"Probably private security contractors," Paige said, "not soldiers. Maybe the same kind they used against us in Ouray."

Bethany double-tapped the formation near the house, and the view centered and tightened on it dramatically.

"That's gotta be Allen Raines's place," she said.

She minimized the satellite frame, opened a browser and clicked on Google Maps. Within seconds she'd isolated and zoomed on Rum Lake, and then she typed an address into the search field. The hourglass flickered. A red thumbtack appeared. Same house the Humvees were parked at. Bethany was reaching to open the satellite window again when Travis grabbed her wrist, the move startling her.

"Look," he said.

He pointed with his other hand to the center of town. In the past half second, little icons and labels had popped up along Main Street, identifying certain businesses. Both Paige and Bethany inhaled audibly when they saw the one Travis had indicated:

Its symbol was made up of a tiny fork and a knife, and its label read, THIRD NOTCH BAR & GRILLE.

CHAPTER TWENTY-FOUR

They rented a Chevy Tahoe in Petaluma and were on the Coast Highway by eleven on Travis's phone—adjusted now to Pacific time. Seven hours and forty-five minutes left to work with.

Travis drove. The ocean lay to the left, at times obscured by trees but mostly wide open and endless and blue.

"The name of a restaurant in Northern California," Paige said, "contained in a message transmitted through the Breach." Her eyes registered the same vague bafflement all three of them had shared since seeing the labeled icon.

In one sense Travis found it plausible: if the instructions could send Ruben Ward to a specific town, then why not a specific location within that town? But for the most part it threw him. It was, in its way, the strangest detail they'd encountered so far. The exactness of it felt absurd. Ward had been directed to travel across the continent and find a passageway beneath a place that served burgers and chicken wings and beer.

Bethany had already verified that the restaurant

had been there in 1978. It dated to the late fifties and had never changed its name. As far as she'd been able to tell, the place hadn't shown up in any headlines during the summer in question. It'd been business as usual then, and ever since.

Far north along the coast, low clouds crept inland from the sea, pressing and writhing through gaps in the mountains. The same clouds they'd seen from orbit.

"There's something that's bothered me since that first phone call last night," Travis said. "The first thing we knew about the Scalar investigation: its cost. Hundreds of millions of dollars. No matter how I look at it, I can't get it to make sense."

"I've been wondering about that too," Bethany said. "The amount is ludicrous. Even if they were accessing the hardest-to-use databases at that time—the kind where paid workers did the searching instead of computers—or running satellite surveillance every day of the week, it wouldn't come to that cost. Not even close. Throw in the use of FBI agents to check out certain leads, compensate the Bureau for their time, you still don't even get into the ballpark."

"The funny thing is," Travis said, "neither we nor Carrie ever actually knew they used any of that stuff. Satellites, federal agents, any of it. We just made those assumptions based on the huge price tag—*something* had to cost that much. But none of those resources make sense, when you think about it. Satellites to investigate a guy who'd been dead for three years? Database searches? Ward wasn't leaving a paper trail—he walked out of that hospital without a single piece of ID. No credit card, no checkbook; he wasn't even wearing his own clothes. I don't see how you'd track him three *days* later, much less three years. It'd be like reconstructing the itinerary of a bum."

"Strange," Paige said. "With all the other questions rattling around, we never asked the most obvious one: How did the Scalar investigation work at all? How could they have pieced together *any* of Ward's moves?"

"We know they really spent hundreds of millions," Bethany said. "Whatever they spent it on, it apparently worked."

They said no more about it, but the question stayed with Travis as he drove.

They'd figured out their approach even before landing. The single road up to Rum Lake was obviously no good, but there were others that passed within half a mile of the town, through neighboring valleys separated from it by low, forested ridges. The nearest was called Veil Road, and in the satellite frame they'd seen that it was clear of checkpoints.

They slid under the low clouds just before the turnoff, and saw at once where the road had gotten its name. A two-way blacktop, it rose in steep pitches and bends along the valley's ascending length, climbing right into the cloudbank within the first mile. Travis saw the clouds now for what they were: a marine fog layer that nourished the flora of this place—most notably the redwoods, which flanked the road like thirty-story high-rises.

They pulled off where the map showed the ridgeline to be at its narrowest, and headed up the slope on foot.

They dropped out of the clouds twenty minutes later on the other side, and through the trees they saw the town, crisp and clear beneath its overcast lid. Well-kept storefronts with brick facades lined Main Street, probably dating back a century or more. Cottages and log cabins comprised the rest of the place, its southern half pitched upward on an incline against the foothills where the three of them now stood, its northern half ranged down to the lakefront. The town was a natural amphitheater with the lake for its stage; there couldn't be a single building in it that lacked a million-dollar view.

The outline of streets perfectly matched Travis's memory of the roadmap overlay. He picked out Allen Raines's house, high on the northeast fringe of the basin, maybe a third of the way around the lake. It stood just below the fog, eye-level with their own position. The six Humvees were still there, their occupants still moving in and out of the place. No doubt they were gutting the home's interior right to the studs, tearing out insulation batts, ripping up the carpeting and the subflooring. A single sheet of paper could hide in a lot of places. Now that he thought about it, Travis supposed it'd been stored in the most inaccessible place of all: its owner's head. Raines had probably memorized the thing twenty-five years ago and destroyed it.

Travis lowered his eyes to the center of town and picked out the Third Notch. It had a two-story facade, green-painted wood with white trim, all of it getting on in years but well maintained. There were no Humvees parked around it. No contractors on foot, either. Through the big front windows Travis could see a few tables and booths, but all appeared to be empty. There was someone in an apron moving about, not doing a whole lot.

"Place looks a little dead," Paige said.

"The restaurant?" Travis said.

She shook her head. "The whole town."

Now that he looked for it, Travis saw what she meant. Rum Lake wasn't deserted by any means, but it seemed to be at a near standstill. No kids out on bikes. No one walking dogs or just taking a stroll. A Jeep Cherokee with luggage tied to its racks pulled out of a driveway, rolled two blocks to Main and swung west. A moment later it'd crossed the outskirts and headed down the valley road toward the coast. Paige pointed out another house: its owners were hauling suitcases and bags out and stuffing them into a sedan's trunk.

"They know something's going on," Travis said.

"Let's find out what it is," Bethany said.

They walked into the Third Notch ten minutes later. The person with the apron turned out to be a woman in her forties. Her name tag read JEAN-NIE. She was visibly stressed, which might've made sense if the place had been bustling and understaffed. But it wasn't. It was empty except for Jeannie and two kids—a boy and a girl, maybe six and ten respectively, clearly hers. The two of them were playing handheld video games at one of the tables and looked thoroughly bored.

Jeannie was on a cell phone when they walked in. She gave them a small wave and made a face: *right with you*. Into the phone she said, "Well we're waiting. Get everything locked up and come and get us." She hung up without saying good-bye, and turned to the three of them. "Kitchen staff's gone home. I have pizza slices I can warm up, and drinks."

Travis considered his reply. The approach he had in mind wouldn't work well if he jumped right into it.

"Diet Coke or Diet Pepsi," he said. "Either one's fine."

Paige and Bethany both asked for the same. Jeannie stepped into the back room, and the three of them sat at the bar. Travis saw a stack of menus to his left. The cover showed a Paul Bunyan type character wearing a huge belt with three notches carved into it. Travis couldn't imagine being any less interested in hearing a backstory.

Jeannie returned with the drinks and the check, set them down and got to work squaring things away around the register. Her movements were hurried, anxious.

"I heard of this place a while back," Travis said.

Jeannie didn't look up from her work. "Yeah?"

"Guy I used to know told me I should stop by, if I was ever in the area."

Jeannie said nothing.

Outside, the sedan with the stuffed trunk went past.

"He said he left something of mine in the basement," Travis continued. "Said someone here would know what I was talking about."

At last Jeannie glanced up at him.

Travis studied her face for any sign of suspicion. Any hint that she understood the significance of this place's basement, and that a stranger requesting access to it was probably tied to that significance in some way.

But all she did was knit her eyebrows together. "I think it's pretty empty down there," she said. "How long ago was this?"

"Few years," Travis said.

Jeannie shrugged, thought about it another second and then went back to her straightening, as if that concluded the discussion.

"Can I take a look anyway?" Travis said.

She seemed amused at the request, for some reason. She shrugged again and said, "Knock yourself out," then reached under the bar out of sight. Travis heard a coffee can slide on wood, and objects clinking against one another. After a moment Jeannie brought out two keys, each on its own ring. The rings had plastic tabs attached to them, labeled simply *#1* and *#2*. She pushed them across to Travis. "Entrance is outside, around the back."

With that she returned to the register and ignored them.

Travis traded looks with Paige and Bethany, and then the three of them stood, leaving their drinks. They were almost to the door when Travis stopped and turned back toward Jeannie.

"You ever heard of a man named Ruben Ward?" he said.

She met his gaze.

Travis had seen lots of people play dumb before. They almost always overdid it. Their faces scrunched up. They registered too much confusion. Really, *any* confusion was too much; it wasn't confusing to simply hear an unfamiliar name.

Jeannie didn't look confused. She looked puzzled, which was stranger yet. Travis got the impression that she knew nothing about Ward, but that she'd heard the name. Maybe recently.

After a moment she shook her head. "Can't help you."

Travis considered pressing her on the subject, but held back. He turned and led the others out.

They were halfway along the building's left side, moving down an alley floored with cracked pavement and a few lonely tufts of grass, when it happened.

It started as a sound—or what seemed like a sound. Maybe the frenetic hum of an electrical transformer about to fail, or the snapping, static-like buzz you sometimes heard over a field of grasshoppers on a dry summer day. It rose over the span of a second, seemingly from a source very close to Travis—behind him, he thought at first. He spun to look for it but saw nothing there, and noticed as he moved that the sound's direction didn't change at all. It *had no* direction. It was just everywhere, as if he were hearing it through a set of headphones. He saw Paige and Bethany reacting the same way. They were hearing it too. They looked at him and each other, their eyes narrowing in concern—and then widening.

Because they'd just realized the same thing Travis had.

That it wasn't a sound, exactly. It wasn't anything they were picking up with their ears. It was *closer* than that, somehow—already inside their heads.

It was a thought.

They were hearing it the way they heard their own internal monologue.

All three of them came to a stop, facing one another. None of them spoke. Second by second the sensation intensified, its apparent volume and clarity mounting. Travis felt it becoming almost a physical presence, its insectile quality growing sharper. It felt like bugs swarming inside his skull. The effect began to push him toward nausea. He saw it doing the same to Paige and Bethany. Saw them taking careful breaths to keep their stomachs under control.

And then it was over. The sound was gone as if someone had thrown a switch, and there was only the hush of the town again.

The three of them stood there for a long moment, still not speaking. Just breathing, getting their bearings.

"What the hell's happening in this place?" Bethany said. It came out as hardly more than a whisper.

Travis thought of the sea withdrawing before the arrival of a tsunami. Of people's hair standing on end before a lightning strike. Of the supposed panicked behavior of animals in the hours before a major earthquake.

"No idea," he said, his own voice quieter than he'd intended. He nodded to the back of the building. "Come on."

CHAPTER TWENTY-FIVE

A passageway beneath the Third Notch.

They didn't even have to enter the basement to see it. It was there in plain view to any stray dog that wandered through the rear lot. Centered on the back wall, one story below the main level, was the arched entry to a corridor beneath the building. A set of concrete stairs descended to it, hugging the cinderblock foundation. A stamped metal sign was bolted to the bricks just shy of the opening:

> **720 Main St.**
> **Apt. 1**
> **Apt. 2**

An orange security light glowed softly, somewhere in the gloom beyond the arch. The floor down there was more concrete, probably from the same pour that'd laid the stairs.

Travis understood Jeannie's amusement now. He also knew what they would find beneath the restaurant.

* * *

Nothing.

Both apartments were long deserted. They'd probably been declared illegal for residential use: each had only a tiny window, tucked up near the ceiling, all but impossible to crawl out through during an emergency.

Each unit's layout was a mirror image of the other: kitchen and bathroom on one end, balanced by undefined space that served as living, dining, and sleeping quarters. Like a slightly oversized hotel room minus carpeting and a view. Both apartments were empty. Not even boxes of random junk had accumulated—just a few cracked laundry baskets in unit two, nested together and forgotten in a corner.

There was nothing else that could've been called a passageway. No hidden tunnel behind either derelict refrigerator—they checked. No mirror on any wall that could swing out on concealed hinges. The corridor itself was the only thing the notebook could've been referring to.

"*A passageway beneath the third notch*," Bethany said. "And the next sentence started with *Look for.*" She thought about it. "Look for one of these apartments? It wouldn't make sense to word it like that. You don't have to *look* very hard to find these doors, once you're in the hallway."

"Look for John Doe in Apartment One," Travis said. That sounded better. He couldn't think of anything else that sounded right at all. "Maybe Ward met someone here. Was *instructed* to meet someone here—someone who lived in one of these units back then."

Before he could say more they heard Jeannie's voice through the ceiling straight above them, yelling at someone. They were standing in the second apartment, roughly beneath the seats they'd taken at the bar. Travis couldn't quite make out Jeannie's words, but her angry tone was clear enough. It went quiet for three seconds, then started again. There'd been no one else speaking in between. She was on the phone—probably with whoever she'd talked to earlier, reiterating her demand: *get your ass over here and get us out of this town*. Her second spiel ended on a note of finality. Silence followed.

Paige turned to Travis. "Who could they have told Ward to meet here?" Her lower eyelids edged upward. "One of *their own*?"

Travis weighed the idea. He turned and studied the dark recesses of the apartment. It didn't exactly fit the image that'd come to him earlier: the sprawling penthouses above the nerve centers of the world. But that'd been a snap impression at best. A guess based on nothing at all, because they *knew* nothing at all about who they were up against. Power took other forms, he knew. Like anonymity.

He turned to Bethany. "Can you check records for who lived here in 1978?"

She winced. "I can try. Tax records might turn up something—assuming whoever lived here even filed."

"Maybe there's paperwork on old tenants upstairs," Paige said. "I think our approach needs to lose its subtlety."

They pushed back in through the front door and Travis asked about the paperwork.

Jeannie stared at him. The anger she'd put into the phone call was still on her face.

Then she said, "I didn't think you'd stick with the 'good cop' thing much longer."

"Excuse me?" Travis said.

The two kids were watching now, their video games forgotten.

"In back, both of you," Jeannie said.

The kids complied, disappearing into the kitchen.

"Ma'am," Travis said, "whatever you think—"

"That's the idea, right?" Jeannie said. "All morning we get the bad cops—all these hard-asses in their Humvees scaring the shit out of everyone who catches a look at them. Coming into all the shops and grilling us about Ruben Ward, Allen Raines— What do we remember? What have we seen?"

"Raines," Travis said. He'd always intended to ask her about the man, but only after checking the basement. It would've been one thing too many to stuff into the first conversation.

"Yeah, I knew him," Jeannie said. "Everyone knows everyone here. *You people*, we *don't* know, which is why we're not talking to you about him. And putting on street clothes and acting casual isn't going to change that."

"We're not with the others," Travis said. "We came over the ridge on foot to avoid them."

She didn't buy it.

"Get out," she said. "And if your friends are supposed to be fixing whatever's wrong inside that mine, tell them to stop screwing around and do it."

"Mine?" Paige said. She looked at Travis, then Bethany. Each shared her bafflement.

For the first time since they'd come back in, Jeannie's anger slipped. She glanced from one of them to the next, reading their reactions.

Travis advanced and rested his hands on the back of the stool he'd sat on earlier. He met Jeannie's eyes and didn't blink.

"We're not playing good cop," he said. "Please listen to me. What's happening around here is only the ramp-up to what's really coming. Do you remember what time Allen Raines was killed last night?"

She thought for a second. "About a quarter to seven."

"And what time was President Garner killed?"

She started to answer, then cut herself off, thinking about the correlation.

"This is not just something that's happening in Rum Lake," Travis said. "The problem is a lot bigger than that, and as far as we know, everyone who's supposed to be stopping it is dead. Please—anything you can tell us will help. Start with the mine."

For a while Jeannie didn't reply. Maybe she was considering where to begin. Maybe she was debating whether to begin at all.

Travis saw movement at the edge of his vision. The two kids had come to the kitchen doorway, watching with wide eyes. The girl kept her little brother behind her, as if to protect him.

Jeannie exhaled deeply. "It's probably been shut down for most of a century. I don't know anyone who remembers it being open. I moved here in the nineties, a few years after everything happened up there. I only know about it through the stories I've heard, but I've always believed them. They've never changed over time, the way stories do when they're made up."

"Tell them about the ghost," the little girl said.

Jeannie waved her off.

"You told us it was real," the girl said. "You said you and Dad heard it talk."

Jeannie looked annoyed at the girl's insistence, maybe a little embarrassed. But there was something else in her expression, Travis saw. Some inability to refute what the kid had said, because no doubt Jeannie really had told her children those things.

"I don't know what's up there," she said at last, keeping her focus on Travis and Paige and Bethany. "There's . . . something." She was silent a bit longer, then just shook her head. "The stories all go like this: the mine was nothing special until 1987—kids might go up there to drink or make out, but nothing strange ever happened. Then, that year, the government came in and fenced it all off. The nearest shaft entrance is actually on Forest Service land, outside the town limits." She nodded out the front windows. "You probably saw the house up at the treeline with all the Humvees in front."

"Raines's house," Travis said.

She nodded. "His property butts up against federal land. The mine access is two hundred yards straight uphill from that house, deep in the woods. They say the government took over the site and . . . did something up there. Built something, maybe. Down inside the shaft."

Travis looked at Paige. He saw her processing the information and drawing the same conclusion as he was: Jeannie had it wrong. The stories had it wrong. The government—working with Tangent—had only *found* something in the mine shaft. The Scalar investigation's long search for answers had led to this town in the end, and in turn had led to the mine. Whatever was in there, Ruben Ward had created it. Maybe with help.

"They say most of the government's comings and goings were at a different entrance," Jeannie said, "over the ridge to the north. That opening is a lot lower down, accessible by old logging roads. I guess some teenagers from here in town got pretty close to it a few times, when everything was going on. Close enough to overhear workers talking about what was in the mine." A shiver seemed to pass through her. She shook it off. "The workers called it the Stargazer. They were scared of it. They hated being down inside with it, whatever it was—whatever it *is*. They said it had to be kept under control, but they were still working out how to do that. And then Mr. Raines bought that house up on the slope—he paid twice what it was worth to speed up the deal. He moved in, and around that time all the government activity just went away. It was pretty clear Raines was involved somehow. I don't think anyone trusted him, at first. But after a while something became obvious: the man never left this town. And I mean never. I've seen that for myself, living here almost twenty years now. In all that time, Raines never took so much as a drive down to the ocean, three miles away. He'd come down to Main Street for groceries, or to have a sandwich in here. Then right back up to that house. The way people eventually saw it, he was the one keeping the Stargazer under control, whatever the hell that entailed. He got stuck with that job, and he did it. He kept us safe from it, all those years. And if we weren't sure of it before, we are now. It was about six hours after he died that we got the first . . . hum."

Travis had been staring down into the bar. Now he looked up. "Like the one five minutes ago. Feels like bugs in your head."

Jeannie nodded. "Second one was about four hours after the first, then less than two hours, and they've been coming faster and faster ever since."

No wonder the town was emptying out. Twenty-five years of these stories, and now physical evidence that they weren't bullshit. That there really *was* something bad up in the mine.

Travis considered the word: *Stargazer.* A uniquely strange name for something that was deep underground.

Much of what they'd learned was strange—both here and before they'd arrived in Rum Lake. There were giant gaps in the puzzle, and Travis couldn't picture what would fill them. The Stargazer itself was one: it had to have been in that mine since the summer of 1978, some nine years before the Scalar investigators found it, but in all that time it must've been effectively dormant. If it'd been generating these hums back then, this place would've become a ghost town. Yet when Allen Raines had taken watch over the thing, he'd had to stay on top of it day and night, right from the beginning. Those two facts were hard to reconcile. As was a third: even if he and Paige and Bethany could reach the Stargazer, it was unlikely they could do much more than Raines had. Which was to keep the thing in check, assuming they'd see how that was done. But what sort of Achilles' heel was that? If all they could do was babysit the thing, how long could they stay on it before someone interfered with them? Like these guys in the Humvees. A few hours, at best?

He knew he was thinking in circles, and that doing so wouldn't help until they'd seen the Stargazer for themselves. For better or worse, they'd have the whole picture then. He drew hope only from what Bethany had said back in Casper: *If they consider us a threat, then we are.*

The little girl stepped out of the doorway and tugged on Jeannie's arm.

"The ghost," the girl said. "Tell them."

Jeannie's forehead furrowed. She seemed stretched between frustration and sober gravity, as if she believed the story herself but would never expect others to.

"Try us," Travis said.

Jeannie frowned and let out a long breath, giving in. "They say it always happens around the two entrances to the mine. They say anyone who goes near starts to hear voices, whispering right behind them in the trees. Pine boughs around you start to move like the wind's blowing, even when it isn't. My husband and I . . . we like to think now we might've imagined what we heard. The wind really *was* blowing that day. Maybe that's all it was. I don't know."

Travis tried to picture the mine entrance relative to Raines's place, on the satellite image they'd seen. The moment he did, something occurred to him. He turned to Bethany.

"That satellite was looking almost straight down, right?"

She nodded. "*Perfectly* straight down. Default angle unless you command it to do otherwise."

"From that perspective," Travis said, "even redwoods would have lots of gaps between them. Plenty of open ground visible in the image."

Bethany shrugged. "I guess. Probably quite a bit."

"We didn't see any heat signature uphill from Raines's house," Travis said. "No bodies moving through those woods. Not even one." He thought about it a second longer. "I don't think these guys are going near the mine shaft."

"I'm *certain* they're not," Jeannie said. "I've been watching all morning, waiting for them to head up into the trees and get in there—get working on the problem. I've assumed that's what they were sent here to do. But all they're focused on so far is that house. In and out, hours on end now."

The more Travis considered it, the more that made sense, and not because of any strange phenomenon that could be mistaken for a ghost. Simple priorities were enough: these men had been sent to find and destroy the cheat sheet, and failing that, they would at least prevent anyone else from getting into that house and obtaining it—if it still existed at all. And while those who'd sent them probably wanted some muscle close at hand to protect the mine if the need arose, Travis wasn't surprised these guys were staying back. *Being kept back*, more likely, by strict orders. They were almost certainly nothing more than hired guns; why let them sniff around the mine at all? Whatever the Stargazer was doing in there, it was doing without anybody's help. All it needed was for Allen Raines to stay dead, and none of his powerful friends to show up in his place.

"Two hundred yards isn't much," Travis said, "even with tree cover. But maybe it's enough. Maybe we can get in there from the uphill side without them seeing us."

The sound of a loud engine faded in. A second later an old pickup went by, heading out of town, its bed loaded with boxes and bags.

Travis put aside the mine for the moment, his thoughts going back to earlier questions. He turned to Jeannie. "What about the man I mentioned before? Ruben Ward."

"I never heard that name until today," Jeannie said, "when the others came in and asked about it."

"And none of these old stories talk about the summer of 1978?" Paige said.

Jeannie shook her head.

"*Do* you have paperwork for who lived here back then?" Travis said. "I know it's a long shot—"

"It's possible," Jeannie said. "There are old file boxes in the office—"

She stopped and cocked her head.

Travis listened too, and heard another engine rumbling. Another loud one, though it sounded different from the truck. Jeannie appeared to recognize its tone.

"Shit," she whispered. "I only meant to complain."

"What are you talking about?" Travis said.

"When you went downstairs I called the number they gave me earlier. I yelled at them for sending in the good cops."

The engine grew louder, drawing very near now. Its growl spoke more of power than age. A second later it cut out and brakes whined, somewhere just out of view past the edge of the glass front wall.

"That's one of the Humvees," Jeannie said. "They know you're here."

CHAPTER TWENTY-SIX

Storage room, back right," Jeannie said. Her hand shot out toward the corner of the building opposite where the Humvee had stopped. "No screen in the window."

Paige and Bethany were already moving. Travis took a step after them, then pulled up short. He looked at Jeannie and the two kids.

Jeannie shook her head. "We're fine if you're gone. You left three minutes ago."

Travis nodded, spun and ran after the others. He'd almost cleared the room when Jeannie called after him. He stopped again and faced her.

"Cell phone number," she said. "I'll find the old paperwork."

From outside came footsteps and men's voices.

Travis said the number aloud once. Didn't wait to see if she'd caught it all. He sprinted for the back room, and in the same second that he slipped into it, he heard the front door open.

Paige already had the window up: an old single-pane affair with about ten layers of paint on its frame. It was on the side wall, leading out to the back stretch of the alley they'd walked down earlier. Bethany slipped through; the alley's pavement was only a couple feet lower than the floor. Travis motioned for Paige to go ahead of him, and took hold of the raised sash as she let go of it. He went through after her, got his feet on the concrete and stood upright, his hand still holding the sash in place.

He considered just leaving it up—an open window in a back room shouldn't stand out as unusual, if any of the men from the Humvee came to check this part of the building. Travis relaxed his hand on the bottom of the sash.

It immediately slipped downward a quarter inch, its sides lightly shuddering against the frame. If he let go entirely it might stay where it was, or it might hold for five seconds and then drop, making all the sound in the world as it went.

He heard Jeannie's voice, through the doorway and down the hall. "Is 'Go to hell' too subtle for you people to grasp?"

A man replied, his tone coming from a deep, broad chest cavity. "Where are they?"

"Probably bullshitting the shop owner next door. They're *your* people, why don't you call them?"

No reply. Just boots thudding around on the ancient wood floor.

Travis leaned back inside and looked around for something with which to brace the window.

There was nothing.

He'd have to shut it, and not quickly—he couldn't trust it to stay quiet at any real speed. There were long vertical abrasions where it'd rubbed against its frame over the decades, probably on humid days when the wood had expanded. Days like this one.

He began to ease it downward, making about an inch per second.

"You saw which way they went?" the deep voice said, still somewhere up front by the bar.

There was no audible reply. Travis pictured Jeannie just pointing, too pissed to speak. She would send them along Main Street back in the direction of their Humvee, to keep them from walking past this alley.

He had the window half shut now. Twelve inches left.

Paige and Bethany were right beside him, watching the progress with gritted teeth.

Nine inches. Eight.

"Sorry to bother you when you're this busy," the deep voice said. The boots clumped away toward the front door.

Six inches.

Then a bird started screaming, somewhere above Travis. He looked up sharply at the sound.

A blue jay. Right on the cornice ten feet overhead. It scolded in loud, double squawks. It probably had a nest up there. The cries went on for four seconds and then the bird flitted out of sight onto the roof.

Silence followed, outside and inside. The boot steps toward the front door had halted.

Then they began again—thumping quickly over the hardwood toward the back room.

"Shit," Travis whispered.

He lowered the window the last six inches in the next second, risking the sound. It made none.

Paige and Bethany had already covered the distance to the back corner of the building across the alley—ten or twelve diagonal feet. Travis followed, got past the edge and stopped alongside them, his back against the old cedar siding. They listened.

At first there was only silence.

Then came the scrape and whine of the window going up. The sill creaked as heavy weight leaned onto it. Travis waited for the clamber of a body coming through, and the scuff of soles on pavement, but all he heard was a fingertip drumming idly on wood. After a moment it stopped. There was a click and a wash of static, and then silence again.

"Anyone copy at the Raines house?"

Static as the man waited.

Then a tinny voice: "Go ahead."

"Leave three men up there, send the rest down here for a coordinated search. Bring every Humvee."

"Got it."

"Put the three that stay behind on lookout. Eyes on the slopes below the treeline. These people didn't come in a vehicle."

"You want to take Holt up on his offer? Grab law enforcement from nearby jurisdictions? We could have an army in here pretty soon, taking orders from us."

The fingertip drummed again. Less than a second.

"Make the call."

A click ended the static and then the window came down hard, and muffled steps faded away behind it.

* * *

The three of them ran along the row of back lots until they'd passed four more alleys. They stopped behind a building that nestled against a side street, and listened.

Far away, across and above town, the Humvees at Raines's house fired up one by one and began to move. Then their sound was lost to the roar of the one near the Third Notch.

Travis nodded quickly and they sprinted across the street to the next block. They continued into it past the first building, then turned down an alley and moved farther away from Main Street, at last coming out between a little art gallery and the town's post office. The street they now faced ran parallel to Main. Across it were small homes tucked close to one another, and beyond lay three more blocks of the same, the whole spread rising toward the exposed hills. Those hills could be easily climbed—the three of them had come down them fifteen minutes ago—but it would take a good sixty seconds to reach the redwoods from the concealment of the highest backyards. That hadn't been a problem when nobody was watching. Now that at least three sets of eyes *would be*, an undetected crossing was pointless to even think about.

Travis thought about it anyway. If they could get up into the trees and hide, they could circle around to the mine, probably a mile away through unbroken forest.

Paige gazed up at the woods too, and the open ground beneath, clearly running all the same calculations.

"We've probably got three minutes before the first highway patrol units roll in here," Paige said. "It'll be a steady stream after that; anything we try to do will just get harder and harder." She paused. "Three minutes. That's not enough time to think of even a *bad* plan."

Travis stared at the empty hillsides a moment longer, then dropped his gaze to the residential blocks nearer by. Dozens of homes, most of them probably empty by now. A natural gas explosion might make a nice diversion; five or six at once might even generate a smokescreen behind which they could climb. Or maybe he could hotwire a car, douse its interior with gasoline, and send it rolling down to the lake in flames. It would probably crash into something before it got there, but that in itself would be a fine distraction. It might buy them a fifty-fifty chance of gaining the trees unseen, provided they were way up at the edge of town and ready to run at the moment of impact.

But none of those things could be done in three minutes. Not even close.

"You're right," he said. "We don't have time to plan anything."

"So what do we do?" Paige said.

All Travis could think of was a panic option. It was the furthest thing from a plan. He couldn't even properly envision how it would play out—he had yet to actually *see* the nearby Humvee and the number of men inside it. Probably more than one. Probably fewer than five.

He could hear it now, grumbling along in low gear, hunting the alleys that branched off of Main

Street. It would pass *this* alley in another twenty seconds or so.

It hardly mattered that these guys had no description of their prey. The fact that the three of them were on foot would be enough. None of Rum Lake's few remaining occupants were out for a stroll just now.

"Stay close to me," Travis said, "but stay in the alley. And be ready to run if this doesn't work."

He said no more. He turned back toward Main, two hundred feet away along the alley's length. Stared at the gap where the Humvee would soon appear. He was pretty sure he could get there first.

He ran. As fast as he could. Heard Paige and Bethany following behind, and the heavy diesel engine somewhere ahead and to the side.

One hundred feet from the alley's mouth now. Fifty. Ten.

He burst right through it without slowing, and saw the huge vehicle in his peripheral vision. Twenty-five feet away. Matte black. Soaking up the overcast glare and reflecting away almost none of it.

Travis kicked the sidewalk with the front of his foot, and sprawled. He hit the concrete with his hands and tumbled once, scraping every part of his body that struck. He heard the Humvee's engine throttle down hard. Heard the faint whine of shocks as the driver hit the brakes and the thing's five thousand pounds rocked forward onto its front suspension.

Travis got up without coming to a stop. He snapped his gaze toward the Humvee and reacted to it. He went for a mix of surprise and relief, but didn't let it linger more than half a second. Instead he advanced on the vehicle, his legs shaky, his hands waving frantically overhead as if to flag it down—as if he were too brain-addled to see it'd already stopped for him. He was fifteen feet away when the driver opened his door and got out. The guy with the deep voice. Had to be. Six-three and easily two hundred fifty pounds. MP5 submachine gun slung over his shoulder, right hand on its grip, finger outside the trigger well. Travis could see the weapon's left side, and its three-setting fire selector switch, just like the ones he'd seen on the force two decades earlier. The settings were labeled S, E, and F, for German words that meant "safe," "single-shot," and "autofire." This one was set to "safe"—for the moment. Travis glanced through the Humvee's windshield and took in the other occupants. One more up front. Two in the back.

He took another visibly awkward step. Ten feet from the driver now. The guy was just drawing a breath to speak.

Travis recalled something else from his time as a cop—a training exercise called cone versus gun. The setup was simple. One man would play the cop and stand with an unloaded pistol holstered on his hip—safety on, holster strap in place. Another man would be the assailant, facing the cop from twenty feet away, an ice-cream cone in his hand to represent a knife.

From a standing start, the assailant would charge the cop. How close would he get before dying?

Most of the trainees had guessed ten feet: the guy would cover half the distance by the time the gun was leveled at him and clicking. Travis had felt generous and said he'd get within five.

Then the assailant had burst forward, and an instant later the room was full of low, surprised whistles.

The ice cream was mashed against the cop's neck before he could pull the trigger even once.

Same result on the second run. And the third, and the tenth. Didn't matter who played which part. Didn't matter if one was a trainee and the other a hardened veteran. After a few iterations, certain truths became evident. First, twenty feet wasn't that damn far, and the last third could be covered in a single, diving lunge, the body tipping forward and the arm shooting out in a movement that erased several feet at blink-speed. Second, there was a concentration issue. It took focus to snap loose a holster strap, draw a pistol, thumb off its safety, raise it, aim it, and fire. It took *lots* of focus, in fact, and focus was in short supply when someone was charging toward you like a runaway log truck. Your body was preconditioned to tense under those circumstances. Your hands wanted to go up in front of your face, not to your hip. You had to work against those instincts every time, even after you'd trained yourself to expect them. Even when the attacker was a friend with an ice-cream cone.

"No closer," the driver said. His thumb went unconsciously to the selector switch.

Travis didn't have a knife. Didn't even have an ice-cream cone. He also didn't have twenty feet to cross.

He charged.

CHAPTER TWENTY-SEVEN

It happened in less than three seconds, and it *felt* like less than three seconds. At no point did it seem to slow down. At times in Travis's life, eruptions of violence had sometimes taken on special clarity. A simplicity made of goals and obstacles and means, playing out in a few beats of his pulse. He'd heard Paige put it in similar terms.

None of that happened here.

It was all motion and panic; flinching bodies and jerking limbs and the startled beginnings of shouts. Travis crossed the distance in a burst of momentum, got his left hand on the MP5's barrel guard, balled up his right and slammed it into the big guy's Adam's apple with all his forward speed. The man's free hand went to his throat, and his gun hand loosened, and Travis took his attention off the guy completely. Arms were moving inside the vehicle. Reaching for door handles. Reaching for weapons Travis couldn't see. He knocked the driver's hand away from the MP5, gripped the gun with both of his own, thumbed its selector to full-auto, and yanked it down away from the huge torso. The strap pulled tight, but there was enough play for what Travis had to do. He put the weapon's barrel into the gap between the open driver's door and its frame. Right at the front, above the hinge, head-level with all three men inside. Like an archer pointing a drawn arrow through a loophole in a fortress wall.

He aimed for the front passenger and pulled the trigger. Felt the cyclic, full-auto recoil as the thing roared. Saw the guy's head come apart, and shoved the stock hard clockwise to spray the back-seat, hitting both heads there probably five times each. He let go of the trigger and hauled the gun back out of the gap, its strap still tight around the big man—who'd recovered enough to reach for the weapon again. Travis pointed it straight at him and fired, and its last four rounds entered right below his jaw. The guy went limp and dropped where he stood, his weight on the strap tugging the gun out of Travis's hands.

Silence, except the vehicle's idling engine.

Travis looked up the length of Main Street. No sign of the other Humvees just yet.

He raised his eyes to the distant Raines house, just visible over the nearest shopfronts, and saw the three spotters up there going apeshit. Grabbing one another's arms and pointing down toward the action. Drawing two-way radios and shouting into them.

Time to get going.

Travis turned and saw Paige and Bethany at the mouth of the alley. Paige looked only a little shaken. Bethany more so.

"Seconds are going to count," Travis said.

Paige nodded, shoved Bethany forward and ran after her.

Travis opened the back door on the driver's side and Bethany got in first, heedless of the bodies—all the blood was farther back, covering the rear windows and the storage area behind the seats. Paige climbed in after her, and by then Travis was at the wheel, slamming his own door and shoving the vehicle into drive. For half a second he considered reversing instead, backing up and taking the nearby cross street. Then he thought of the spotters up high again, on their radios, and knew it was pointless. There would be no hiding from the other Humvees. He floored the accelerator and the vehicle shot forward along Main, toward the street at the far end that led to Raines's house.

"Get the guns off those guys in back," Travis said.

"Already on it," Paige said.

Travis reached with his right and unslung the front passenger's MP5 from his shoulder. He set the weapon in his own lap and patted the guy's pockets for extra magazines. He found two in a big pouch on his pant leg.

Three blocks from the end of Main now, doing sixty. A second later the first of the other Humvees appeared ahead. It rounded the corner Travis meant to take, at the end. Another followed half a vehicle length behind it. Then came four more. The whole procession advanced, roughly single-file, accelerating to meet him.

If these guys had had time to form a plan, they

might've spread out like horsemen riding abreast. No way could Travis have rammed through that barrier; his vehicle weighed exactly as much as any one of theirs. But in the few seconds available, as the closing distance shrank toward zero, the column simply stayed in a straight line, bearing toward Travis in an impromptu game of chicken.

At least maybe it looked like that from their point of view.

Travis jerked the wheel to the right at the last possible instant, veering past the leader. As he did, he saw the rest of the line begin to destabilize, the Humvees braking or jogging to one side or another—little movements that betrayed their drivers' confusion. But Travis was passing the formation almost too quickly to notice those things—or to care. Sixty miles per hour, he'd read somewhere, was just under ninety feet per second. With these vehicles moving the other way at the same speed, he was passing them at closer to one hundred eighty feet per second. In hardly *more* than a second they were all behind him, just shapes in his side mirror, stopping and turning and trying not to slam into each other like cops in an old movie.

Travis braked hard and took the turn at the end of Main doing thirty, then gunned it again along the secondary street. He could already see the curve ahead that would take them uphill toward Raines's. No doubt the three men still up there had their guns in hand by now. Travis guessed this vehicle's shell could withstand 9mm fire, but he wasn't certain of it.

He took the curve and saw the incline rising above

him, steep as any street in San Francisco. There were houses to his left and right, but just ahead the way opened up on both sides to a broad, empty grassland. Raines's house was three hundred feet above that point, the redwoods almost at its back wall.

Travis saw the three spotters. They had their guns. They were positioned way up next to the house itself, maybe ready to duck inside it if they needed cover.

They wouldn't. Travis didn't give them a second glance. He pulled hard right on the wheel and left the road altogether, angling up across the slope to miss the house by two hundred feet. As the redwoods drew nearer, he sized up the gaps among them. At a distance, the trees had been just a visual screen, but at this range he could see several openings that would admit the Humvee. They probably wouldn't get far into the woods, but any distance was better than none.

They were still a hundred feet from the trees when the spotters at the house opened up. A burst of a dozen shots hit the window right next to Travis; the pane bulged inward as the glass sandwiched between the lexan layers shattered. Other salvos pattered against the vehicle's metal sides. Travis aimed for the biggest opening in the trees, and a second later they were through it, deep in the shadows and the green-filtered light beneath the boughs. He angled back to the left; Jeannie had said the mine access was straight uphill from the house. He dodged a trunk that loomed out of the dimness, and saw a gap between two others, just ahead, that for half a second looked wide enough to pass through. Then it didn't. He stood on the brake and felt the huge tires slide in the sandy soil. He cranked the wheel right, felt the vehicle rotate without actually changing course, and a moment later, sliding almost sideways along its path, it rocked to a halt.

Travis shoved open his door, heard Paige and Bethany scrambling out of theirs. Far away down the slope, men were shouting and heavy engines were racing; the Humvee column was less than thirty seconds behind.

The three of them ran. Clambered up the needle-carpeted slope. Scanned the way ahead for any sign of the shaft's opening. It occurred to Travis for the first time that the thing might be difficult to spot. It might be choked with ferns and low scrub; it might look like nothing but a patch of undergrowth at any distance beyond ten feet—it might be impossible to see that it was an opening at all. He worried about that for five seconds and then Bethany screamed "There!" and shot her arm out ahead, and Travis saw that his concerns had been groundless. The shaft access was an upright opening, like a garage door but a third smaller. It formed the end of a rough, squared concrete tube that jutted straight out from the hillside, its end cracked and worn and showing rebar.

They sprinted for it as the engines roared behind them. Tires skidded and metal thumped hard against wood, and then doors were opening and voices were shouting again, no more than a few dozen yards back. Beneath all those sounds Travis suddenly heard his cell phone ringing. Jeannie, calling with the information from the old files. He ignored it, pointed his MP5 behind him and fired a quick burst. He heard feet slip and men curse as they went for cover. The access was right ahead now, fifteen feet away, pitch black beyond the tunnel's mouth.

"Watch out for a drop-off," Travis said, and then they were inside, blind for a second as their eyes tried to adjust.

An instant later Paige sucked in a hard breath and stopped—she threw both arms out to block the others.

There was a drop-off.

Ten feet in, the concrete floor ended as neatly as a high-dive platform, empty space beyond the left half, black metal stairs descending beyond the right half. Paige led the way down. Ten steps, then a landing made of the same metal gridwork, and another flight. And another. At the bottom of the fourth they touched down on concrete again— another horizontal tunnel. It stretched twenty feet and terminated against a slab of solid metal, eight feet square, visible in the pale glow of an overhead mercury lamp.

There were giant hinges on the slab's left side, and there was a keypad on its right.

Travis stared.

He felt his thoughts begin to go blank.

High above, sounds reverberated through the stair shaft. The sliding of feet and hands on loose soil outside. Then the scrape of boots skidding to a halt on concrete.

Paige and Bethany ran forward, getting clear of the shaft. Travis followed, but at a walk; he'd barely noticed the sounds. All his attention was on the giant door.

Which was green.

CHAPTER TWENTY-EIGHT

What the hell do we do?" Bethany whispered.

Paige could only shake her head.

There was a handhold inset in the steel just below the keypad. Her sense of futility manifesting in her body language, Paige took hold of it and pulled. The door didn't so much as rattle in its frame.

Behind and above, in the shaft, more footsteps thudded into the concrete tunnel. Voices spoke in low, soft tones, some of which carried unusually well in the strange acoustics.

"We called it in," someone said. "They want them alive, whoever they are."

Someone else cursed softly, then said, "Okay."

Paige turned from the door and faced Travis, and seemed thrown by the look in his eyes. He imagined he appeared numb. He sure as hell felt that way.

"What is it?" Paige said.

Travis took a deep breath. He steeled himself for the likelihood—it should've been a certainty—that the dream had been *only* a dream. That this was the mother of all coincidences, and a cruel one at that.

Up in the shaft, something like a backpack dropped to the concrete. Tough fabric with metal objects clattering inside. A zipper came open.

"Travis?" Paige said.

He stepped past her to the keypad. Above the buttons was a simple readout, like a VCR's clock. There were glowing blue dashes where digits could be entered. Five of them.

"There's a dozen masks in one of the back storage holds," someone up above said. "Go get them all."

Then came a faint but sharp sound from atop the stairwell. Some tiny metallic thing being pulled free of something else. Like a key drawn from a lock, but not quite.

Travis blocked it all out and thought of the dream. The old man—the Wilford Brimley look-alike—staring at him from a few inches away. Asking over and over what was behind the green door. *We already know the combo*, the old man had said.

And then what?

What *exactly* had come after that?

High up in the vertical shaft, something bounced hard against the wall—by its sound Travis pictured a can of shaving cream, though he was pretty damn certain it wasn't. The thing ricocheted again and again, hitting the stairs, the walls, the landings, making its way down. Travis turned with Paige and Bethany and watched it hit the bottom, less than twenty feet from where they stood. They could barely see it in the vague light there, but there was no real mystery as to what it was. It came to rest and did nothing for two seconds. Then it jumped and skittered and started blasting thick gas into the air. Tear gas or pepper gas or some variant. Another canister came rattling down after it. Then another.

"*Shit* . . ." Bethany whispered. Her voice gave away a tremor.

The gas churned and curled toward them in delicate wisps.

We already know the combo.

Travis closed his eyes.

A second passed.

He opened them again and turned back to the keypad.

At the corners of his vision he saw Paige and Bethany watching him, confused.

He entered the numbers carefully but quickly: 4–8–8–5–4.

The instant he punched the last one the keypad flared with green backlight. Something very heavy thudded inside the door, and with a hiss of air pressure the huge slab kicked open an inch.

Both Paige and Bethany flinched. They looked back and forth between Travis and the keypad. Then Paige stowed her bafflement and grabbed the door's handhold again. Travis gripped it too, and they pulled it outward more easily than he'd imagined was possible. There had to be an unseen counterweight somewhere beyond the hinges, balancing the whole thing so that it pivoted smoothly.

In a few seconds they had it open a foot and a half. Travis saw darkness beyond, tempered by another mercury light somewhere above. He also saw the thickness of the door itself: at least five inches of steel. He stood aside and ushered Paige and Bethany through first, then glanced back along the short corridor behind them.

The ragged front of the gas cloud was three feet away.

Someone up in the higher chamber said, "Did you hear something?"

"I don't know," came the reply.

Travis followed the others through the opening, turned and took hold of an identical grip on the door's far side.

"*How about this?*" he shouted, and leaned back and dragged the door shut with a booming *clang*.

A second later the heavy mechanism inside the door thudded again, and when Travis tested the slab by shoving his shoulder against it, it felt as though he were pushing on the base of a cliff.

It crossed his mind that the guys upstairs probably knew the combination too—if not, their superiors could sure as hell give it to them—but almost before the thought had formed, he saw that it didn't matter.

Waist high on this side of the door was a sliding bolt latch, similar in shape to the little ones you could get in a hardware store for three or four bucks. This one had probably cost more—its bolt was thicker than a baseball bat. Travis grabbed its handle, rotated it upward out of the notch it rested in, and rammed the bolt sideways into its seat in the frame.

*   *   *

For a few seconds none of them spoke or moved. Travis stood there with his hand still resting on the bolt, Paige and Bethany close by and staring at him, waiting for him to explain.

By the echoes of their breathing, Travis sensed they were in a much wider space than the corridor they'd just come from. The tiny light above this side of the door shone mostly straight down, casting a glow over the three of them, but leaving deep darkness everywhere else.

Travis turned from the latch and met their stares.

He described the dream in every detail he could recall. The strange little room swimming and warping, as if he'd been drugged even before the dream began. Richard Garner tied upright to a dolly. He himself bound in the same way. The old man asking what was behind the green door, and saying the combination aloud. The empty syringe on the tray. And right at the end, the drug's harsher effects kicking in, spreading pain up to his heart and then everywhere else.

That was it. He couldn't remember any more. He was pretty sure there hadn't *been* any more.

As he finished telling the story, a series of indistinct thumps began to transmit through the steel door. Travis pictured men in gas masks on the other side, pounding and kicking the slab. After a moment he heard what might've been shouts, but they were so faint he could've been imagining them. He put it all out of his mind.

Paige turned and paced at the edge of the light pool, hands in her hair.

"Eliminate what it wasn't," she said. "It wasn't an ordinary dream that happened to contain the code for this door. Not a chance." She shut her eyes. "So what the hell was it?"

"I don't think it was a dream at all," Travis said. "I think what I saw and heard was really happening—to someone else. I think Richard Garner is still alive, tied up in that little room, wherever it is. And there's somebody tied up there with him, being drugged and interrogated. I think I was seeing through that person's eyes."

He knew how that sounded to both Paige and Bethany. It sounded the same to him.

"The part about Garner being alive is plausible, anyway," Bethany said. "I've heard from more than one person that there's a mock-up of the Oval Office somewhere else in the White House—a mock-up of the part you see on TV, anyway. They say there's even a defocused projection to simulate the background behind the windows. If Garner anticipated any threat last night, he could've broadcast from there; the missile would've probably still knocked out the TV signal."

"I can accept that he survived," Paige said. "I can even accept that there was some kind of internal action against him right after that, with Holt in charge of it. But the dream—"

"I don't understand it either," Travis said. "Is there a Breach entity that could account for it? Something that ties you into someone else's senses for a little while?"

"I've never heard of one that could do that,"

Paige said. "What are you thinking—that if something like that existed, someone could've used it on you? That someone wanted you to hear the combination?"

"I don't know," Travis said. "I don't see how that would work, it's just . . . it *did* work. Whatever it was, it worked. The door combination was right."

"There *are* entities that interact with the brain across distances," Bethany said. "Blue flares, for example."

Paige nodded absently, but didn't look swayed. Blue flares were a fairly common entity type; a couple hundred had emerged from the Breach since the beginning. As with nearly all entities, no one knew what their creators had used them for, but their defining characteristic was that you could make them heat up just by thinking about them—if you focused hard enough and consistently enough. In tests people had gotten them up to over eighteen hundred degrees Fahrenheit in less than a minute, from distances as great as one hundred feet, and with walls in the way. But heating up was all they did. They didn't connect one person's eyes and ears to someone else's mind.

"If there *were* an entity like that," Paige said, "how would someone outside Tangent have control of it? Why wouldn't I have heard of it?"

Even as she asked the question, her expression changed. Travis saw her feeling the edges of the same possibility he'd begun to consider.

"Your father recruited a group of powerful people in 1987," Travis said, "to act against what Ruben Ward set in motion. Would it be surprising to learn Peter supplied them with Breach technology, if he thought it would help them? Maybe even things he kept off the books in Border Town?"

Paige bit her lip. The idea didn't sit well with her, but she couldn't dismiss it either.

"I know I'm reaching," Travis said. "I don't know what else to do. I saw a five-digit number in a dream, and it opened a door in the real world. *Something* made that possible."

Paige nodded, still looking uneasy. "I'm sure we'll find out what it is. One way or another."

For a while no one else spoke.

The vague thumps against the steel door had ceased.

Bethany frowned. "The dream itself—or whatever it was—doesn't make sense to me. The old guy was asking what was behind the green door, but he already had the combination. Couldn't he just come and see for himself? More to the point, wouldn't he already *know* what was here? Wouldn't these people *know* about the Stargazer? *Holt* sure as hell should know; he's working with *them*—the ones who sent Ruben Ward here to create the damn thing."

On that point Travis couldn't even reach. She was exactly right: Holt should know. It made no sense at all for him and his associates to be out of the loop.

"So why *didn't* they use the combo?" Paige said. "They had it, and it definitely works—we just proved that. Why not send these contractors in here hours ago to take a look around? They were two hundred yards away at the house. Or if Holt didn't trust them enough, he *could've* come here himself. None of it adds up."

Travis nodded slowly. More gaps in the puzzle. The whole middle of the image was nothing but a void.

Every instinct told him that was about to change.

He wasn't half as sure they'd like what it changed to.

CHAPTER TWENTY-NINE

They found a long switchplate on the wall, just visible in the gloom three feet from the door. Five switches, all down. Travis flipped them up one by one, and the chamber lit up in discrete zones until the whole thing was blazing.

It was bigger than he'd expected—a nearly perfect cube of space, forty feet in each dimension—but its size lost hold of his attention almost at once.

What grabbed it was the layout.

The place looked like a loft apartment cut out of solid stone. There was a kitchen area in the far right corner, complete with cabinets, a range, a deep sink, and a huge refrigerator. A few recent issues of *Newsweek* lay on the counter. Ten feet away was a couch facing a flat-panel television on the wall, and beyond that, filling the nearer corner, was a bedroom suite. It included a bathroom of sorts—not really a separate room but just a vanity butted up against a glass-block shower enclosure, and a walled-off area containing a toilet. A stacked washer and dryer stood nearby. The wiring for all of it—switches and outlets and overhead lights hanging out of the dimness high above—ran in black conduits fixed to the stone walls. The conduits converged on a breaker box near the kitchen, from which a much thicker conduit plunged through the chamber's floor.

That was the right side of the room. The left side had a computer desk at the far end, its data cable climbing the wall and disappearing through the ceiling. Travis hardly noticed it. His eyes had been drawn to the rest of that wall—and the array of additional flat-panel monitors that covered it, three screens high and ten wide. They were each the same size as the television in the living room, but while that one remained dormant, all thirty of these had come on when Travis flipped the light switches.

They carried video feeds from the forested slope surrounding the mine access, a strange equivalent to Defense Control in Border Town, with its dozens of angles on the empty desert. In some of these shots of the redwoods, the access itself was visible, with contractors milling around looking pissed. On closer inspection Travis saw that the rough opening appeared vacant in some of the images. After a second he realized what he was really seeing: the *other* access Jeannie had told them about, across the ridge and lower down.

Travis looked at the screens a few seconds longer, then turned his focus to the room's most commanding feature.

The pit.

It was exactly centered, measuring maybe fifteen by fifteen feet—a square donut hole, in proportion to the chamber's floorspace. A steel-tube handrail boxed in its entire perimeter except for a three-foot gap where a flight of stairs descended. The same kind of stairs they'd come down a few minutes before. From where he stood, Travis could see only a few feet of the hole's depth, but he knew it went a long way down. This was the actual mine shaft. The concrete floor around it bore the scars of its long-abandoned function: corrosion-stained outlines, dotted with masonry bolt holes, where the footings of heavy equipment had rested. Twin grooves worn faintly into the surface, three feet apart and parallel to each other, extended from the pit back to the green door and right under it. There'd been a rail track here at one time, for heavy-duty carts and maybe a gantry crane.

The last thing Travis took in was a red metal locker fixed to the wall at the near end of the bank of monitors. It was shaped more or less like the one he'd had in high school, but was half the height and positioned at chest level. It had a standard drop-latch with a hole for a padlock, but no lock had been put into it. On impulse Travis went to it, lifted the latch and opened the door. Nothing inside. He closed it and turned back to Paige and Bethany.

"He lived here," Paige said. "Allen Raines. He had the house down at the edge of the woods, but *this* was his home."

Travis nodded. The illusion would've been perfect. From town, people would've only seen Raines park his vehicle at the house and walk in the front door. They wouldn't have seen him continue right through the place, out the back and up into the trees; from a flat viewing angle the undergrowth and low boughs would've hidden him completely.

"It must've mattered," Bethany said. "Being right inside here almost all the time, instead of down at the house. It must've made a difference, in terms of his handling of the Stargazer."

On the last word her eyes went unconsciously to the pit.

Travis nodded again, and started toward the railing.

He was halfway there when the snapping buzz started back up, the same as it'd been in the alley. The field-of-grasshoppers sound, deep inside his head. The only difference was that it was stronger now—a *lot* stronger—this close to its source. It brought Travis to a halt, and after a few seconds he found his balance deserting him. He saw Paige and Bethany swaying on their feet too. He put his hands forward and let himself lean in the same direction, ready to control the fall if it came. As before, the sound—the thought—intensified until it felt almost physical. Like there were things moving inside his head. Skittering little legs and wings and mandibles, descending the brainstem now, boring toward his throat. Bethany shut her eyes and gritted her teeth and sucked in a deep breath, and Travis was sure she was about to scream at the top of her lungs—

And then it was gone again. A perfect cutoff, like before. Paige put a hand to her stomach, eyes widening for a second. Bethany released the pent-up breath. She looked rattled all to hell. Looked like she might scream anyway, but didn't.

Travis dropped his arms to his sides and steadied his breathing—he realized only now that it'd gone shallow.

He went to the rail.

Paige and Bethany stepped up to it beside him.

They stared down and said nothing for probably half a minute.

The pit had to be six hundred feet deep. Maybe deeper. Mercury lights every thirty feet or so lit up the descent. The stairs wound down in a squared spiral, following the shaft walls and leaving a wide-open drop in the middle. Seen from up here, that open space shrank to a tiny square by the time it reached the bottom. There was no way to discern the structure of what was down there—to know whether the shaft accessed a horizontal run, or did something else altogether.

The only visible detail was a soft red glow that shone onto the lowest flights of stairs, its source apparently somewhere off to the side. Its brightness waxed and waned in random patterns, and even its color seemed to vary within a narrow range: deep red for the most part, but for fleeting instants it seemed closer to neon pink.

Travis looked at the stair treads just beneath him. He followed them down and around through half a dozen flights. Each step had a layer of dust covering its ends, left and right, but was clear in the middle. They'd seen regular use.

"These stairs weren't part of the mine's original architecture," Travis said. "Workers weren't lugging tons of ore up sixty flights back in the day. The stairs were built later on, for Raines's use. Power consumption and maintenance probably ruled out a lift, but a person could go up and down these all the time, with the right pacing. Take it slow, don't kill yourself." He paused. "Whatever Raines was doing to keep the Stargazer in check, it required him to go down there and deal with it directly."

He didn't need to finish the point aloud: the three of them would have to deal with it directly too.

"When we see it," Paige said, "do you think it'll be obvious what we're supposed to do? Do you think we'll just know?"

"Only one way to find out," Bethany said.

But they didn't go that minute. They did three things first, none of them difficult.

They searched the chamber for any kind of paperwork that might help. Maybe, by a long shot, the cheat sheet would turn up.

It didn't. They checked the kitchen cabinets, the desk drawers, the space beneath the mattress, the vanity, even the couch cushions. Nothing.

Next they switched on the computer and Bethany scoured Raines's files. There were hundreds of songs and audiobooks and movies and television shows that'd been downloaded from iTunes. The web browser's history showed lots of visits to mainstream news sites, YouTube, and a scattering of blogs. There were very few document files on the computer—just instructions for various programs that'd probably come with the system. There was nothing about Tangent or Scalar or the Stargazer. Nothing useful at all.

The third thing they tried came to Travis as Bethany was reaching to shut off the computer.

"Hold up," he said.

He followed the data cable with his eyes, up to where it punched through the ceiling.

"How does the system get online?" he said. "Cell transceiver, right?"

Bethany nodded. "It must be hidden up in the trees, like the surveillance cameras."

Travis took his phone from his pocket and switched it on. As expected, there was no signal at all.

"Jeannie called me right before we came in off the slope," he said. "She must've found out who lived downstairs in 1978." He indicated the data line. "Is there any way to plug that into my phone? She might've left a voicemail."

Bethany thought about it. She slid the computer's case out from under the desk, pulled two thumb tabs and removed its side panel. She leaned close and scrutinized a card attached to the motherboard.

"No problem," she said.

While she rigged the connection, Travis gazed at the wall of monitors. The contractors were still gathered near the squared tunnel that led into the hillside. Still pissed. One of them was on a phone, yelling at someone.

Travis noticed a few angles he'd overlooked before. They were interior shots of the tunnel right outside the green door, just resolvable through the gas cloud from the canisters. Other images showed an identical door that must be built into the second access—it was clear of gas, and no one stood outside it yet. Now as he watched, two

men in ventilator masks made their way to the
first door. Each had something in his hand, but
through the haze the objects were impossible to
identify at first. Then the men used them. The first
held a tape measure. He pressed its tab into the
gap on the hinged side, and walked the tape sideways until it stretched across the width of the door.
The second man turned out to have a hammer, a
standard-sized claw type. He rested an ear against
the door and used the hammer to tap very lightly
on the steel. Travis heard the tapping on this side,
but only faintly. A few seconds later both men re-
treated back toward the stairs.

"We're in business," Bethany said.

She held his phone out to him, the computer's
cable attached to an exposed board within it.

Jeannie had left a voice mail. In 1978 only one
person had lived in either of the apartments beneath the Third Notch. A woman named Loraine
Cotton. She'd moved in during the fall of the previous year and stayed through all of 1978.

Bethany patched the data line into her tablet
computer and quickly pulled up Loraine Cotton's
history. She seemed, by every measure, to be an
actual person. She'd been born in 1955, which
made her 23 when she lived beneath the restaurant. At that time she'd just gotten a biology degree
from Oregon State, specializing in forest ecosys-
tems, and had apparently come to Rum Lake on
a grant to study the redwoods. Her choice of such
a dismal apartment made more sense in that light;
she'd probably only gone inside the place to sleep,

if even then—maybe she'd tented in the woods part of the time.

Loraine's career path had changed pretty dramatically in March of the following year, 1979. She'd moved up to Bellevue, Washington, and taken an entry-level job at a small company that'd just moved its operations there: Microsoft. By the turn of the millennium she'd been worth over half a billion dollars.

"She's on Twitter," Bethany said. She pulled up the site and navigated to Loraine's profile. "Doesn't tweet much. Once every few days. Last one's the day before yesterday: says she's on vacation—Kings Canyon in the Australian Outback."

Travis paced, rubbing his forehead.

"A passageway beneath the Third Notch," he said. "Look for Loraine Cotton in apartment whichever. The message from the Breach sent Ruben Ward to meet her. It's like she was intended to be another pawn. One that was going to last a lot longer than three months."

"And have massive financial resources at her disposal after a while," Paige said. "If whoever's on the other side of the Breach had a presence on our side by that time, maybe they recognized the potential of a company like Microsoft—even back then."

"Plenty of regular humans recognized it," Travis said. "They all own islands now."

He stopped pacing. He stared at the floor for a second, thinking hard. Something in what they'd just learned about Loraine Cotton had set off a *ping*, but he couldn't get his mind around it. He gave it another ten seconds' thought but got no-where. He let it fade. Maybe it would come to him on its own.

He looked at a clock above Raines's refrigera-tor. Twelve thirty. Six hours and fifteen minutes left before Peter Campbell's estimated deadline. All at once it seemed like all the time in the world, but Travis took no relief from that fact. If things went well down in the shaft—if they saw what they had to do, and were able to do it—then he imagined it would all unfold pretty quickly. And if things *didn't* go well—if they went bad in ways he couldn't guess at the moment—then that would probably unfold pretty damn quickly, too.

They went.

The going was easy on the stairs. They were well constructed and solid and the mercury lamps put out plenty of light. Travis led the way. Every few flights he leaned over the handrail as he descended, and got a slightly closer look at the deep floor of the pit. Still no details. Just the slowly pulsing red-and-pink light.

They were some two hundred feet down when Travis noticed a break in the pattern of stairs far below—maybe two hundred feet lower still. It was as if the squared spiral had been compressed by ten feet at a single point. Like an accordion held open vertically, with just one pleat of its bellows pinched shut in the middle. He stopped for a moment and stared at it, and realized what it was: a horizontal walkway where a flight of stairs would've other-wise been. A single stretch that went sideways instead of down. From this high angle he couldn't see the shaft wall at that spot—the flights above it blocked it from view—but he knew what was there.

The three of them stopped again when they were only fifty feet above the level walkway, facing it from the opposite wall. From this vantage they could easily see the opening there, where a side tunnel branched off the shaft into pitch darkness.

They stared at it a few seconds and then continued downward, but Travis kept his eyes fixed on it as they made their way around. He couldn't admit it out loud, but something about the opening unnerved him. Some ancient fear coded right into his DNA was setting off an internal klaxon, telling him it was a bad idea to walk past a dark cavity in a rock face. He had his MP5 slung on its shoulder strap, the same as Paige and Bethany, and was on the verge of taking hold of its grip as they came down the last flight before the tunnel. Only logic kept him from doing so. This was an abandoned mine in the present, not Olduvai Gorge a million years ago. Nothing with claws was going to erupt from the darkness and try to have them for lunch. That's what he was thinking when he was two treads above the walkway, and then a man's voice out of the blackness said, "Stop right there."

CHAPTER THIRTY

There was no sound of a gun being cocked. Just a tone confident enough to imply one.

Travis stopped.

Paige and Bethany stopped behind him—he heard their breathing cut out at the same time.

"Keep your hands away from the weapons," the man said.

"We're not going to drop them," Travis said. There was caution and then there was stupidity.

"I'm not going to ask you to," the man said.

A moment later there came the soft crunch of a careful step, followed by another. Travis saw a hint of movement in the darkness, clothing catching the indirect spill of mercury light ten feet back in the tunnel.

Then the man said, "You're Travis Chase."

The unreal quality of the moment passed quickly. The analytical part of Travis's mind kicked in, firing off questions. Who was still alive who could both recognize him and be inside this place? Had the voice sounded familiar? He had no immediate answer for either one.

"Who are you?" Travis said.

"I think you'll remember me. I'm coming out now. My weapon's holstered."

More footsteps. Then a shape materialized out of the gloom, and a second later the man was standing right at the tunnel's opening, hands out at his sides in a nonthreatening stance. He glanced up the flight at each of them in turn, then looked at Travis and waited for him to speak.

Travis knew him. He'd met him just over a year ago under very tense circumstances, and spent a few hours in his general vicinity. He couldn't remember if they'd spoken directly—if so, it would've been just a few words. Paige and Bethany wouldn't recognize him at all; they'd been in the same room with him for ten seconds back then, but their faces had been pressed to the floor, and there'd been a lot of shooting going on.

"Rudy Dyer," Travis said. "Secret Service for Richard Garner."

Travis introduced Paige and Bethany. The three of them filed down onto the walkway and into the open space at the tunnel's mouth. Between themselves and Dyer they formed a rough square a few feet apart from one another, in which everyone could see everyone else. Travis had his back diagonal to the walkway's railing. He turned and looked over the edge at the bottom of the shaft, now just two hundred feet below. From here he could resolve the lowest flight in the spiral. It didn't terminate against a solid floor, but instead tied into a flat walkway like this one, which led out of sight to one side. Though he couldn't be sure, Travis had the impression there *was no* floor at the bottom of the shaft. That instead the vertical channel punched down into some broader chamber beneath it, whose bottom might be dozens of feet further below, and whose width and length he couldn't determine.

He stared a moment longer, the red glow almost hypnotizing at this range. It saturated the bottom walkway and the steps there, and every visible inch of whatever lay beneath it all.

Travis looked up and saw Dyer gazing down at it too. Then the man trailed his eyes upward until he was craning his neck to stare at the top two thirds of the shaft, rearing above them like a chimney seen from deep inside. Travis got the impression that Dyer was looking at it all for the first time.

"You came in through the other access," Travis said.

Dyer nodded, at last leveling his gaze and turning to face the group. "I only got here half an hour ago. I was in Barbados with my wife and daughter when I got the news last night."

"How did you know the door combination?" Paige said.

"Garner gave it to me, just after he took office again last year. He told me—" He cut himself off, looking puzzled about something. Travis realized the same puzzlement had been there, under the surface, from the moment Dyer had stepped out of the dark. The man looked from one of them to the other. At last he said, "Are you guys it? None of the others made it?"

"Others?" Travis said.

Dyer nodded. "This mine is the rally point. Everyone still alive is supposed to show up here."

Travis thought of the people who'd been killed in unison with Garner, all over the country. The power players Peter had met with, all those years ago.

Still looking confused, Dyer said, "No offense, but I didn't think you guys were part of the group. You'd be just about the *last* people I'd expect to meet in this place. How did *you* get the combination?"

Travis met Paige's and Bethany's eyes. Their bafflement matched his own. Clearly Dyer knew a lot more than the three of them did—he'd learned it directly from Garner.

Travis looked at Dyer again. The man stared and waited for the answer.

"We're honestly not sure how we got the combo," Travis said. "We think Breach technology was involved, but if so, it was a kind we've never heard of." He shook his head. "Look, you seem to have the whole picture of this thing. We've been piecing it together slapshot since last night, and we're missing big chunks of it. If you know it all, please tell us."

Dyer frowned. He seemed to struggle with some deep indecision. "This is all happening wrong," he said. "It's not supposed to be like this."

"Tell us what it *is* supposed to be like," Paige said.

For a moment Dyer just stood there. He looked troubled by the idea he needed to express. Then he said, "The whole point is *not* to tell you. *That's* what it's supposed to be like. No current member of Tangent is supposed to know anything. Not for a few years yet."

Travis found himself getting tired of the confusion. "You're right," he said. "It *is* all happening wrong—the people you expected aren't here. But *we are*. I assume your purpose is the same as ours." He nodded over the rail behind him. "To do whatever can be done about the Stargazer."

Dyer looked more thrown by that than anything so far. "That must be an old nickname for it. Whatever you want to call it, I don't think much *can* be done. Just management, like Allen Raines was doing."

"You're not here to stop it?" Paige said.

Dyer shook his head.

"What about the deadline?" Bethany said. "A little over six hours from now."

"That's the deadline," Dyer said, "but it has nothing to do with what's in this mine."

Paige looked frustrated. "Just tell us everything. We already know the basics. We know Ruben Ward got instructions from the Breach in 1978. We know he spent that summer carrying them out. We know my father picked up on it later, and the Scalar investigation spent six years following Ward's trail. Which led here, to whatever Ward created in this mine. So tell us the rest. Tell us what needs to be done, and we'll help you do it."

Dyer stared at her. His expression went almost blank, as if his thoughts had turned inward to process what he'd just heard.

"You've got the first few points right," he said.

"The rest is way off. Ward didn't create anything in this place, and the Scalar investigation never picked up his trail. For all practical purposes, he didn't leave one."

Travis remembered their conversation on the Coast Highway. Their uncertainty as to how the investigation could've accomplished anything at all.

"But they spent hundreds of millions doing something," Bethany said.

"Probably more like billions," Dyer said. "Most of the cost was likely hidden one way or another."

"The cost of *what*?" Bethany said. "What the hell did they do?"

Suddenly Travis knew. He realized he might've known hours ago, if he'd given it more thought. Might've guessed, anyway; he couldn't have known for sure until they reached this place.

"Holy shit," he whispered.

Dyer nodded, seeing his understanding.

"They did the only thing they *could* do," Dyer said. "They knew from the beginning that Ward's trail was long gone, and so was the notebook with the instructions written in it. Trashed or burned before he killed himself. They were never going to see it again."

"They needed a do-over," Travis said.

Dyer nodded again. "They needed another Ruben Ward. And this is the place where they tried to get one. At the bottom of this mineshaft they created the second Breach."

PART III

THE TUMBLER

CHAPTER THIRTY-ONE

Paige started to speak, then stopped. Her mouth opened and closed a second and third time, but nothing came out. At last she just stepped to the rail beside Travis and stared down into the pit. Bethany did the same. They watched the light playing—slowly flaring and receding.

When Paige's voice finally came, it was softened almost to a breath. "The colors are different."

"Almost everything about it's different," Dyer said, "hard as they tried to duplicate the original."

"Do entities emerge?" Travis said.

"No. But other things do."

Every head turned to Dyer. Every eye widened a little.

"Understand," Dyer said, "everything I know comes from Garner. I've obviously never been in Border Town. I've never seen the first Breach—or this one. Garner said the one you oversee is an opening to something like a wormhole, however loosely that term is defined."

Paige nodded.

"He also said it's a wormhole being used for a specific purpose," Dyer said. "Someone out there, or some*thing* out there, either designed it or harnessed it for transporting the objects you call entities."

"Something like that," Travis said.

"Well the second Breach tapped into a very different kind of wormhole," Dyer said. "Maybe a more common kind, according to some of the scientists who worked on it. The term they used for it was *primordial*. A natural wormhole that could've formed out of the energy of the big bang itself. They say the universe might be riddled with them. And this one, at least, has no physical objects moving through it."

"So what comes out?" Bethany said.

"Transmissions," Dyer said. "Garner called them parasite signals."

Travis's eyes snapped to Paige's, then Bethany's.

Dyer saw the looks. "You felt them too."

All three nodded.

"No one knows exactly what they are," Dyer said. "They figure the other end of this wormhole is bonded to someplace where there's life. Some equivalent to bugs, maybe. The way I heard it, things like that would evolve to make use of the tunnel, if they could. Like things here evolved eyes to exploit sunlight, and ears to take advantage of soundwaves in the air. These things, even if they couldn't physically pass through the channel, could transmit natural signals into it. There are any number of ways they'd benefit by doing that, and—"

He stopped. Frowned. "Look, this Breach is dangerous as hell, and it gets *more* dangerous if it's not managed, but I can take care of that later. None of this is the reason Garner brought me into the loop. It's not why I'm here. For now, it's enough to know that this second one didn't do what everybody hoped it would. There were no Breach Voices, and there was no effect up front like the one that hit Ruben Ward. That stuff just didn't happen the second time around. Different tunnel. But in a way—I guess indirectly—opening this thing got them the answers they were looking for. They learned what was really going on."

He went quiet again, shut his eyes hard and rubbed the bridge of his nose. "I'm going to tell you everything I know. I don't see any choice at this point. If I'd gotten here and found any of the others alive, they would've been in charge, and my orders would've been to help them. But Garner gave me different orders to follow if none of them made it. The only real priority now—"

A sound cut him off: a violent, concussive bass wave, like a shotgun blast amplified many times over. It came from the chamber four hundred feet above, and echoed down the shaft in strange harmonics that set the metal stairs vibrating. Everyone looked up. They listened as the reverberations faded.

Only silence followed.

Travis thought of the men with the tape measure and the hammer, getting a sense of the steel's bulk.

"They're trying to blow the door," he said.

"Who are they?" Dyer said. "Private sector guys?"

Travis nodded. It occurred to him that, until now, Dyer had been entirely unaware of any hostile presence outside the mine. Having come in the back entrance, he'd encountered none of them.

Now as Dyer took the information into account, his gaze seemed to dart back and forth over nothingness in front of him. The look of someone considering a large number of variables and making a fast decision. He jerked his head to indicate the tunnel leading away off the drop shaft, back in the direction he'd come from.

"This way," he said. "Right now."

The tunnel wasn't as dark as it'd seemed at first glance, against the brighter mercury lamps in the vertical run. There were dim orange lights here, widely spaced, and after a few seconds Travis found his eyes adjusting. In the same short time, Dyer picked up the pace to just under a sprint, cursing softly under his breath.

"This was supposed to be the one place they wouldn't know about," he said. "That's why it was the rendezvous point."

"They knew about it hours ago," Travis said. "They even had the door combo."

He described the dream, leaving nothing out. He included their own speculation that Garner was still alive, and that the dream had been real—seen through the eyes of someone held captive with him, and sent to Travis by way of an unknown entity.

If any of it threw Dyer, he didn't show it. He seemed about to reply when another thudding blast made them all flinch and stutter-step.

It hadn't come from the upright shaft behind them.

It'd come from the darkness far ahead.

CHAPTER THIRTY-TWO

They came to a stop just inside one of the orange pools of light. Travis studied Dyer's face and was surprised by the stress it showed, even taking the circumstances into account. Dyer didn't strike him as a man prone to fearing for his own safety, yet at the moment he looked deeply afraid.

It crossed Travis's mind that he himself had given no thought to escaping this place, until they'd set off a minute ago. All his focus, at first, had been on getting inside, and then it'd shifted to reaching the bottom of the mine and figuring out what to do there. He supposed that on some level he hadn't really expected to make it back out.

But Dyer wanted out. That much was obvious. And it really *didn't* look as though he was afraid for himself. There was more to it. *A lot* more, Travis thought. A missile commander in some bunker under South Dakota, with a launch order in hand, might look as tense as Dyer did right now.

The man turned back and forth, staring in both of the tunnel's directions, as if willing either unseen exit to become viable again.

"Christ," he whispered.

"They're not inside yet," Travis said. "The explosives they've used so far are nowhere near big enough to get through those doors."

He imagined the men outside were using whatever small-scale stuff they'd already had with them, stored in one of the vehicles like the gas masks had been.

"They've got Holt on speed dial," Dyer said. "They can chopper in whatever they need, from wherever's closest. They'll have the doors down in half an hour."

His eyes tracked over their three MP5s but dismissed them in about a second. He paced to the wall and leaned his forehead into it, thinking hard but getting nowhere.

"I was told there's a residence at the top of the shaft," he said.

"There is," Travis said.

"Anything in there we can use to set a trap? Gas lines to the stove or dryer?"

"Both electric."

Dyer went back to thinking.

"What's in the Breach's chamber?" Travis said. "Other than the Breach. Is there any equipment? Anything big? Anything useful as a weapon?"

"Wouldn't think so," Dyer said, "given what Garner told me."

"Let's see for ourselves," Travis said.

They were three flights from the bottom when Travis saw that he'd been wrong about something: the shaft wasn't exactly open to the broad chamber below it. Just beneath the lowest step, and the catwalk that extended from it, a heavy barrier of glass or clear plastic had been bolted in place like a floor, separating the vertical stretch from the space that yawned underneath. All around its edges, the barrier had been sealed to the stone walls with some heavy duty compound that looked like tar.

Travis could see now where the catwalk led—what it disappeared into, anyway: a channel about the height and width of a standard doorway, bored through the shaft wall a foot above the bottom, and six inches above the clear barricade. By the time they were descending the last steps before the walk, Travis could see deep into the narrow tunnel. It extended some fifteen feet through darkness, then opened up broadly on its right side. Through the opening streamed the same intense red-and-pink light that shone over everything beneath the stair shaft.

Travis, leading the way, came to a stop at the foot of the stairs. He looked straight down through the transparent floor just under his feet. Even from here he couldn't see the sides of the chasm below it. Its bottom was maybe thirty feet down, and covered with a dark gray layer of something granular and crumbled. Like ground-up asphalt, but not quite.

Travis refocused on the barrier. He could see its thickness under the sealant along the walls. Three inches at least. A person could walk on it without risk. It looked like someone *had*: the whole surface was scratched and scuffed—it must be dura-plastic instead of glass. Had the installers made those marks? Travis took a step sideways while keeping his eyes on the damage, and by the movement of vague reflections on the surface he realized he had it wrong again: the scratches were on the *underside* of the barrier.

He stared at them a moment longer and then continued into the tunnel. His footsteps and the others' echoed everywhere in the pressing space.

They came abreast of the opening at the end.

They stopped.

They said nothing.

Hanging off the side of the corridor, into emptiness, was an elevator-sized enclosure made of the same plastic as the barrier in the shaft. Rectangular panels of it were bolted into a steel framework. Even the floor was clear.

The structure offered a perfect view of what lay beyond: a vast biscuit of space blasted and carved out of the mountain's core. Thirty feet from top to bottom, at least a hundred feet in diameter. The viewing booth looked out over it from up near the plane of the ceiling.

This had been the original ore deposit, Travis was sure. Miners had cleared this cavity with dynamite and pickaxes in the early twentieth century. The notion registered and faded in the same instant. Two other things filled all his awareness.

One was the second Breach. Its familiarity and exoticness overlapped, each inescapable. Positioned straight out ahead of the viewing structure, near the furthest point of the cavern's arc, the thing had the same size and shape and texture as its counterpart in Wyoming. A ragged oval torn open across thin air, ten feet wide and three high, forming the flared mouth of a tunnel that plunged away to a vanishing point beyond. The tunnel itself was perfectly round, its height matching the opening's three feet but drawn far inward from its sides. Mouth and tunnel alike were made of something like plasma—like flame rippling and playing along the underside of a board.

Only its colors set this Breach apart, but they were enough to make the difference jarring. Travis stared and didn't blink. The tunnel was a deep bloody red, with strands of ethereal pink twisting and writhing along its length every few seconds. Those colors spread out across the flared mouth, flowing against its edge: a five-inch border that shone brilliantly white.

All of it combined to illuminate the second thing that had Travis's attention.

The cavern's floor.

Which was carpeted with dead insects the size of human hands.

He'd seen them from the lowest flight of stairs, but hadn't realized it. The details were only obvious where the light was brightest—in the thirty or forty feet around the Breach. Fractured carapaces and cracked wings and segmented, chitinous bodies—the chamber could be waist deep in them for all Travis knew.

He noticed something else: the plastic shielding here was scratched like the panel below the stairs—and again only on the opposite side.

He became aware of Bethany's breathing, off to his left. Intensifying and speeding up. Travis recalled her telling him once that she hated bugs. Deeply, irrationally hated them—a serious phobia she had no intention of coming to grips with. Now she stepped into his peripheral vision and pointed to a spot halfway between their position and the Breach. He followed. And saw.

One of the bugs was alive. It lay atop the detritus, fanning its wings in slow, delicate beats. It was visually similar to a hornet. Needle-thin waist, compound wing-structures, bristled thorax with some kind of stinger at the tip. Head to tail it was maybe six inches long.

Travis saw another just like it ten yards to the left—also alive. He picked out three more in the next few seconds.

Bethany steadied her breathing and spoke. "I thought they couldn't come through."

"They can't, exactly," Dyer said. "How they get here is tricky. That's where the parasite signals come in. Bugs just like these ones transmit them from the other end of the tunnel. The way Garner described it, the signals can seek out conscious targets on this end. Living brains—the bigger the better. They get in your head and use it as a kind of relay, probably amplifying the signals, which are . . . kinetic. *Tele*kinetic. They can trigger complex reactions in certain materials. Can rearrange them, at least on a tiny scale. Down at the level of molecules."

"You mean the movement we felt inside our heads?" Paige said. She sounded more than a little rattled by the idea.

"No," Dyer said. "Supposedly that feeling is just your nerves going crazy. The rearranging happens somewhere else—some random spot outside your body, but not far away."

"What do you mean?" Travis said. "What do they rearrange?"

"Simple elements. Carbon, nitrogen, hydrogen, a few others. They assemble them to form a cell—basically an embryo. Like one of ours, but even smaller, and much less complex. The signals build it in about ten seconds, and then they cut out and the embryo is on its own, and the rest is straight-forward biology." He waved a hand at the mass of hard-shelled bodies beyond the glass. "Only takes the embryo a few weeks to develop into the full-sized form—probably a perfect copy of the trans-mitting parasite at the other end of the wormhole."

Travis let the concept settle over him. He was struck not by how strange it was, but by how it paralleled much of what he'd read of biology in the past year. Propagation was life's first objective. To spread. To *be*. It evolved stunningly elaborate ways of doing that, from the helicopter seeds of maple trees to the complex, two-stage life cycle of the Plasmodium parasite that carried malaria between mosquitoes and vertebrates—Travis had struggled to accept parts of that process as possible, even though it was hard science that'd been nailed down decades ago.

"Most of these things don't live very long after they form," Dyer said, "and a lot of the ones that do can barely move. It's pretty clear they're not built for this world. Wherever they're from, maybe the gravity's weaker and the air's thicker. Who knows? But the thing is, some of them *can* move.

And fly. Garner said there were serious injuries to the workers here in 1987. They set up these barricades as soon as they got a sense of what was happening, and pretty much by accident they figured out how to rein it all in."

"Someone has to be a lightning rod," Travis said.

Dyer nodded. "That's close to how Garner described it. For whatever reason, if someone comes down here even a few times a day and makes a nice, easy target of himself, the signals never hunt any further. If they *do* have to look further, they eventually look *much* further, even through hundreds of feet of rock, somehow. And in that case they don't stop at one target—they don't seem to stop at all. The signals get stronger. The intervals between them get shorter. Peter Campbell and the others who were here at the beginning used equipment to work out the signal strength, and even some of the timing. There was some kind of reliable curve you could draw on a graph, showing how bad it would get if you left it untended too long. It would get out past Rum Lake after a while. It could extend for hundreds of miles."

Travis stared over the tumble of insect debris and imagined Allen Raines's life for the last twenty-five years, centered entirely on this place. Bound to it as if tethered to a stake.

A sound intruded on the thought: a high metallic whine from far above in the stair shaft. It lasted a few seconds, then stopped, then proceeded in starts and fits.

"They're drilling the hinges," Dyer said. "Probably planning to stuff shaped charges into them."

Travis turned and surveyed the cramped space around them. Observation booth on one side, rock-lined tunnel on the other. No tools or equipment of any kind lying around. Nothing that could help them lay a trap.

"I don't know what to do," Dyer said. "I just don't."

The bigger-than-himself fear was back in his eyes. Travis let it go for the moment. He turned again to the plastic-built compartment and, for the first time, stepped into it. He stood right on the see-through floor, a quick thrill of vertigo spinning up through his nerves. He looked down and across the cavern floor, studying the bugs. Many more of the hornetlike things were visible now, lazily beating the air with their wings, drawing forelimbs over heads full of terrible composite eyes. Was he imagining it, or were there a lot more of them moving now than at first? In a glance he could see dozens, and that was only where the light was strong. How many more were beginning to stir in the darker regions?

All that could explain this sudden activity was the fact that the four of them had just arrived. Their voices, transferring through the plastic, however faintly, had roused these things from some lethargic state.

Travis looked at the trace scratches crisscrossing the window in front of him, and then without warning he raised his fist and pounded it hard and fast against the panel.

He heard the others startle behind him.

"*What are you doing?*" Bethany said.

Out in the chamber, every hornet shape jerked at

the sudden racket. They didn't cock their heads—probably didn't have their ears there—but splayed their bodies out instead, wings going flat and rigid, all movement ceasing in a matter of seconds. To Travis, the posture looked like the embodiment of tension and alertness.

It looked like they were listening.

He kept pounding the panel. Another second. Two.

On three the first of the insects lifted off. It was one Travis hadn't even seen—it came up out of the deep red, somewhere to the left. By the time Travis had swung his gaze toward it, there were others in the air. Lots of others. Dozens and then well over a hundred. Where they rose directly past the Breach, its glare shone right through their bodies, as if they were hollow shells made of thin paper. Light enough to fly—even on Earth.

They converged toward the booth before they'd ascended even a few feet, the whole mass of them moving as if guided by a single mind. Travis finally stopped pounding and stepped back, and an instant later the first of them hit the windows. They flew more like moths than hornets. They made great swooping circles and scraped the plastic in glancing blows. Within moments there were enough of them swarming the panels that it was hard to see out.

"Was there a *reason* you did that?" Bethany whispered.

"Yes," Travis said, without looking back.

He dropped the magazine out of his MP5, drew it close to his eyes and studied the metal edges at the top where it socketed into the weapon. He found one that suited his purpose.

Then he stepped into the booth again, fit the chosen edge to the nearest of the screws holding a panel in place, and began to loosen it.

CHAPTER THIRTY-THREE

It wasn't likely to work. He knew that. It was just all they had. If it failed they'd die—but if they did nothing they'd die anyway. Not much of a dilemma.

The idea was simple enough: prep the window to be removed with a good shove, wait for the contractors to enter the mine and reach the bottom of the stairs just outside this tunnel—and shove. The bugs would spill in. They would attack everyone. The four of them would expect it. The contractors wouldn't. As a group, the contractors would present a much larger and louder target—as well as a fleeing one. It was hard to imagine the men wouldn't reverse course in the mother of all hurries, all the way back to whichever access they'd come in through. With a decent amount of luck, the bulk of the swarm would go with them, and briefly scatter whoever was waiting outside the mine. Whatever portion of the bugs stayed down here in the tunnel might be manageable; Travis pictured their translucent, fragile bodies meeting violently swung MP5s. Maybe it would work. Maybe they'd get a few minutes' opportunity to follow the contractors up into the woods and run for visual cover.

Maybe.

Travis didn't pretend to be optimistic, either for the others' benefit or his own.

He and Paige removed all but four screws, one at each corner, and loosened those as much as they dared. They left them holding on by no more than a few turns each. The panel, a little larger than a beach towel, rattled and swayed in place at the lightest touch.

On the other side, the hornets continued to loop and dive and scrape.

The four of them sat in the tunnel just shy of where it opened to the plastic enclosure. Bethany pressed her hands tightly between her knees and tried to keep them from shaking. She said little.

High above, the drilling continued. During pauses they could hear the same progress going on at the more distant access.

"All right," Dyer said. "Here's what I know."

He was quiet for twenty seconds, lining it all up.

"You've been acting on limited information," he said. "You knew that. You had no choice but to try connecting the dots anyway—the ones you had. Peter Campbell did the same thing, early in the Scalar investigation, and came to the same misunderstanding as you: that Ruben Ward did something bad."

Paige looked at Travis and Bethany, then Dyer.

"He *did* do something bad," she said. "My father was terrified about it."

"In the beginning."

Paige shook her head. "In the end, too, and long after. He was still scared of it five years ago."

"He was scared five years ago, but not for any of the reasons you think."

Paige started to reply, then just stopped and waited for him to go on.

Dyer shut his eyes for a few seconds. A last consideration of how to say it.

"The message Ward received had distinct halves. The first was a description of the place on the other side of the Breach, along with an explanation of why the message had been sent. None of which Garner shared with me. Those are the deepest parts of the secret. What he told me about was the second half: the instructions. They included a list of nine names, nine people who were alive in 1978, and directions for finding them."

Travis looked at Paige and knew what she was thinking. *Loraine Cotton.*

"Ward's task was straightforward," Dyer said. "Take the message to each of these people and convince them it was for real. There were verifiers built into it, to help him do that. Specific predictions of things like aurora activity that summer, down to the minute. Things you couldn't just guess about—things a *human* couldn't just guess about anyway."

"What were these people supposed to do with the message once they had it?" Travis said.

"Follow the instructions that were included for

them. Which were more complicated than Ward's. His part was done by early August."

"Why did he kill himself?" Bethany said.

"For the reason everyone assumed, the day they heard about it. The Breach had fried him. Whatever gave him the means to translate the message—and dumped him into a near-coma for all those weeks—screwed him up in lots of other ways. Serious mood problems. Imbalances. It's a wonder he lasted those three months. Did you know the message included an apology for that effect? Whoever sent it knew it would do that to a human brain. It couldn't be avoided."

The drilling atop the shaft suddenly changed tone. Became deeper, more guttural. The first bit had been swapped out for something bigger. Everyone listened for a moment and then tried to ignore it.

"So by August of 1978," Dyer said, "the nine recipients had their orders in hand. These were nine pretty average people, but that was about to change. The instructions included ways for them to dramatically increase their financial and social status over the following years. The wording was pretty careful—the message's senders may have anticipated that other people might see it along the way. It didn't necessarily say 'Invest in Apple on this exact date, or apply for this particular job,' but it was in the ballpark. It read like a childishly simple riddle, if you knew to look past the surface, and for these nine people it was the recipe for becoming extremely rich, and politically connected, in just a matter of years."

Travis thought of the three names Bethany's data-mining had turned up. Three of the people Peter Campbell had met with here in Rum Lake, in December 1987. All three had been worth tens of millions by then, with ties to Washington.

And all three had begun amassing that wealth and power in the late seventies or very early eighties.

Suddenly Travis understood what the *ping* had been about, a while earlier when they'd learned about Loraine Cotton: they'd recognized that her steep financial climb started just after Ruben Ward met with her, and as a direct result of his doing so. But Travis hadn't noticed the similarity with the other three. Hadn't tied in the fact that their climbs had begun around the same time as hers. He'd overlooked it because those people were supposed to be *Peter's* allies, whom he'd chosen in 1987. It hadn't seemed to matter when and how they'd become powerful.

"Whoever's on the other side seems to have at least some rudimentary knowledge of our future," Dyer said. "They had it as of 1978, in any case. Some understanding of which technologies, even which companies, were about to break in a big way."

"There are entities that can access the future," Paige said. "With certain restrictions."

"However it worked," Dyer said, "the information was dead-on. These people were all major players by the mid eighties, which allowed them to begin following the next instruction: get close to the people who control the Breach. Stay informed on all that surrounds it, and gain as much influence over it as possible. That last part they were free to take their time with. They wouldn't have to *use* the influence until quite a ways down the road."

"How far down the road?" Travis said.

"Seven minutes past three P.M. mountain time, June 5, 2016."

The three of them stared. None spoke.

Travis's mind automatically sought a meaning for the date, but came up with nothing. It was a few months shy of four years from now. Beyond that, nothing about it stuck.

"What happens at that time?" Paige said.

"The Breach inside Border Town opens," Dyer said. "Really opens, I mean. Becomes a two-way channel that a person can pass through from this end. But only one specific person, whom the instructions also name and describe. They made it very clear that no one else was to come through. Putting that person in front of the Breach at the right time falls to the other nine. That's their entire purpose. It's what all the power and influence are for."

The notion of someone actually stepping into the Breach affected Travis to an extent that surprised him. Through the fabric of his shirt he could suddenly feel the stone wall at his back, radiating its chill.

"Who goes in?" he said.

Dyer looked at him. "You do, Mr. Chase."

CHAPTER THIRTY-FOUR

The tunnel seemed almost to move beneath him. To rock gently left and then right, like a boat in a passing wake.

"The message that came through the Breach was about you," Dyer said. "It named you. It specified your time and place of birth."

A memory came to Travis. An image of the dark alley near Johns Hopkins, between the town houses. Ruben Ward staggering somewhere ahead of him, aware that he was being followed.

The man had called out: *Who the hell are you?*

And he'd answered: *Travis Chase. Let me help.*

There'd been an audible response on Ward's part. Some expulsion of breath Travis had pegged for confusion, and then dismissed.

You're only a kid, Ward had said. And a moment later: *The instructions didn't say anything about this.*

Travis looked around at the others—Dyer just watching him, reading his response, Paige and Bethany staring with blank faces, still processing the information.

Then Paige's expression changed. She looked at Travis and mouthed a single word: *it*.

Travis acknowledged her with a nod neither Bethany nor Dyer saw.

It.

Jesus.

No doubting the connection now.

Was that what the filter was about, then? Was it some consequence of entering the Breach from this end? An unavoidable result, like the brain damage Ruben Ward had suffered when the thing opened?

Whoever it affects, it's not their fault. Not really. Under the wrong conditions, anyone could end up the worst person on Earth.

Travis looked at Dyer. "Did Garner ever say anything about a filter? Did that word ever come up, regarding the message?"

Dyer thought about it, but seemed to draw a blank. He shook his head.

Travis considered the notion for another second and then let it fall away—for the moment. The present conversation drew his full attention again.

"I was a child when that message arrived," Travis said. "How the hell could it be about me?"

"I'd tell you if I knew," Dyer said.

"Does Garner know? Does he know what happens when I go through?"

"He knows something—whatever the first half of the message says."

"We saw part of it," Paige said. "I won't go into the *how*, but we saw two separate lines from the notebook. One was about finding Loraine Cotton here in Rum Lake. The other was from earlier in the text. It said, 'Some of us are already among you.'"

Dyer's eyes tightened involuntarily. He'd clearly never heard that before.

"I don't know," he said at last. "Like I told you, Garner kept all that to himself. All he said about it was that it mattered. Like the biggest things in history matter. Things we can't afford to get wrong." He paused. "They *wouldn't* have gotten it wrong. Everything was on the right track, at the beginning. The nine knew all they were supposed to, and were gaining power. No one else knew a thing. By the end, right before 2016, they'd have been well positioned to get you into Tangent, Mr. Chase, under whatever necessary pretense. To give you an idea of *how* well positioned, consider that Garner himself was one of the nine. In 1978 he was a retired Navy SEAL thinking about putting his law degree to use. The instructions rerouted him into politics. Everything was rolling smoothly. And then it wasn't."

"Scalar," Paige said. There was a note of pain in her voice.

Dyer nodded. "Your father's learning about the notebook, from Ward's wife, threw everything off. He launched the investigation, came up empty, and got started on the project to create this second Breach the following year. Before it was long under way, a few of the nine had already gotten wind of it. They knew why Peter was doing it, and couldn't blame him. Of course he'd want to find out what the message had said. Given the secrecy, how could it sound anything but ominous to him? Garner and the others debated meeting with him and telling him everything, but held back. What if he didn't agree with their goal? Their advantage would be lost, just like that. So they waited instead, and watched over this project as closely as they could. They weren't sure what would result from it, but they were confident it wouldn't generate another Ward." He shrugged. "In the end they actually exerted some influence on the construction. Peter had a team building the new ion collider in a secure location a few hundred miles from here—it could be taken apart and moved once he found a place to set it up for good. Secrecy around the search for a final site was incredibly strict. No one in Washington was privy to the memos. The nine were worried they'd end up never knowing how all this turned out, so they used indirect methods to suggest this mine shaft, by way of one of the engineering firms involved. Loraine Cotton knew the mine from her time as a biologist here."

Dyer nodded at the red light streaming in nearby. "They installed the collider in about three months in 1987, and switched it on. You know how that went. Garner and the others figured that was the end of it. But it wasn't. Even while he was containing the mess here, Peter began preliminary steps toward trying again somewhere else. And again and again, if need be. He was that rattled by not knowing what Ward had done. He couldn't justify ever giving up. So Garner and the rest finally rolled the dice. A few of them met with Peter and told him the whole story."

"How did he take it?" Paige said.

Dyer rubbed his eyes and leaned his head back

against the stone. "Like he'd accidentally released plague rats from a lab." He exhaled slowly. "Peter agreed entirely with their aim, and that all of his work on Scalar had to stop. But by then it wasn't as simple as that. Things were worse than Garner and the others realized. They'd been watching Tangent's dealings for a few years by then, especially as Scalar began to ramp up. They never thought Peter knew about them—but he did. And he'd countered their moves with his own. He'd been watching *them*. Remember, he had Breach technology at his disposal. Serious advantages no one outside Border Town knew about. He'd also involved contacts he had within the FBI, for things like background checks and financial record searches."

"Oh shit," Travis said. He could see the rough shape of the problem.

Dyer nodded. "Peter did that stuff long before Garner and the others came to see him. Before he knew any better. By the time they *did* meet with him, there were a handful of people in the United States government who knew all nine of their names, and knew they'd taken an unusual interest in Scalar—which a select few also knew about. You see the danger, right? And you see how even stopping the investigation in its tracks, ceasing work on new Breaches, wouldn't make that danger go away. There would always be those few people out there, along with whoever they'd talked to, who might put the pieces together. Rumors of an alien message, its instructions carried out on Earth in 1978. Nine powerful people deeply involved with it somehow, all of whom had radically improved their standing right after the message arrived. There would always be the risk of someone connecting the dots and re-acting out of fear. Of huge-scale action being taken against Garner and the others, and maybe against Tangent itself. All of that could happen years before 2016. Years before the culmination of their work."

Dyer waved a hand to indicate the unseen chamber six hundred feet above. "So they all met to talk about it. Peter and the other Scalar investigators, and Garner and the rest of those who'd received the message. They came here in mid-December 1987 to figure it all out. The location worked because it was still secret to anyone in D.C. Only the engineers knew where this place was, and they'd all signed nondisclosure forms that threatened capital punishment. Between that and how damned scared of the place they were, by that point, they weren't likely to ever talk. So, good place for the meeting. Peter and the others brought a report with them. A plan for how to proceed."

"The cheat sheet," Paige said.

Dyer looked puzzled.

"That's what others in Tangent called it," she said.

"A one-page plan," Travis said. "Jesus, now I know why. It could've probably been a one-*line* plan: *Stop everything and cross our fingers.*"

"More or less," Dyer said. "In the end it was all they could do. Like submarine combat. Rig for quiet and go dead in the water. Hope like hell they just lose you after a while."

He went silent, and for a moment the four of them listened to the drilling up top. Droning, patient, relentless.

"I guess they didn't," Travis said.

A second later the drilling stopped.

CHAPTER THIRTY-FIVE

They listened. A minute passed. No sound anywhere, except the scrape and rattle of insect bodies against the viewing booth. The drilling at both accesses had finished.

"Not much longer now," Paige said.

They waited. Time slipped by. Sometimes they heard a metallic tapping from one access or the other. Mostly they heard nothing at all.

"This dream you had," Dyer said. "You actually think it was real?"

"The door combo was real," Travis said. "That's all I have to go on."

Dyer looked thoughtful.

"What?" Travis said.

"The drug you described," Dyer said. "That's real too. It's called phenyline dicyclomide. They use it for interrogations. It's been around for about twenty years, but they perfected it in the last ten, in places like Gitmo. Intel guys call it hypnosis in a vial."

"It makes you talk?" Travis said.

"It can. But its selling point is that it makes you *act*. It hits you in two stages. The first one lasts a couple minutes. Mild hallucinations, with an amnesia effect; you don't remember much of anything from before the drug kicked in. Then comes the second stage, maybe five minutes long, during which your short-term memory is fractured down to a second or less. Someone can speak to you, and you can forget each word as it passes. Very disturbing effect—with two kickers. One, you can still follow commands. Even complex ones that are too long to remember. If I've got your laptop sitting there, I can tell you, 'Log into your e-mail account and your banking site,' and you'll probably do it. Passwords and all. You'll be forgetting the command even while I'm saying it, but you'll follow it anyway. It's a conditioning thing—it functions like a habit. They say you hear the command well enough to obey it, but don't remember it well enough to resist."

"Why am I not even vaguely surprised we develop shit like that?" Bethany said.

"The second kicker is even better," Dyer said. "While your memory is crumbling by the moment during Stage Two, you can still remember Stage One. Stage One is really *all* you remember, during that time. Usually they'll keep you in darkness, with no sound, so there's not much to remember anyway. But if they want to, they can make use of the effect. They can feed you information in Stage One that you'll use in Stage Two. They might say, 'Your brother is flying into LAX tomorrow, United terminal, five thirty in the afternoon.' Then when your memory starts to fracture and you're open to commands, they give you a phone and say, 'Call your brother's usual driver and arrange to have him picked up.' You'll do it, because you remember hearing that he's coming in. Just like that, they find out who his driver is."

"Sounds useful," Travis said.

Dyer nodded. "If they're employing that drug on Garner and one of the others, I'm not surprised they know the door combo by now."

"Couldn't they just know everything?" Paige said. "Couldn't they command Garner to start telling the whole story?"

"Getting directly into someone's secrets is tricky," Dyer said. "Like with real hypnosis—a person's moral restraint weighs in. They say you can make someone in a trance state bark like a dog, since it's no big deal, but you can't make him kill his best friend. I think secrets are in the same vein—if it really matters to keep them, people do. So it's one thing to type a password by habit; it's something else to start spilling information you've protected for years." He paused. "But they can use the drug over and over, and it can wear you down after a while. So yeah—in time they might know everything." He looked at Travis. "If they learn your name, I think the game's over. If not, there's still a chance."

Something seemed to occur to Dyer. His eyebrows drew toward each other. "This room you saw Garner in—was there light brown carpeting with gold stars in a wide-spaced pattern? A star the size of a cookie every couple feet?"

Travis visualized the little room again. He let the image form for a second or two. "That's exactly what it had," he said.

"And you heard jet engines running?"

"The three of us were on a jet at the time. That was just background noise . . . seeping into the dream."

"I don't think it was," Dyer said. "That carpet is aboard *Air Force One*."

For a moment Dyer's expression flared with hope, but almost as quickly it lost its edge. Doubt faded in. His face became a tug-of-war between the two.

"Garner reassigned me to the Treasury branch of the Service after he brought me in on all this," he said. "He needed me out of harm's way if shit happened. But my BlackBerry still gets automatic updates of the plane's flight plan. If we get back outside, I can find out where it is." He frowned. "I just don't think that's going to make a difference."

"Why wouldn't it?" Travis said. "You could just call someone and tell them Garner's being held aboard the plane. You're in the Secret Service— contact someone at the top. Contact *everyone* at the top. They can't all be aligned with Holt on this thing."

"No one's going to believe any of it," Dyer said. "Think about it. Think how that phone call would sound."

"Then make up something more credible. Say whatever it takes, just get them to raid the plane. Once they find Garner, it'll all come undone."

"There is no one on this planet with the authority to raid that plane. Stuart Holt is the president of the United States." He pressed his hands to his temples. Shook his head. "What happened last night was the endpoint of years of planning. Nothing will have been left to chance. Six agents are listed as killed in the attack on the White House, but if Garner didn't die in the explosion, I doubt those agents did either. I'm sure they were murdered because they weren't part of the arrangement. Which means everyone else *is* part of it. Everyone who matters, anyway. Holt's probably got a skeleton crew aboard *Air Force One* right now. A tiny circle of loyalists, seeing all of this through. No official outside that shell is going to break in through it."

His eyes darkened then. Some kind of cold acceptance settled in. "We don't have to worry much longer anyway, about Garner being interrogated. That's where the deadline comes in."

Travis shared a look with the others. "What do you mean?"

"They all agreed, back in 1987, on a panic option. They figured if the hammer came down, it'd be some huge simultaneous move against all of them. Their thinking was, if some of them survived, they might have time to call in hired muscle and try to free the others. So they agreed on a timeline. If any were taken alive, they'd endure torture for exactly twenty-four hours, and then kill themselves. They have hydrogen cyanide caplets sewn into their tongues."

"Christ," Bethany whispered.

"Six hours from now," Dyer said, "Garner will

bite out the caplet and swallow it. Whoever's being held with him will do the same. That'll be it."

The metallic tapping stopped.

Nothing replaced it.

The minutes drew out.

Travis watched the others try to keep their nerves steady. Paige, sitting next to him, took his hand.

They waited.

He found himself going back to the message from the Breach. The understanding that it was about him, and always had been. Even when he was ten years old.

He couldn't grasp the concept. Couldn't get within a mile of it. After a while his mind settled on a more material problem. He understood he was only thinking about it for the distraction it offered. He thought of it anyway:

Even if everything went perfectly in the next few minutes, how would he get inside Border Town in 2016? It would be the best-defended military outpost in the world by then. He'd infiltrated the place once before while it was under someone else's control, but only with the help of an entity—one of the most useful ever to emerge from the Breach.

His stream of thought came to a dead stop.

He stared at the tunnel wall straight across from him, and then at nothing.

"Holy shit," he said softly.

The others looked at him, but he said no more. He just let go of Paige's hand and scrambled to his feet and ran for the stairs.

CHAPTER THIRTY-SIX

W*hat are you doing?*" Paige shouted.

Travis was two flights up already. Paige's voice echoed crazily after him, rebounding off the walls.

Travis looked down as he climbed, sprinting, taking the treads three at a time. Paige was just emerging from the tunnel, Bethany and Dyer behind her.

"Follow me!" Travis yelled. "But not all the way. Stay a hundred feet below the top."

"They're going to blow the door anytime!" Dyer yelled.

"I know," Travis said.

In rough shouts as he lunged upward, he explained the idea. The hope. He glanced down again as he finished, and saw that Paige's eyes had gone wide. She thought it all through for another two seconds.

"Oh my God," she said.

Travis turned his attention back to the stairs, and after a moment he heard the others' footsteps following.

*   *   *

He passed the dark tunnel Dyer had emerged from. Two thirds of the shaft's height still soared above him. The bright square of Raines's residence chamber appeared very small yet. He kept running, climbing. His lungs already felt like they were submerged in acid. His thighs and ankles were going numb from the shock of repetitive impacts.

He lost his sense of time going by. Even his sense of steps and flights going by. There was only the top of the shaft, the open square full of halogen light, turning and turning above him, growing by imperceptible degrees.

He thought of the little girl at the Third Notch, insisting her mother tell the story of the ghost.

He thought of Jeannie's inability to dismiss what the kid was saying. The woman had believed, against all her logic, that there really was something haunting the mine entrances.

They say anyone who goes near starts to hear voices, she'd said, *whispering right behind them in the trees. Pine boughs around you start to move like the wind's blowing, even when it isn't.*

He thought of his own words to Paige, regarding the power players her father had allied with. The notion that Peter might've given them Breach technology.

Maybe even things he kept off the books in Border Town.

Travis looked up. The top of the shaft was huge now, filling his vision. Three flights left. Two. One.

*   *   *

He vaulted up over the lip into the chamber without slowing, and crossed the room in a burst, blurring past the wall of monitors. He crashed to a stop against the red metal locker mounted waist high on the wall, lifted the drop-latch and tore open the door.

The locker looked empty.

He reached in at the bottom and found that it wasn't.

There were very rare entities—kinds that'd shown up only two or three times in all the years the Breach had been open. A few had emerged only once. Travis had always believed—was sure every current member of Tangent had always believed—that the transparency suit was in the latter group.

The feel of nearly weightless fabric bunching in his fist, where only thin air was visible, told him otherwise.

He drew the suit from the locker, carefully getting hold of its two halves—top and bottom. It was like pulling clothes out of a hamper in pitch darkness.

Certain he had both components, he pressed them together under his arm and turned back for the stairwell. As he did, his eyes picked out images on the wall of screens. The first thing he saw was that four of the monitors had gone to blue—one for each of the dual cameras inside the two accesses, all of which had been knocked out by the initial explosions. Then he noticed movement in some of the still-active frames. Men were lugging yellow fifty-five gallon drums into the north access, where

Dyer had come in. Travis stepped closer and saw boxy attachments stuck to each barrel's top, wired in with thick red and black cords. He darted his gaze around to find a view of *this* access—the one that led to the far side of the blast door ten feet away from him.

He saw it: the squared concrete tunnel sticking out of the slope among the redwoods.

There was no one going in.

There was no one anywhere near it.

A second later he found a screen showing the Humvee he and Paige and Bethany had driven up into the trees. It was right where they'd left it, jammed sideways near a trunk. Other Humvees were visible in the frame with it.

There were men crouched on the downhill side of each vehicle.

They were all covering their ears.

CHAPTER THIRTY-SEVEN

E very inch of the sprint felt like too much to ask for. Each vaulting step seemed like it should be the last.

He went back over the lip at the top of the stairs. Jumped with no thought for which tread his foot would land on—the time required for that kind of thinking was also too much to ask for.

It turned out to be the fourth step above the landing. His arch came down right on the drop-off, and only his forward momentum kept him from dumping all his weight onto it and breaking his ankle. He threw his other foot down with more control, rammed it hard and flat onto the steel landing, and brought his forearm up to catch the wall before he shattered his face on it.

The arm took a lot of the blow, but not all. The rest of his body was hurtled against the stone an instant later, the impact wringing the air from his lungs. He sucked it back in and used it to scream for the others to cover their ears, then pivoted toward the next flight and jumped again. He was arcing through the air, aiming for the next landing and clamping his hands over the sides of his head, when it finally happened.

It felt like having a boxcar dropped on him.

The airspace around him seemed to solidify and compress inward in a single, monstrous clap. He saw the stairs beneath him jump and vibrate. Saw the effect race down the shaft, a shockwave trailing a vacuum in its wake. The bass followed, making an eardrum of his whole body. He heard it with his knees and his spine and his fillings.

He kept his feet under him as he plunged ahead toward the landing, and threw both hands forward from his ears to catch the wall. He became aware of the transparency suit falling away below his arm, and had just enough time to notice it'd dropped toward the sidewall, not the open center of the shaft.

Then he hit, and his arms folded, and his forehead slammed against his wrist on the wall and everything went black.

Hands, shaking him by the shoulder, frantic.

"*Travis.*"

Paige, whispering.

He opened his eyes. The shaft was swirling with gray-white concrete dust. Ten feet above him, a broad rectangular shape stuck out over the top of the shaft.

The green door. Bent and twisted at its edges. Hurled out of its frame into the room, lying with maybe a quarter of its mass over the shaft's edge.

Travis looked at Paige. Her eyes were wet and

her cheeks were smeared. Relief just outweighed fear in her expression.

Travis turned over and sat up. He looked at the flight he'd jumped down past. He got up on his knees and leaned forward and pawed at the landing and the lowest stair treads, and for a terrible few seconds believed the suit's halves had missed them anyway. Maybe they'd caught the air and gone under the rail—or right between the treads—and slipped down into the depths of the shaft, where a painstaking week wouldn't be enough to find the damn things.

Then he saw them: misshapen pockets of clear air amid the churning dust, clumped near each other halfway up the flight. He reached up and grabbed both, withdrew to the landing again and looked at Paige and the others.

"I'm going to engage them outside in the open," Travis said. "That gives me the best advantage, especially with the dust down here."

He turned and sat on the second step, felt for which half of the suit was the bottom, and began to pull it on. He heard Dyer take a quick breath at the sight of first one leg and then the other vanishing.

"The three of you should find shooting cover in the chamber up top," Travis said. "Weapons trained on the doorway. It's like the Thermopylae Pass. Anything comes through that you can see, kill it."

He unslung his MP5 and handed it to Dyer.

Dyer looked puzzled. Then, assuming Travis was asking him to trade, he drew his own sidearm from his shoulder holster and held it out.

Travis shook his head. "I'm good."

"What are you going to use?" Dyer said.

"Something quieter," Travis said, and pulled on the suit's top half.

He took the stairs quickly but carefully, no longer able to see his feet. He'd worn the suit before—its twin, anyway—but that had been more than three years ago, and the thing still held all its novelty for him. The material was comfortable and breathable, and there was no question it had some capacity to shape itself to its wearer. As Travis had been told, it generally kept the form of whoever had last worn it, then actively adjusted to anyone new. He felt it doing that now, as he ascended. Where it covered his face, it drew taut along his jawline and relaxed a bit over his nose. It sucked in around his shoes and ankles. It molded to the precise dimensions of his hands. He guessed it would've done the same for a hand with seven digits instead of five. Maybe even for a body with four arms, or some altogether different structure.

He stepped off the top stair into the chamber. The green door lay at his feet among the curling dust. Straight ahead, its frame had been torqued and blown half free of the stone that'd encased it. The giant bolt latch lay off to one side, bent like a pried-out roofing nail.

Travis turned from the opening and sprinted toward the back right corner of the room. The kitchen.

He found what he wanted in the third drawer he opened: a ten-inch chef's knife right out of a horror film. He took it and ran for the blasted-out doorway.

He climbed the access stairs in perfect silence. By the third flight he was above the dust. He waved his free hand in front of his face and saw that none had stuck to the suit. He rounded the next landing and started up the topmost flight. The horizontal tunnel above was full of indirect daylight; it led directly out onto the forested slope.

He heard men talking just outside. Then the faint thud of boot treads stepping onto concrete. Once, then again and again in rapid succession. More than one person walking. Travis put the number at three.

He lifted the hem of the suit's top and carefully raised the knife into the space behind it. This was one of the suit's most useful tricks: its capacity to hide handheld objects. A silenced pistol would've been a godsend just now. Travis had seen for himself the brutal effectiveness of that combination. He'd come within half a second of taking a bullet to the head as a result.

He crept up the stairs and saw the men in the tunnel as soon as his eyes cleared floor level.

Three, as expected.

They stood at the midpoint between entry and stairwell, heads cocked, listening for any sign of movement down in the mine.

Travis stepped onto the concrete, the knife still hidden. The three men nearly blocked the tunnel ahead of him, but there was enough room on the left to slip by. Travis advanced, twisted sideways, eased past the formation.

He looked out through the tunnel's mouth and saw no one else close by. The Humvees were forty yards away down the hillside, and every man Travis could see was among them, standing or crouching.

He turned back to face the three listeners. For a moment longer they just stood there, waiting. They were arranged in a rough triangle, two forward and one lagging back, all three staring ahead into the darkness at the top of the shaft. Travis took a position directly behind the loner. He brought the knife out from under the suit and raised it slowly until it was eight inches behind and to the left of the man's neck—nowhere near the edge of his peripheral vision.

He held the blade level, with the cutting edge facing back toward himself.

With his other hand he pulled the suit's hem outward once more, ready to hide the knife again in a hurry.

"I don't hear anything," one of the men up front said.

Travis slipped the knife beneath the loner's jaw and yanked it straight back with all his force. It sliced through skin and cartilage and tough rubbery cords of muscle about as easily as it would've passed through ground beef. The man's body spasmed hard and his hands jerked to his throat, and a ragged choking noise came from his mouth.

The other two men spun, raising their weapons instinctively.

Travis brought the knife down to his waist—blocked from view by the still-standing victim—and raised it back into concealment within the suit.

"*Gordy,*" one of the other two said, his eyes taking in the wound but unable to comprehend how the hell it'd gotten there.

Gordy dropped. One shoulder landed first and his head went back and to the side, and the awful gash drew open and began founting blood in thick pulses.

The man who'd said the name sank fast to his knees and reached for him. The other guy stood back, hyperventilating, looking around instinctively for a threat he couldn't perceive.

He settled on the tunnel's mouth, ten feet away. The only logical place the attack could have come from. He stared at it, eyes darting, MP5 held tense.

Travis sidestepped around him in a wide arc, got behind him and brought the knife back out, then sliced him carotid to carotid.

He didn't rehide the knife. He simply stepped forward and slashed the third man's throat before number two had hit the ground. Just like that, there were three bodies convulsing and dying on the concrete, one of them maybe five seconds further into the process than the other two. Nothing about the encounter had been loud enough to carry to the men downslope.

Travis scooped up one of the dead men's MP5s, flicked the selector to full-auto and walked to the tunnel's open end.

"*Heads up!*" he screamed, his voice high enough that it could've belonged to any man, and opened fire with the weapon. He raked the stream of bullets randomly across the Humvees far below, heard shouts of alarm and confusion and saw bodies dive out of sight. He didn't bother aiming for them. He dinged up the sides of the vehicles until the machine gun ran dry, then dropped it in the dirt and sprinted away laterally across the slope. He knew his feet were kicking up sand and needles, but between the ground vegetation and the fact that no one was looking, he didn't worry. He exerted only enough effort to keep his footfalls close to quiet, and the knife hidden up inside the suit.

Fifty yards from the access he stopped. He turned straight downhill and moved at a careful walk, entirely soundless now and kicking up nothing. He descended until he was level with the Humvees, and saw the men crouched behind them on the downhill side. Anxiety in every set of eyes. Universal confusion over the screamed warning, the gunfire, and now the silence.

Travis counted fourteen men. He also counted two fewer Humvees than had chased them up here earlier; the others must have gone to the north access.

Getting at these fourteen from behind would be a joke—they were all looking uphill, over the vehicles' hoods or through their passenger compartments. The men were clustered in twos and threes, the Humvees spaced dozens of feet apart among the redwood trunks. One little group at a time, these people could be handled with no more difficulty than the first three.

Travis stared at them and wondered why he didn't feel worse about this. Why he'd felt nothing for the guys he killed on Main Street earlier, or those in the tunnel. Maybe necessity just pushed remorse aside. Maybe that was an animal thing from way back. Maybe he had more of it than he should. He considered that idea for another second and then pushed it aside too, and started across the slope in a long arc that would put him below the Humvees.

CHAPTER THIRTY-EIGHT

It took ninety seconds. When he'd finished, he dropped the knife and sprinted uphill to the access. He shouted the all-clear to the others, ran back to the Humvees and got one started.

They rolled down out of the trees and saw the town full of police vehicles far below. Crown Vics and SUVs and pickups, state and local, every flasher strobing blue and red in the overcast gloom. The big guy in the Humvee had ordered them in here earlier, to help search the town for the three of them.

Travis braked on the narrow road near Raines's house and put the vehicle in park. He switched on the two-way radio mounted to the dash and heard a man's voice in mid-sentence.

"—any assistance needed, please advise us on that, over."

There was a long hiss of static and then the same man began speaking once more: "Say again, any civilian unit, this is CHP, please acknowledge. I see one of you just out of the woods now."

"They heard the shooting," Paige said.

Travis nodded. "And their signals must not be getting to anyone on the other side of the ridge."

He grabbed the radio's handset and depressed the talk switch. "CHP and local departments, stand by for now. No assistance required. Echo unit, meet us on the highway; we're bringing out a subject for extraction, over."

He let up on the switch and shut off the radio.

"Nice," Dyer said.

Travis, sitting in the driver's seat and still wearing the transparency suit, glanced around at Dyer and then Paige and Bethany.

"Take the wheel," he said to Dyer. "You look exactly like someone who'd be driving this fucking thing."

He clambered out of the seat and into the back, where Paige and Bethany had already taken the hint and ducked out of sight below the windows.

"Pull into the first good-sized parking lot we see," Travis said.

It was five minutes later. They were back in bright sunlight, heading south on the Coast Highway. The Pacific lay to the right, low grassy hills to the left. Here and there the land dropped into flat stretches that might have been flood plains, or even extensions of the seafloor in ancient times. Farm buildings and other isolated structures dotted most of them, but Travis recalled seeing others developed into mid-sized towns on the drive up.

They needed to swap the Humvee for something else. There was no question it had a LoJack or some equivalent on board, and that someone would start tracking it at any time. The ruse back in town had bought only minutes, and probably not many.

Travis was in the passenger seat now. He'd pulled off the suit's top and had it bunched in his lap. He looked at his phone. A quarter past one. Five and a half hours until Richard Garner killed himself.

Travis turned to Dyer. "Skeleton crew aboard *Air Force One*, you said."

Dyer nodded. "If they're torturing captives, I doubt they brought the press corps along. Doubt they brought *anyone* they don't need."

"If we can get within a mile of any airport where it lands," Travis said, "getting aboard in this suit would be fishing with depth charges."

Dyer said nothing. He simply drew his Black-Berry from his pocket and opened an application, his eyes darting between its display and the road. A few seconds later he said, "Two flight plans. One's already expired: the plane landed at an un-designated site in eastern Wyoming, just over an hour ago."

"Border Town," Paige said.

"Holt's touring his new property," Travis said.

Dyer scrolled down through the text on his screen. "Second flight's coming almost straight to us. Plane takes off from Border Town in half an hour, arrives at Oakland International in two and a half."

"He's visiting the points of conflict," Bethany said. "Probably has people aboard the plane that he trusts to check out the aftermath and make assessments."

Travis managed his first smile in some time. "They're going to be busy today."

Half a minute later they saw a supermarket with a sprawling lot a quarter mile off the highway. Beyond it lay suburbs and a few blocks of low-rise commercial buildings—the western sweep of some unseen city further inland.

Dyer swung off the highway, then into the market, and parked out at the edge of the lot. Something like half the spaces were occupied. There were probably two hundred cars to choose from.

Travis pulled the suit's top back on. Then he opened the huge glove box in front of him and saw three different wrenches and half a dozen screwdrivers, both slotted and Phillips types. He grabbed the biggest slotted one.

"We'll wait here until you get something hot-wired," Paige said.

He nodded and got out into the sharp wind coming off the ocean, and shut the door behind him. It would occur to him only later that she couldn't have seen the nod—that from her point of view he'd simply left without acknowledging her words.

He stood surveying the nearest row of vehicles, and settled on the oldest thing in view: a mid-'90s Ford Taurus forty yards to the right, probably antique enough to lack any special security measures in its ignition. He sprinted for it.

Just inland from the lot, a train horn blared. Seconds later the rumble and clatter faded in, and he looked over his shoulder and saw it: a little six-car freight coming up from the south.

He reached the Taurus, gripped the screwdriver by the end of its shaft and swung it like a hammer. Its handle connected with the driver's side window and burst it inward in a spill of crumbs. He unlocked the door, brushed most of the glass away and got in. Five seconds later he had the ignition smashed open and the starter wires isolated. He was about to touch their stripped ends together when something made him stop. Some sound right at the edge of his awareness. Something to do with the train, he thought. The racket of its wheels suddenly sounded wrong, though he couldn't say how—or why it had struck him as important. Why it made the skin on his arms prickle. He listened for another second and then disregarded it. Whatever the hell was spooking him, sitting idle here wouldn't help matters.

He sparked the wires and heard the starter motor kick over, and then the engine roared.

He opened the door and got back out. The train had already passed, churning away to the north, its clatter going with it. It'd faded for another second when Travis's skin began to crawl again.

Now he knew why.

He could hear the sound even over the grumble of the Taurus's engine. A sound that'd been perfectly masked by the passing freight.

Rotors.

He spun and looked around wildly, but for a few seconds he couldn't pin the direction. The staccato hammering of the chopper's blades seemed to come from everywhere, bouncing off the broad storefront and from the panels of every nearby vehicle.

Then he saw it. A quarter mile south. Coming in right out of the sun glare.

For a moment he thought it was a police chopper. It was black and there were bulky shapes hanging off the sides that might've been cameras or loudspeakers.

An instant later he saw he was wrong—he recognized the flattened, broad profile of a Black Hawk. But not the standard transport model; it was some special variant with stub wings jutting off the fuselage.

And missiles clustered beneath them.

Travis turned and sprinted for the Humvee, screaming Paige's name. Screaming *Get out*, over and over. He could see her through the heavy glass, seated in back on the side facing him.

She couldn't hear him.

He screamed louder, the soft tissue lining his throat going ragged.

In the direction of the chopper, high in his peripheral vision, white light erupted and something shrieked.

He was thirty yards from the vehicle now, moving as fast as he could move, screaming as loud as he could scream.

Paige turned toward the sound of his voice at last, centering her focus on it so perfectly that, for an instant, Travis forgot she couldn't see him. She was looking right into his eyes when the missile hit the Humvee.

CHAPTER THIRTY-NINE

The vehicle simply vanished. One millisecond it was there, and the next it'd been replaced by a hurricane of flame and shrapnel and whipping soot. The air shattered and a superheated wind slammed into Travis. It picked him up and threw him backward eight feet. He landed off balance and tumbled and ended up lying on his chest, staring straight ahead at the roiling fire.

He was curled on the grass way off the edge of the lot. He couldn't remember getting there. He was still in the suit. There were police and fire vehicles all around the blackened shell of the Humvee. The flames were gone and there was a thick gray column of smoke coming off the wreck, trailing almost sideways in the shore breeze.

He realized he was crying. Holding his knees against his ribs and saying *No* with every fractured breath. Some deep, barely flickering, analytical part of his brain understood that he was bargaining more than denying. He wasn't just saying no; he was looking to actively undo what'd happened, as if the right thought—the right string of words or maybe the right mental image—could take it all back if he focused on it long enough. He couldn't say why, but his mind stuck on that notion for a minute or more while he lay there, and while the clot of emergency vehicles grew and the traffic on the front street congested.

64°.
  2:18 P.M.
  64°.
  2:18 P.M.
The sign at the edge of the little bank parking lot kept alternating, flashing its message at him. He stared at it from the bus-stop bench. He could recall walking to this spot, but only vaguely. He remembered the crowd of onlookers around the supermarket getting too thick. People edging in on the grass where he was lying. No choice but to move.

The bank was four blocks inland from the market. Sometimes the wind shifted just right and he caught the stink of diesel smoke and tire rubber from the Humvee.
  64°.
  2:19 P.M.
He was no longer crying. He'd gone numb for a while, but he was no longer numb, either. Some other feeling was coming in, heavy and cold as a glacier. He hadn't felt it in a very long time.
  64°.
  2:20 P.M.
Oakland International Airport.

Air Force One would be there in about an hour and a half.

He could be there sooner.

In some fold of his thoughts, dulled almost mute, the idea of getting to Richard Garner still tolled.

Much closer, keening like a siren against his eardrum, was the idea of getting to Stuart Holt.

CHAPTER FORTY

He got another screwdriver from a hardware store down the block, tucked it under the suit and walked out. He got a survival knife with a sheath from an outfitter across the street, hot-wired a '93 Blazer with tinted windows and headed south on the highway.

He saw from the long-term lot at Oakland exactly where *Air Force One* would situate itself. A cluster of CHP cruisers already half encircled the huge apron on the tarmac, behind the cargo terminal and far from any active runway. Patrol officers stood at their open doors. The crackle and hiss of their radios carried in the calm between takeoffs.

Travis had the sheathed knife clipped to his waistband under the suit. He walked right through the crescent of police units, close enough to hear one of their radiators ticking as it cooled. He found a spot in the shade under a FedEx plane seventy feet away, and sat waiting.

* * *

A C–5 Galaxy lumbered down out of the sky at around 3:20. It rolled onto a nearby apron and dropped its tail ramp, and its crew offloaded the large, boxy helicopter known as *Marine One*. Then they offloaded another, identical to it, rolled out a few specialized lift vehicles, and got to work setting up the rotors, which had been folded back for transport.

Travis could tell by the body language of the waiting police that *Air Force One* was inbound, even before he saw it. A quick burst of speech crackled over every radio, and every pair of eyes turned south and skyward.

For the first five minutes after the giant aircraft rolled to a stop on the apron, nothing happened. Then Air Force personnel in dress uniforms drove a motorized stairway to the plane's door, and one ascended the steps and stood at attention just left of the access.

The door was sucked inward an inch and then swung fully out of sight into the shadowy interior.

Two men in suits and ties emerged and stood on the landing atop the staircase, their hair and clothing flapping in the wind as they talked. They watched the Marines working on the two choppers, still hard at it, and then stepped back inside the 747. No one else came to the door. The dress guard stayed rigidly in place.

Travis stood.

He left the shadow of the FedEx plane and crossed to the foot of *Air Force One*'s staircase.

He saw no movement inside the doorway at the top.

He climbed just slowly enough to keep his footsteps silent.

Light brown carpeting. Cookie-sized gold stars a few feet apart.

He'd entered at a kind of choke-point—a corridor just behind the cockpit leading aft to broader spaces. Dangerous to stay here; no way to dodge aside if someone came walking through. He risked a quick glance forward and saw two pilots at the controls, and a navigator just visible off to the right. Travis turned and made his way aft, out of the corridor.

Skeleton crew. Dyer had called it. The rest of the upper deck, behind the cockpit, was deserted. There was a short seating area and a suite of small offices at the back end, all doors open and secured to the walls. No one inside any of them.

Travis descended to the huge main cabin level. Something like a fourth of it stretched forward from where he stood at the interior stairway; the rest extended back toward the tail.

He went forward first. More empty offices and a large galley that called to mind a restaurant kitchen. All the pans and bowls and utensils were stowed and locked down, and the lights were off. Whoever cooked for the president wasn't along on this trip.

He returned to the stairs and headed past them toward the back end, and encountered the first passengers he'd seen since stepping aboard. Beyond a short hallway a huge array of seats opened up, filling the cabin from side to side and running to maybe the midpoint of the plane, sixty feet behind the stairs. The seats were large and comfortable-looking; probably standard first-class issue for a 747. Travis guessed there were eighty to a hundred of them in all. On a normal trip they'd probably be filled with the press corps and any number of aides or even elected officials traveling with the commander in chief.

All but eight of the seats were empty now.

Two of the occupants were the guys who'd stepped outside earlier to look at the choppers. Both were currently seated at windows where they could watch the Marines' progress. The other six had more or less the same appearance as the first two. All were men between forty and sixty. They struck Travis as hard-edged guys just starting to soften up. Like they'd been soldiers and field operatives for most of their adult lives and had only recently ended up in plusher work environments. Intelligence guys, maybe.

Travis walked down the aisle past all of them, entered a six-foot-wide corridor and looked in through a broad doorway on its left side. A conference room lay beyond. Long polished-wood table. Big leather chairs randomly strewn around it.

Past the table, a granite counter ran the length of the room's back wall.

The counter was lined with Breach entities, and on a low-slung gurney in front of it lay a dead man.

* * *

Travis entered the room and crossed to the body. He recognized the man at once. His name was Curtis Moyer, and he'd been a technician in Border Town. His duties often kept him in the lowest levels of the complex, just above B51. He would've likely been down there this morning when the bunker buster hit.

Jesus, he'd survived the blast. He'd been as far beneath it as Travis and the others had been above it, and he must've been on the north side of the building, away from the collapse. His injuries had been severe, though. One leg was broken and torn in multiple places. His shoulder looked like it'd been dislocated, too. Internal damage had probably been what eventually got him—he was staring straight up now with glazed eyes.

But he'd still been alive when the squads from the helicopters found him—and they'd kept him that way for a while. An IV pole stuck up from the gurney's side, with three drip bags of different chemicals hanging from it. One was morphine. Travis raised his eyes from Moyer to the row of entities—all that the intruders had recovered from the wreckage, at least up to the point when *Air Force One* had left to come here. Travis understood why they'd kept Moyer alive as long as possible: they'd questioned him on the entities they found, and written the key details on slips of paper that now lay in front of each one. Maybe they'd gotten his cooperation in exchange for the medical treatment. Maybe just for the morphine.

The entities were mostly common types; a group of three blue flares appeared to be the rarest of the bunch—until Travis's gaze reached the end of the counter.

Where the Tap was sitting.

For a few seconds he couldn't imagine how it'd gotten here. It'd been in the vault in the back wall of his and Paige's closet, and Paige had been unable to reach it before they fled Border Town.

Then he considered the time scales involved, and began to understand. The guys in the choppers had made their way into Border Town around 9:20 in the morning, local time. That'd been hours before *Air Force One* even arrived there. Plenty of time for those men to notice a built-in safe in such a visible location—right at the drop-off to the abyss. With safety lines or other precautions they could've gotten to it easily, and among their military hardware there would've been things that could've compromised the safe's lock or hinges.

Travis stepped closer to the Tap. He watched the room's lighting scatter and reflect in its depths.

The sheet of paper in front of it contained all the main points of how to use the thing. Moyer had left nothing out.

Suddenly Travis heard footsteps coming from further aft—the small portion of the plane he hadn't checked out yet. He turned just as two men entered the conference room.

One was the Wilford Brimley stand-in from the dream.

The other was President Holt.

CHAPTER FORTY-ONE

Travis's hand went to the knife's grip just
above his waist, and felt it through the material of the suit.

He could kill both men without any risk to
himself—could do it right now, and by the time
the eight in the seats came running, it'd be over.
There'd be all the time in the world to swipe the
blade clean and resheath it under the suit before
any of them got here. No problem, after that, to
pick them off one by one as he'd done among the
redwoods. Them and anyone else he might come
upon farther back toward the tail. Almost any way
that it shook out, two or three minutes from now,
everyone on the plane could be dead except the
pilots, Garner, and whoever was being held with
him. For a dramatic finish, Travis could then help
Garner to the open doorway at the front of the
aircraft, and several dozen California state cops
would see a dead man step out into the sunlight.

That would sure as hell be the end of the cover-up.

But as a plan, Travis didn't like it.

Even with the story broken wide open, Garner

would be in serious danger. Federal authorities of one kind or another would descend on the scene and exert control, and there would be no telling whether they'd stood with Holt or not. Garner would be entering that situation from a position of uncertainty and weakness. He'd be at the mercy of others. Lots of others.

There was a better approach to take, and it would be just as brutally simple to execute. All it would require was a little patience.

Travis let his hand fall away from the knife.

The Brimley look-alike was holding a few sheets of yellow notepad paper and a red pen. He dropped the pen on the table and spread the sheets out side by side, and he and Holt stood looking down on them, saying nothing.

The pages were scrawled with red handwriting. Travis stepped close enough to discern the words while staying at a safe distance from either of the men. He began to read, and within seconds realized what he was looking at.

These were interrogation notes.

The scribbled lines comprised all the information that'd been drawn out of Garner and whoever else they had, in repeated drug sessions going back to probably late last night.

Travis scanned all the text in about sixty seconds.

These guys had learned almost everything—at least regarding the second half of Ruben Ward's message. The instructions. They knew that the original nine recipients had gained financial and political power *based on* the instructions. That they'd been told to use that power to acquire knowledge of—and influence over—the Breach and whoever ended up overseeing it. The last note read:

Someone is designated to pass into the Breach in 2016. Name???

Travis looked up from the pages and realized that both Holt and the older man were focused on that final line.

The old man exhaled hard and paced away from the table. "Five hours on this last point and we've got nothing. He's not going to give up the name. It's the linchpin. He knows how important it is."

"Let's not write it off yet," Holt said.

"I've done more interrogations with phen-d than anyone, and I promise you—"

"Porter—"

"I promise you, he's not going to tell us. Worst of all is the longevity involved. Thirty-four years, this has been his deepest secret. Forget it."

Holt started to respond, but a sound cut him off. Someone's ringtone, out in the seating area ahead. Through the doorway and beyond the hall, Travis saw one of the men in the window seats take out his phone. He answered, listened for a long time, said a few words and then ended the call. He pocketed the phone, stood, and came and leaned in the doorway.

"Your contractors found a scrap from a wallet in the burned-out Humvee, with a Social Security number. Victim was a Secret Service agent named

Rudy Dyer." He looked at Holt. "You know him, sir?"

Holt nodded slowly, thinking. "Heard of him. Garner was close to him, as I recall."

That piece of information hung in the air. All three men seemed to grasp its significance at the same time.

The older man—Porter—put it in words first: "If Dyer was involved in this thing, it's because Garner wanted him to be. Which means Dyer was, what, a backup plan?"

"Something like that," the guy from the window seat said.

"In that case he'd have to know as much as Garner knew," Porter said. "He'd at *least* have to know who goes through the Breach in 2016—otherwise what good would he be?"

He looked thoughtful. He drummed his fingertips on the back of one of the leather chairs for a few seconds.

Then he turned and walked directly toward Travis. The movement was so unexpected and sudden that Travis dodged him by only the width of an arm. Porter stepped right into the space where he'd been standing and grabbed the Tap off the counter. He held it toward the others, and gestured at Moyer's body.

"You believe him?" Porter said. "You believe this thing really does what he described?"

"It's Breach technology," Holt said. "Compared to whoever built it, we're monkeys throwing shit." He was quiet a moment. Then: "Yeah. I believe him."

"Then let's use it," Porter said. "Any one of us can

go back a few hours in our heads and order someone into that parking lot before the Humvee arrives.
We can take Dyer alive and interrogate him."

Holt seemed to get the point. "You think he'd
give up the secret easier than Garner."

"He's newer to it," Porter said. "In my experience, that matters. Sometimes a great deal."

Holt looked at the Tap, Porter still holding it out.
Holt's expression faltered.

"Fucking thing goes inside your brain," he said.

Porter shrugged, his face deadpan. *It is what it is.*

Holt considered it a moment longer, then turned
to the man in the doorway. "Let's see what you
guys find in this mine shaft they're talking about.
If you come away from there with no new information, then we'll use the Tap."

The other two nodded. Porter turned and set the
Tap back on the counter, then pulled out one of the
chairs and sank into it.

Travis stood still for a moment, considering
what he'd heard. Porter was clever, seeing the Tap's
potential so quickly. Maybe his idea about Dyer
would even work—but it didn't matter. None of
these people would live to put it into action.

Travis crossed out of the room and continued aft.
He turned a corner, came abreast of a darkened
little space off the hall, leaned in and saw that it
was a weapons cache. Heavy duty plastic-and-steel
wall cases held Benelli M4 shotguns and Glock 19
pistols, with neatly arranged ammo stores beneath
them. All the cases were closed tight, and each had
a palm-scanner below its door handle.

Travis returned to the hall and followed it to its end: an open set of double doors into a private residence filling the aircraft's tail. He stepped inside.

The space was beautiful. Its look matched that of the Oval Office and probably most of the White House's interior. No doubt the same people maintained both. There was a broad, open kitchen to one side, a living area on the other, and a hallway leading back to unseen rooms. Travis crossed the entry and slipped into the hall. He passed a full bathroom, then a bedroom suite with a large walk-in closet. Only one door left. Travis stepped to it and saw exactly what he'd expected to see:

A windowless room. A portrait of George Washington on the wall. And Richard Garner tied upright to a dolly like Hannibal Lecter without the face mask. The top of the dolly was zip-tied into an exposed wall strut behind Garner; someone had roughly broken away part of the wall's surface to expose it.

There was nobody else in the room.

No other victim.

Had that person been offloaded somewhere already?

It crossed Travis's mind that Curtis Moyer might have been the second victim, but he discarded the idea: the timing didn't work. Travis had experienced the dream well before *Air Force One* landed at Border Town, according to Dyer's BlackBerry. Moyer couldn't possibly have been in this room at the time.

There was a desk in the corner, which Travis hadn't seen from his viewpoint in the dream—he'd been standing too close, directly beside it. Apparently this space was a study.

He focused on Garner. The man's eyes were half open, staring downward at nothing. He wore a pair of dress pants and a dress shirt—probably the clothes he'd worn when he spoke to the nation last night. His coat and tie were gone, and both arms of the shirt had been cut away at the elbows. Needle marks dotted the exposed skin of his arms.

Garner blinked a few times. He opened his eyes a little wider, then let them relax again. He seemed to be getting past the lingering traces of the drug's effect.

Travis stepped close to him and whispered, "Mr. President."

Garner flinched and turned toward his voice. Looked right through him into the hallway five feet beyond.

"Who's there?" Garner whispered.

Travis moved so that his voice would come from deeper within the room.

"Travis Chase," he said.

It didn't take long to explain. Garner already knew everything except the specifics of the past several hours. When Travis reached the end and told him what'd happened to Paige and Bethany and Dyer, the man shut his eyes tight and said nothing for a long time.

"I'm sorry," Garner whispered at last. "For every part of this thing."

"Holt's going to be sorrier," Travis said. He left it at that.

He was standing now roughly where he'd been in the dream. To see the room in real life, from this angle, felt surreal.

"Who did they have in here with you?" he asked. "Who else were they interrogating?"

Garner looked thrown by the question. "No one," he said.

"There had to be," Travis said. He hadn't yet detailed the dream; now he did. He watched Garner for some spark of recognition, but none came. The man simply shook his head, as confused by the story as Travis himself had been when he opened the green door.

"We wondered if there was some entity that could've been responsible," Travis said. "Something that would let a person transmit what they were seeing and hearing. Would let them send it to somebody else, if only for a few seconds."

"I've never heard of an entity like that," Garner said. "And there was nobody here with me at any point. I'd remember."

For a long moment Travis stared into space and said nothing. He couldn't recall ever being this lost for an explanation. The dream couldn't have been *just* a dream. It'd really shown him this room, though he'd never set foot in it before. And the door combination had worked. How could any of that be reconciled with what Garner had just told him?

"You should get out of here," Garner whispered. "You've got the suit; it's all you need to get inside Border Town in 2016. Which is all that matters."

"You know I'm not leaving you here," Travis said.

Garner looked insistent. "It's not worth the risk. You matter. I don't."

"Are the pilots aligned with Holt? Are they in the loop?"

Garner shook his head. "Holt ordered them to stay in the upper deck, and he brought me inside before they boarded."

"All things being equal," Travis said, "you'd be better off regaining control of this plane while it was airborne, wouldn't you? You'd have more sway over how things unfolded from that point on. You'd dictate where it landed, and who'd be there to meet it. You could broadcast a video stream to television networks, from altitude, and explain what you needed to explain. Everything would happen on your terms. That would be better than if the whole thing broke open while you were sitting here on the tarmac."

"Much better," Garner said.

"Okay," Travis said. "For now we sit tight. Let these people check out Rum Lake and then get back aboard. And at wheels-up I'm going to kill them all."

CHAPTER FORTY-TWO

Travis didn't leave the study from that point on. It made sense to stay close to Garner, and to be ready to change the plan in a hurry if there was any threat to the man's life.

He watched the hallway most of the time, poised to move to one of the study's corners if someone wandered in.

Other times, when he was sure no one was coming, he took stock of the room. He knelt and studied Garner's restraints: heavy-duty plastic zip ties binding his wrists together behind him. Way too thick to be broken by just straining at them—they were probably rated for a thousand pounds. More of them held Garner's shoulders and ankles to the dolly's steel-tube frame.

Travis looked at the hole punched in the wall higher up, allowing the dolly to be zip-tied to the support strut behind it. The break revealed the wall's surface to be standard plasterboard—strange for an airplane, but this one was obviously something of an exception. The strut the zip tie encircled was metal—probably aluminum—with crisp, machined edges. The material was strong as hell, of course. The plane was made of it.

"When you need to cut me loose, there are nail clippers in that desk," Garner said. He nodded at it. "Tray drawer, top right. Ton of clutter, but they're in there."

From outside came the sound of the choppers' turbines powering up, first one and then the other. A minute later their rotors began slapping the air in heavy thuds, and then they throttled to full power and lifted off.

For the next two hours nothing happened. The plane's interior had gone dead silent, though Holt, at least, was probably still aboard. Probably Porter, too. Travis expected them to come back and have another go at Garner with the interrogation drug, but they didn't. Maybe they really had written off their chances of learning more.

The rotors faded back in and then rose to a machine-gun rattle. The choppers landed outside and powered down. Soon afterward voices picked up again somewhere forward in the cabin. Two minutes after that, a series of hydraulic rumbles reverberated through the 747, and its engines began to whine. Travis drew the survival knife from its sheath, and hid it behind the suit's top.

Holt and Porter were sitting in the conference room as the plane taxied. Outside the windows, hazy twilight had settled over the terminals and runways. Porter was reading the simple handwritten notes for the Tap—the Tap itself remained on the counter along the back wall. Travis moved past the room and into the seating area ahead. The other eight men were there, like any regular airline passengers about to accelerate to two hundred miles per hour in a big metal tube. They weren't buckled in, but they sat face forward with their heads against the padding behind them.

Five had taken window seats, all on the port side. The other three had sat along the aisle, also to port. Each was in his own lateral row. Each could see only the men ahead of him, unless he turned around. The plane nosed to the starting line of its takeoff run and its massive engines built to a scream, rendering sound within the cabin pretty much meaningless for the next thirty seconds.

By the end of those thirty, before the plane had even tilted upward and begun to climb, all eight men were dead.

Travis didn't bother wiping the blade clean or hiding the knife under the suit again.

He strode back to the conference room as the plane banked and climbed. He held the weapon out to his side, letting it drip. He went right through the doorway, making for Porter first. The man saw the hovering knife in his peripheral vision and turned fast to look at it. Confusion broke over his face and then fear, and then the blade went tip-first into his trachea all the way to the spine, and Travis twisted and flicked it sideways on the way out.

Holt looked up in time to see the man spasm and

collapse. In time to see the knife withdraw and remain bobbing in the air, then circle the end of the table to his side and come floating toward him. He jerked backward, almost tipping his chair over, and scrambled out of it. He ended up in a kind of defensive crouch in the corner, his neck hunched behind a tight barrier he'd made with his hands.

Travis came on slowly. Patiently.

"What is this?" Holt said, getting barely above a whisper. "*What is this?*"

"I came to ID the other two victims in the Humvee," Travis said.

Holt's eyes left the knife and tried to pinpoint the location of Travis's voice.

"Their names were Paige Campbell and Bethany Stewart. They were two of the best people I ever met. They passed up normal lives to make the world better, or at least to keep it from getting worse. They gave up a lot to do that. For the most part they even gave up sunlight."

"Whatever you want, I can get it for you," Holt said. "I'm the most powerful person in the world."

"All appearances to the contrary," Travis said.

"You need to think about this," Holt said. His voice cracked. "You really do."

"I really don't," Travis said, and he shoved the discarded chair aside, stepping past it toward where the man crouched.

Before he got there, his vision began to flash green and blue.

CHAPTER FORTY-THREE

Travis stopped mid-step. He swayed forward until he caught his balance. He looked around fast, as if his eyes could outrun the effect. They couldn't.

Green. Blue. Green. Blue. The flashing saturated everything in his field of view, like intense stage lighting at a rock concert.

Green. Blue.

He knew what it meant—but it was impossible. How could he be catching up to the present from within a Tap memory if he hadn't *used* the Tap?

Green. Blue.

The knife fell from his hand, bounced and spun on the carpet. Holt looked confused.

Travis staggered backward, stumbled against one of the chairs, turned and leaned down and steadied himself on the table.

Green. Blue.

He was about to be drawn out of this memory against his will. Any second. But drawn out to *what*? And to *when*? When and where had he put the Tap into his head?

Green. Blue.

Black.

He flinched and opened his eyes. He was back in the study, at the plane's tail. Holt and Porter were standing in front of him, Richard Garner just beyond them and off to the side, still bound to the dolly. Travis looked down and saw that he himself was bound to a dolly now, right where he'd been in the dream.

Which hadn't been a dream.

Neither had it been a projection sent to him by somebody else.

It hadn't been either of those things.

He had less than a second to think about it, and then his memory simply wiped itself away. Vanished like a sand picture in the blast of a leaf blower.

Where was he?

How had he gotten here?

What the hell was he tied to?

An old man who looked like Wilford Brimley leaned into his viewpoint, scrutinizing his face.

"Can you understand me?" the old man said.

But before Travis could reply, his memory blew away again, no more than a second after it'd begun to form.

Where was he?

How had he gotten here?

Garner watched Travis struggle against the drug. As strange as it was to experience the effect yourself, it was almost more so to see someone else endure it.

He watched Travis's eyes keep losing the room and finding it again. Rediscovering his surroundings every second or so as his memory fractured.

Porter was leaning in with his nose six inches from Travis's.

"Tell us who goes through the Breach," he said—framing it as a command, not a question.

Travis blinked, no doubt having lost the statement already. He stared at Porter and said nothing.

Porter repeated the instruction. And again. And again. Carefully and patiently. Working it into Travis's subconscious like a dog trainer setting a patterned response. He'd been doing this for years.

"Tell us who goes through the Breach."

Garner had undergone the questioning himself all night and all day. Sessions like this every hour or so, seventeen in all. The needle marks on his arms helped him keep count.

He'd given up a lot of information. He knew it. He also knew he'd held on to the only piece that would matter in the end. He knew by the frustration he'd seen in their eyes, each time the narcotic's power dissipated and his memory stabilized. They hadn't gotten it from him. He'd been protecting it too long to surrender it now, even under the drug.

It would be different with Travis. If he knew the answer, he'd learned it today.

Porter gave the command a sixth time: "Tell us who goes through the Breach."

Travis's eyelids drew close together. He seemed to grasp the instruction, even beneath the crumbling memory.

"Tell us who goes through the Breach."

"I do," Travis said.

Porter narrowed his eyes. He drew back a few inches.

"I go through," Travis said. Something like amusement crossed his face. "Lucky me."

"Is he playing with us?" Holt said. "Is the effect wearing off?"

Porter looked at his watch. "It's probably starting to. We used up three sixteen while he was in the memory."

"Get the Tap back out of him," Holt said. "While you can still make him cooperate."

Porter nodded. He leaned in again and said, "Think the Tap out of your head." He repeated it, his speech precise and direct. He said it a third time and Travis shut his eyes and seemed to concentrate hard on something. A few seconds later he gasped. His face twisted in pain. Then the Tap began to emerge from the same pinprick hole it'd gone in through, a bright green tendril snaking and darting. Porter held up his hand and let it collect in a mass on his palm.

"Try again in an hour," Holt said. "We'll have the whole four or five minutes to question him then. We'll get it."

By the time they left with the Tap—re-formed into its cube shape—Garner could tell Travis's memory was solidifying. The drug's influence tended to recede very rapidly, from full strength to no effect at all in about a minute. The clarity growing in Travis's eyes showed he was well into that time.

Where was he?
Some little room.

He was tied to something—a dolly, it looked like.

He took a deep breath, and felt a fog clear from his mind as he did. Another breath—even clearer.

He looked up and saw that Richard Garner was with him, also tied to a dolly.

He thought the room was a study, though for the moment he wasn't sure how he knew that.

There was a deep droning sound coming through the walls and floor. Jet engines.

This was *Air Force One*. This room was back in the tail. He was certain of that, though again he didn't know how.

While he wondered, it occurred to him that someone had just left the room. Two men, he thought. And they'd taken something with them.

The Tap? Had that been it? He was all but sure of it, and a second later he was sure of something else:

The Tap had just come out of his head.

The headache said so, and the trickle of blood at his temple confirmed it.

His next breath pushed out the last of the haze, and the day's memory came down on him in a single rush.

He and Paige and Bethany, flying to Rum Lake. Evading the contractors by entering the mine. Meeting Dyer. Seeing the second Breach. Using the transparency suit to get away. Then the supermarket. The missile. The mindless drive down to Oakland afterward, with little thought in his head but gutting Stuart Holt like a fucking pig. He recalled boarding the plane, scouting it out, finding Garner back here at the tail. Then killing the others, and—

And catching up to the present.

From within a Tap memory.

He thought about that. He stared into space and tried to put it together.

The Tap memory had ended in the conference room aboard this plane.

Where had it begun?

When had it begun?

He couldn't recall any starting point.

Worse yet, the Tap had burned all his real memories of the time span in question. It always did that. He had no way to remember what had *really* happened during the period he'd just relived.

"Coming around?" Garner said.

Travis nodded.

"They used a drug on you," Garner said.

Travis nodded again. "Phenyline dicyclomide."

Garner looked surprised.

"Dyer told me about it," Travis said.

"Do you understand what they did to you just now?"

"Not really. Parts of it, maybe."

"The drug has two stages," Garner said. "Mild amnesia for a couple minutes, then four or five minutes of total short-term memory fracturing."

"Dyer said they can give you commands during Stage Two," Travis said, "and sometimes they feed you information in Stage One that they want you to use—"

He cut himself off.

He thought he suddenly understood part of it.

Garner nodded, seeing his expression.

"You never made it inside the mine, in real life,"

Garner said. "You and Paige and Bethany got as far as the blast door, and you were trapped there. You didn't have the combo. They used gas grenades and captured you all."

Travis had been looking at the floor. Now he looked up sharply at Garner. "Paige and Bethany are alive?"

Garner nodded. "Tied up just like us, in the closet of the bedroom suite. They're fine."

All the emotions that'd torn into Travis earlier like serrated blades now reversed themselves. They withdrew in a searing instant of release that seemed to hit him as hard as the missile's shockwave had. His breathing spasmed and his eyes flooded. He couldn't stop himself. Didn't care to, either. The most he could do, after a moment, was quiet the shuddering breaths. He lowered his head and let the tears stream and made hardly any sound.

Garner stayed quiet a moment longer, then continued.

"Until they chased you three to the blast door, Holt's people hadn't even known the mine existed. Neither had Holt. Once they found it, they figured it mattered, and they located the other access and blew them both in. Inside they encountered Dyer, by himself. They traded gunfire with him—and killed him. When they realized who he was, and that he must've been working with me, they figured he'd probably had all the information they were after. Including the one thing they couldn't get from me."

"My name," Travis said, his voice still cracking.

Garner nodded. "They were sure Dyer knew it,

and they considered using the Tap on themselves to go back and interrogate him. They even got the door combo out of me so they could enter the mine quietly. That information was far less important to me than your identity—I'm sure I didn't give them much of a fight."

Travis looked up and blinked hard at the tears. Garner's image swam and then resolved.

"Holt was afraid of the Tap," Travis said. "He was hesitant to even let his subordinates use it."

"That's exactly right," Garner said. He stared for a moment, visibly confused as to how Travis could know that detail. Then he set it aside and continued. "They realized they could use you instead, to spare themselves the risk. They gave you the drug, and in Stage One they fed you the door combo, and in Stage Two they put the Tap in your head and commanded you to relive the day. If it worked like they hoped it would, the memory fracturing would keep you from knowing you were in a Tap memory at all. You wouldn't *remember* using the Tap—or living through the day the first time around. You'd drop into some point in time this morning and think it *was* this morning. You'd think it was real."

The plane. En route to Rum Lake. Waking up aboard it—*that* was when the Tap memory had begun. The whole day after that had been fake.

"Later on you'd reach the blast door," Garner said, "and this time you'd know the combo. You'd never know *how* you knew it—you'd remember Stage One like it was some strange vision you'd had—but under the circumstances you'd certainly try punching those numbers in."

"And end up meeting Dyer," Travis said.

Garner nodded. "In all likelihood learning what he knew, given that you served the same interests. And when you came back out of the Tap memory, they could interrogate you for that knowledge. You'd be less conditioned to protect it than I am. Far less, I'm afraid."

"Jesus, *did* I give it up? Did I tell them I'm the one who goes through the Breach?"

"You did, but they thought it was sarcasm." Garner frowned. "An hour from now they'll figure out that it wasn't. I'm sorry, but there's almost no chance of your protecting that secret against someone as skilled as Porter."

Garner sounded defeated. It was impossible to blame him. For a long moment Travis felt the same.

Then he thought of something he'd seen earlier, while wandering the plane in the transparency suit.

A second later he thought of something *else* he'd seen, and managed a smile.

Holt and his people couldn't possibly know he'd gotten such a detailed look at the aircraft. They wouldn't have guessed in a million years that, in the Tap memory they dumped him into, he would end up boarding the plane and scoping it out nose to tail. That lack of imagination on their part had been a mistake. A big one, potentially.

He flexed his wrists against the zip tie that bound them behind him, and put his knuckles to the plasterboard an inch away.

Then he shoved. Hard. Once, twice, three times. He heard the board flex and protest, and on the fourth push its gypsum core cracked softly in a fist-sized hole, the paper surface tearing with it.

"What are you doing?" Garner said.

"You'll see."

With his fingers he felt the edges of the hole, and snapped away piece after piece until he'd exposed several inches of the vertical aluminum support behind him. The one his own dolly must be secured to.

Then he contorted his wrists until he had the encircling zip tie stretched between them, and pressed it against one edge of the aluminum strut.

One crisp, machined edge.

It was as sharp as a blade.

He began sliding the zip tie up and down against it.

Garner finally understood, but still didn't look hopeful.

"That won't free your shoulders or your ankles," he said.

"No," Travis said. Then he nodded to the nearby desk. The one so close beside him he hadn't noticed it in his first glimpse of this room. "But I'll be able to reach the top right drawer there, and get ahold of the nail clippers inside."

Garner's eyes registered deepest confusion for three seconds. Then he smiled too.

"You found what Allen Raines had in his red locker," he said.

"Found it and used it," Travis said. "Tell me about the weapons cache in the hall. Will your palm print work on the scanners?"

"It will. But an alarm goes off as soon as you open a case. They'll be on us before we can get anything loaded."

Travis laughed softly. "I wouldn't worry about that."

CHAPTER FORTY-FOUR

Holt was in the conference room, reading the interrogation notes again, when he felt the heat on the side of his face. For three or four seconds he ignored it, assuming the plane's climate control system had begun venting warm air from the ceiling ducts.

Then it felt more than warm.

He turned in the direction it was coming from—the back wall—and his legs involuntarily kicked and shoved him away from the table.

Above the counter where the Breach entities were lined up, the plastic facing of the wall had begun to warp and melt in one area—a big half-circle blooming from the counter's back edge.

Centered right beneath the melting place were three entities, all the same type. Holt had read the paper slip that detailed their function, but couldn't remember it now. The objects were roughly cigar sized and made of something that looked like polished blue stone.

They'd been blue earlier, anyway.

Right now they were closer to pure white, incandescing like lightbulb filaments.

At that moment a line of flame erupted where the melting plastic had begun to pool atop the counter, the material breaking down into constituent oils. A tenth of a second later the entire melt zone was engulfed and sending noxious black smoke toward the ceiling.

Holt shoved himself up from the chair, turned, and began screaming at the others in the seating area ahead. He'd just gotten out the word *fire* when an alarm began shrieking, seeming to come from everywhere. He reached the doorway and saw the others already moving, running for the fire extinguishers positioned along the outer walls. The extinguishers' mounts were strobing bright red—it was impossible to miss them.

Holt stepped aside as the first of the men sprinted past him into the room. One by one they went in, dodging around the chairs and one another, and blasting carbon dioxide at the flames. With their bodies in the way, Holt could no longer see the fire, but the men's audible responses told him they were having trouble with it. They kept triggering the extinguishers, the sound not quite drowning out their curses and shouts.

Porter arrived at the rear of the pack, carrying two extinguishers. He shoved one into Holt's hands and then ducked in past him. Holt followed. As he did, he heard another alarm begin blaring somewhere. Back toward the tail, maybe. God knew what it was; flames and smoke aboard an aircraft probably set off all kinds of emergency indicators.

He shouldered past the edge of the crowd and at last saw why the fire was proving difficult. The carbon dioxide was all but evaporating in the envelope of blazing air around the three entities. How hot *were* the damned things?

Even as he wondered, he saw one of them flicker. Then the other two. Within the following seconds all three began to dim visibly. The white-hot color was fading before his eyes.

Then the throat of the man next to him exploded out from under his head.

A gunshot.

From behind.

Holt spun—saw some of the others turning too, even as a storm of gunfire kicked up—and for maybe a quarter of a second he discerned the figures standing in the doorway. Garner. The other man. Both women. All leveling and firing Benellis from the aft arms locker.

Holt saw Garner's weapon swing toward him. Saw its barrel aim straight into his viewpoint from ten feet away.

Holt shut his eyes.

It was over by the time Travis's shotgun ran dry. He saw the last body drop, and as planned, the other three spun and trained their weapons on the seating area—reloading as they did—on the chance that some straggler might yet be coming in.

At the same time Travis lunged forward into the conference room. He dropped his own gun, grabbed one of the fallen extinguishers and began spraying down the remaining flames. The blue flares were already cool enough that they no longer got in the way.

Within a moment there was no fire at all. Just pooled bubbling plastic and a foot of gray vapor swirling under the ceiling. Travis gave the wall another long blast for good measure, then turned, ducked out of the room, and took his first breath since going in. As he emerged he heard a man shouting from somewhere forward of the bulk seating. Footsteps thudded on stairs, and then one of the flight crew came sprinting back.

"*Where is it?*" the man screamed. He started to repeat it, but the words caught in his throat. He'd seen the shotguns the other three were carrying, and for a second his expression flooded with fear.

Then it simply went blank.

He'd seen Garner.

After a long moment the man swallowed and said, "Sir."

Garner accompanied the airman back upstairs to speak with the rest of the crew. Twenty seconds after they disappeared, all the alarms cut out.

Travis and Paige and Bethany sank into three of the row seats, side by side, and Travis leaned his head back and shut his eyes.

"Did they interrogate you?" Paige said.

He nodded.

"Are you okay?" she said.

He opened his eyes and looked at her. He took in every detail of her face: the strands of hair hanging past her forehead and in front of her ears, the subtle, rhythmic movements of her throat as she breathed.

"Yeah," he said.

* * *

Garner came back down five minutes later. By then the twilight outside had deepened nearly to black, and the landscape below had lit up in soft blues and oranges: bright street grids and dotted parking lots.

Garner sat down just across the aisle from the three of them. He exhaled deeply and for a moment said nothing. Travis couldn't remember the last time he'd seen a person look so weary. He turned to Travis and said, "Tell me everything Dyer told you, so I know where to start." He indicated Paige and Bethany. "They need to catch up on it too."

Paige looked from Garner to Travis, confused. "Who's Dyer?" she said.

Travis spent twenty minutes explaining it. By the time he'd finished, Paige and Bethany looked rattled, but both clearly understood it all.

"Dyer told you everything," Garner said. "Everything I told *him*, at least."

"The second half of Ruben Ward's message," Travis said.

Garner nodded. "I never would've told you any of this—*either* half of the message—until as late in the game as possible. I would've waited until days before you're supposed to enter the Breach, if I could have. There was just nothing to be gained by telling you sooner, and plenty to lose. It adds unpredictability to bring *anyone* new into the fold. Even you." He paused. "But I guess that horse is already out and galloping."

For a long time, fifteen seconds at least, Garner

said no more. He rested his hands on his knees and looked down at them.

"I'm sure all three of you have at least a grasp of the physics implied by the Breach," he said. "The rough theories—guesses, if you like—as to how wormholes function. Maybe you've read Stephen Hawking, and know that space and time aren't really separate things. A wormhole can cross both of them."

Travis nodded, as did Paige and Bethany.

Garner looked up and met their gazes.

"On the other side of the Breach is a starship," he said. "It's orbiting the binary star 61 Cygni, a little over twelve hundred years in our future. The ship was designed and subassembled by General Dynamics in Coffeyville, Kansas, in the first half of the 2250s, and built in low orbit over the next twenty years. It was christened July 17, 2276, the EAS *Deep Sky*. It has a crew of eight hundred thirty-nine people, including an executive officer named Richard Garner, and a commander named Travis Chase."

CHAPTER FORTY-FIVE

Travis waited. He understood that Garner was neither lying nor joking.

"Ballpark figure," Garner said. "When do you think the last veteran of the American Civil War died? Don't crunch the numbers. Just take a shot from the hip, any of you."

"The 1930s," Travis said.

Paige nodded. "My guess too."

"Around there," Bethany said.

"There are disputed claims," Garner said, "but the most agreed upon candidate is a Union veteran named Albert Woolson. He died in August of 1956."

Travis traded looks with the others.

"It doesn't sound right, does it?" Garner said. "The mind tends to chop off the tails of the bell curve when it makes an estimate. But do the math. Three million people fought in the Civil War, most of them very young, many young enough that they had to lie about their ages to serve. You could safely estimate a few tens of thousands of them were fifteen or sixteen when the war ended in 1865.

Which means they were born around 1850. Out of that number of people, a handful could be expected to live to a hundred. A much smaller handful would make it a bit further, or would've been a little younger than fifteen when they served. Either way, the mid 1950s would be your best guess, even if you could never know for sure." He offered a smile. "It *is* right—it just doesn't *seem* right. It's strange to consider that Civil War vets and atomic bombs overlapped each another in history by more than a decade."

He looked forward again. "It's stranger still to learn that the first humans to become effectively immortal—ageless, anyway—were born just before the Great Depression. You're familiar with the Methuselah Project? You must have seen the political attack ads during the midterms."

Travis and Paige and Bethany all nodded.

"Turns out it works," Garner said. "It comes in about fifteen years ahead of schedule, in fact, according to the message from the *Deep Sky*. The first real stabilization and reversal of age symptoms is achieved around 2035. Which means a tiny scattering of people born in the late 1920s will live long enough to benefit from it—will live to see their biological age rolled back until they look and feel about twenty-five, indefinitely. Many more from the 1930s, forties, and fifties will make the cut, and damn near everyone born after that will. Most of the *Deep Sky*'s crew don't yet exist in our time, but some do, and some were already adults in the year 1978—including all nine of the people Ruben Ward was instructed to take the message to that summer."

Travis felt as if two halves of a drawbridge had just dropped together and locked with a heavy thud. He looked at Paige and Bethany and knew what they were thinking, to the last word:

Some of us are already among you.

"Who better to trust the message with," Garner said, "than themselves?"

Paige started to respond, then stopped and frowned, as if something that'd been bothering her for the past couple minutes had finally surfaced. "It's one thing to send us a message through the Breach, but why are they sending dangerous things like entities? If they created a wormhole to tell us something—"

"They didn't," Garner said. "They didn't create the wormhole. Or the entities passing through it. That stuff is all archaic, even on the timescale of the universe. Whoever created it disappeared long ago. Probably a billion years back. These old transit tunnels full of relics are all that's left of them. The *Deep Sky*'s original purpose was simply to study the tunnels—a whole network of them, discovered earlier by the first robotic probes that went out to neighboring stars. The *Deep Sky* was built from top to bottom as a dedicated research ship, with the means to investigate and even exert some control over wormholes. In the end, the crew used that capability to cause the Breach to open here on Earth, in our time. They rerouted a single tunnel to some degree—enough to make sure that the VLIC's first shot in 1978 would connect with it, and not to a primordial one teeming with parasite signals. It took an ungodly amount of power to move the tunnel, and as soon as they'd done it, they had to begin generating and storing *more* power to move it again—this time so *they* could tap into it on *their* end. That process—repowering—would require a little over thirty-eight years, and be completed on June 5, 2016, by our calendar. During all the time in between, they had no way of stopping the flow of entities through the system. The most they could do was set up a kind of reverb effect in the tunnel, a very specific disturbance in which they could encode a message."

"The Breach Voices," Paige said.

Garner nodded. "Along with the initial impulse that would make a translator of whoever was standing closest when the Breach opened. That was some kind of neurotechnology that's probably a few centuries ahead of ours—and obviously not perfected, given the damage it did to Ward."

Travis let all the information settle in his mind, to the extent that it could.

"The tunnels are abandoned?" he said.

Garner nodded again. "Ancient ruins. Though many of the systems engineered into them are still running. Including defensive measures. Safeties."

"Like what?" Paige said.

"The message covered it all pretty briefly. I got the sense that it would take a textbook to really explain it, but the basics were straightforward enough. One of the safeties is the resistance force inside the Breach, which doesn't allow you to enter from our end. All the tunnels have that, to protect against the threat of outsiders—like us—tapping in at some random spot and immediately traveling throughout the network. Which makes sense, when you think about it. If you strung the universe with these tunnels, you'd never know when some hostile race might evolve somewhere, punch in and show up in your backyard."

"So how do you go through it?" Bethany said.

"You need a *tumbler*," Garner said.

Everyone waited for him to go on.

"That's the best stab at translating the word from their language—whoever built the tunnels. Tumbler, as in the mechanism inside a lock. The way it works is, any two points connected by a tunnel need to be authorized before someone can travel between them. Think of it as *unlocking* them. And the only way to do that is for a single individual— a single conscious mind—to think the same complex thought outside *both* entry points first. You see how that works? It means at least one person has to make the trip the old-fashioned way—in a ship—before the tunnel lets anyone through. So you'd open one entrance, think a specific thought near it—an exchange from Twelfth Night, say— and then chug across space at ship speed to the *other* entrance, and think the exchange again. Same mind, same thought—that's what the tunnel listens for. Until it hears that, it won't open."

Travis thought he understood the concept, and the reasoning behind it. "It means no new civilization can come out of the blue and expand their presence in space too quickly, right? They can't push their boundaries any faster than ships can travel."

Garner nodded. "And a person stuck with that job, unlocking a tunnel's two ends, is the tumbler. In this case it's you. I'm sure you can guess why."

Travis considered it. He stared at the seatback in front of him, then turned to Garner. "Because I've already made the trip. There's one of me on that end already, and one of me on this end."

Another nod.

"Will that actually work?" Travis said.

"Same mind, same thought," Garner said.

"So what *is* the thought? Did they put it in the message?"

Garner shook his head. "They'll give it to you in person. After you go through to their end."

He watched Travis for the confusion he obviously expected. Travis saw Paige's and Bethany's eyes narrow too.

"How will you go through the tunnel if you haven't unlocked it yet?" Garner said. "That's another safety—one for the tumbler's own protection. The term for it translates to something like 'scouting.' You get to do it just once, back and forth—a single round-trip. The logic of it goes like this: a tumbler usually has to unlock a tunnel's first end, then travel for a very long time across space to unlock the *second* end. But *before* he unlocks the second end, he can choose to enter the tunnel there, just once, and go through it to take a good look at the first end again. To scout it."

Travis saw the point—was pretty certain he did, anyway. "After all that time had gone by, while you were crossing space in a ship, it'd be risky to reach the far end of the tunnel and just open it blindly. What if things back home had changed by then? What if there was something dangerous waiting to come through?"

Garner managed a smile. "Hell, you might open

the tunnel and get a magma flow. Or seawater pressurized at a mile's depth. A lot can change, given enough time, and it could take thousands of years for a ship to travel the distance required. It could take longer. The *Deep Sky*'s crew isn't worried about that in this case, obviously. As far as I can tell, they just want to speak to you before you fully open the tunnel. About what, I have no idea."

"So the other me," Travis said, "the one aboard the *Deep Sky*, will unlock the far end of the tunnel first, and once that's done, I can make a single trip to their side and back. A scouting trip."

"That's the plan, as I understand it."

Travis stared at him, thinking it all through. Random questions remained. Trailing ends. One in particular.

"Tell us about the filter," Travis said.

Garner looked surprised. "How can you know about that?"

"Beyond that word, we *don't* know about it," Travis said. "I'll explain the *how* later."

He held Garner's gaze and waited for him to speak.

"I don't know much more than you do, I'm afraid," Garner said. "The filter was always the strangest part, to me. And the scariest, I suppose."

"Why?" Paige said.

Travis noticed Bethany looking around at everyone like she'd missed something. Which she had; they'd never told her anything about this. Travis caught her glance and said, "I'll tell you later."

She nodded, but the confusion stayed in her expression.

"The filter was the one thing Ruben Ward chose

to leave out of the written message," Garner said. "He never dictated it to Nora during his stay at Johns Hopkins, and only spoke briefly of it to the nine of us, later that summer. He was afraid to share the details, he said. He worried that if we knew about that part, we'd back out. He said it was something absolutely necessary, but also terrible, and that it was best if no one but you, Travis, ever learned about it."

"Do you think it's something that happens to me when I go through the Breach?" Travis said. "Something that changes me? Am *I* what gets filtered?"

Again Garner looked surprised, but only mildly so this time. "That's more or less what I've imagined all these years. But it's no more than a guess—mine is as bad as yours."

Travis nodded. As he had in the mine shaft, he let the subject slip from his thoughts. There were only so many ways he could hold it up to the light. He looked at Garner again.

"The nine of you were supposed to get me into Tangent," Travis said. "Get me in and then, as you said, tell me everything at the last possible moment."

Garner nodded.

"So what did you think," Travis said, "when I ended up in Tangent *without* your help, in the summer of 2009?"

"That very strange things happen in connection with the Breach. And that it couldn't be a coincidence."

"It wasn't. I'll explain that later too."

"I'd appreciate it."

Travis considered something else. "You were prepared to hit Border Town with a nuke, back then, when Aaron Pilgrim took control of the place."

"The Breach would've survived. You can't imagine the forces that stabilize it. All that stopped me was that you wouldn't leave the place. I had no choice but to go along with the approach you suggested."

For a while after that, nobody spoke. The heavy engines droned and the lit-up nightscape slid by, far below.

"Why are they doing this at all?" Paige said. "The crew of that ship. Does the message say why they're opening the tunnel in the first place?"

Garner nodded slowly, looking down at his hands again. "That part it explains in simple terms." He grew quiet for a few seconds, then continued. "There was a war. It happened on Earth around 3100, right around the time the *Deep Sky* arrived at what turned out to be its last destination—61 Cygni. That star is just over eleven light-years from here, which means the ship's crew, once they were on-site, got all their updates from home with more than a decade's delay. Correspondence from loved ones, news stories, everything. When the war started, they had to watch their world come apart on that same delay, knowing that whatever they were seeing was already eleven years gone. The crew considered returning, trying to intervene somehow, but gave up the idea without much debate: the *Deep Sky* doesn't exactly have a hyperdrive button on its bridge. Its top speed is around twenty percent of the speed of light. It'd taken fifty-five years to get out to that star system, and it would take fifty-five to get back. In any case, it wasn't long before they saw the final headlines, announcing the all-but-certain deployment of weapon systems more or less guaranteed to end the world. The message doesn't clarify what exactly those weapons were—only that they worked. All transmissions from Earth ended right after that, and never started up again."

Garner shut his eyes. "They opened the Breach so they could come through and have a second chance at history. If you think about that, you might begin to appreciate our paranoia in keeping this secret. Think of the power structures in this world. All the horrible things people do just to keep control of their few bars of the jungle gym. Now imagine some of them learning that one day soon a door is going to open, and people will come through it who know the next thousand-plus years of our history. Everything we're going to invent and discover. Everything we're going to get right and wrong. People who, just by their arrival, will render all current political power on Earth obsolete. You know who'd be most threatened by that? All the people best positioned to stop it from happening in the first place." His hands had become fists in his lap. He looked down, noticed, and slowly relaxed them. "To hell with all of them," he said. "It *is* going to happen. For better or worse."

Paige seemed to react to Garner's final sentence. She turned to Travis, her expression haunted by a fear she didn't need to voice.

CHAPTER FORTY-SIX

Travis took the elevator up to the surface and went running in the desert. The night was cool for early June, the breeze coming in from the Rockies fifty miles away. It was close to midnight, and the stars stood out in vivid contrast on the black sky.

He ran six miles in a loop and then slowed to a walk one mile shy of the elevator housing. He was barely winded. Not bad for forty-eight.

He'd covered half the remaining distance back when he stopped altogether. He turned to face north and tilted his head up and found the familiar shape of Cygnus, the swan, seemingly frozen in its slow rotation around the pole star. His eyes went automatically to the faint speck—nearly invisible to naked eyes—of 61 Cygni.

He stared at it until long after his neck had begun to cramp.

The bedroom was pitch-black except for the soft blue light from the nightstand clock. It showed 3:06 A.M. Travis lay on his side, his chest against

Paige's back. They were both staring at the digital display.

It switched to 3:07.

"Twelve hours," Paige whispered.

Travis heard the edge of fear she couldn't quite hide. He held her tighter and kissed the top of her head.

"Save tomorrow for tomorrow," he said.

"This *is* tomorrow."

He insisted on being alone in front of the Breach when it happened. There was no reason to expect any danger to bystanders, but no reason *not* to expect it either.

There was no formality to the event. No grand send-off before Travis stepped into the elevator to head for B51. The group that gathered to see him go consisted of Paige, Bethany, and Garner. They stood together in the corridor on B18, not far from the residence Travis and Paige had moved into when the complex re-opened. To a passerby—of which there weren't many in Border Town these days—it would've looked like four friends standing there talking.

All three hugged Travis—Paige last, and longest. He held on to her and tried to think of nothing but what she felt like. He shut his eyes and let the moment last as long as he dared.

The elevator doors parted on the concrete hallway. The *only* hallway down here at the bottom, its far end open to the vast chamber that held the Breach's protective dome. Travis walked the corridor's length. He passed the heavy door to the bunker where, more than thirty-eight years earlier, Ruben Ward had lain in his half sleep, listening to the Breach Voices and understanding them.

He passed through the opening at the end. He stared at the dome's colossal profile, barely a silhouette against the unlit ceiling and walls of the old VLIC shot chamber, which had been used for its intended purpose exactly once.

The dome's small entry channel, like that of an igloo, lay to the right. Ten feet before it stood a table. Travis crossed to it, removed his phone from his pocket and set it there. He noted the time as he did.

3:06.

He went to the entrance and pushed in through the heavy glass door at its mouth, his eyes already losing everything but the Breach.

Like looking into a depth. Into a furnace.

Those had been his first impressions of the thing, almost seven years ago, echoing the sentiments of one of the first people to see it—and to die because of it.

Travis let the door fall shut behind him and stood staring. The Breach hovered, patient as ever, in its soundproof glass enclosure at the center of the dome. The tunnel and its flared opening looked the same as they always had. Blue and purple. Rippling. Flamelike substance the color of a bruise. Travis went to the glass cage's door and pulled it open.

The Breach Voices sang. They raked his eardrums, seemingly capable of piercing them. He ignored the pain and stepped across the threshold and stood there, three feet from the opening. There was nothing in the way now except the low-profile receiving platform, like a heavy-duty trampoline that rose eighteen inches from the concrete floor beneath the Breach.

Travis waited.

The Voices keened and sighed, multiple tones rising and falling in what sounded like random pitch fluctuations. They were ascending in a harmonic trill when they simply stopped.

The silence made Travis flinch, but almost before he could react to it, other things began happening. The air pressure in the room changed. He heard the door six inches behind him buffet outward and then immediately suck shut again. The glass walls around him seemed to flex and draw in, the Breach's reflection warping in every surface.

Then the Breach itself changed. Rapidly. The distinct streams of blue and violet collapsed into each other. The rippling shallowed, the tunnel's inner surface pressing itself smooth and uniform. The transformation happened in something like ten seconds, and when it was done Travis might have been staring down the interior of a polished steel tube. Even the flared mouth seemed to have solidified.

He waited.

Nothing else happened.

He stepped closer, resting one foot on the receiving platform. He stared straight down the tunnel and suddenly noticed what else was different about it.

He could see the far end.

It might have been a thousand feet away. Distance was hard to judge. It opened into someplace a little brighter than the tunnel itself.

He leaned closer, extended his hand and passed it through the plane of the Breach's opening. For maybe a quarter of a second he thought he felt it resist him, and then his hand simply went through unhindered.

Another step—both feet on the trampoline now. He leaned all the way forward, his shoulders and head crossing the plane and his hands falling to the tunnel's surface just beyond the mouth. He found it to be as solid as it looked—and then found it didn't matter. He tipped the rest of his upper body into the channel and realized he weighed nothing once inside it. For a few seconds he stayed on the margin, his legs and feet pulled down by gravity on the platform, the rest of him floating suspended in the first three feet of the tunnel. Then he pressed his hands to the sidewalls and shoved himself forward, and a second later he was gliding along the channel's length, as frictionless as a puck on an air hockey table.

He shoved again, and then again. Each time his speed stepped up and stayed up; only air drag slowed him—and maybe something else. Something he couldn't quite get a fix on. It felt like the hint of resistance his hand had met briefly at the tunnel's mouth. He sensed it only occasionally—

sliding past one shoulder or the other, or compressing strangely around his feet. That made sense in light of what Garner had described: the idea of a one-time-only scouting trip. The tunnel's resistance force was still as powerful as ever; it was simply letting him pass now in some active, selective way. A little bubble of nonresistance, following him as he glided along.

He waited to feel something, as the tunnel walls continued slipping by. Something like a barrier, or a threshold. Something—anything—that could be called a filter.

But there was nothing.

Just the smooth interior of the channel streaming past.

Much closer now. Maybe a hundred yards from the tunnel's end. Then fifty. Then ten.

He could see details of the space beyond. A brightly lit room of some kind. Metal flooring. An opposite wall, easily a hundred feet beyond the opening. The chamber outside the tunnel must be huge.

He put his hands out again and caught the channel's sides repeatedly, shedding the momentum he'd built up earlier. He came to a complete stop with his head right at the tunnel's threshold. He hovered, staring at the room that lay beyond.

It was massive, and exotically shaped. The floor was a sweeping downward curve, like the inner surface of a barrel laid on its side. The walls to the left and right rose and angled inward, as if toward the barrel's center somewhere high above the ceiling—though the ceiling itself had to be forty feet up. The floor just in front of the tunnel was metal, as Travis had seen earlier, but everywhere else it was glass or some equivalent—it was simply an enormous, curved window, and after the first passing glance at the room itself, Travis found his gaze drawn down and outward to the view.

A planet. Right there. Suspended in deep black space and filling two thirds of the window. It was an amber-and-white version of Jupiter. Distinct bands of color met along ragged, swirled boundaries, and bent around cyclonic formations that were probably bigger than the Earth. Only a crescent edge of the giant world was lit up, catching the glow of a red-orange star that hung beyond it and far to the side. The star was visually the size of a quarter held at arm's length.

A second star, the same color, hovered much further away—it shone as no more than a super-bright point in the darkness. Travis knew these were the two suns that formed 61 Cygni, seen as a single dim speck from the desert in eastern Wyoming.

He stared for probably twenty seconds, his thoughts nearly blank. He noticed that the entire view outside was sliding steadily in one direction, and knew what that meant. Then he bent his legs and drew them forward and got his feet ahead of him in a seated position, and slid out of the tunnel.

Gravity exerted itself at once. A good stand-in for gravity, anyway—the centrifugal force of the rotating ship. He put his feet down on the metal and felt his weight transfer onto them—exactly as it would have on Earth.

"Jesus, it worked," a man said.

Travis turned to see a doorway that'd been out of view from inside the tunnel. Standing in it was Richard Garner, looking about as old as a college kid.

CHAPTER FORTY-SEVEN

T ravis stared at him, and then past him, suddenly wondering who else might step into the frame.

Garner seemed to understand. "It's probably best if you don't meet yourself," he said. "It's not going to split the universe or anything, but I think it would be very distracting."

He had an accent—one Travis was sure he'd never heard before. Nor had anybody else in 2016, he knew.

Garner stepped from the doorway and advanced. He smiled vaguely and shook his head. "I haven't seen someone look this old in over a thousand years."

They stood at the center of the gigantic floor pane and spoke at length. Travis told Garner, in broad strokes, the story of the Breach as it'd played out on Earth. All that had resulted from that day in March of 1978. All that this version of Garner couldn't know about—the aftermath of the plan he and the others had conceived and launched from this ship.

The man looked disturbed, even remorseful, by the time Travis reached the end. He stared away into the starfield below—the planet and twin suns were no longer in view—and exhaled slowly.

"We knew it would go bad in a lot of ways," Garner said softly. "We debated whether to do it at all. But in the end the decision was unanimous. We had the chance to set things right. How could we pass it up?"

He stood staring into the depths a moment longer, and then he drew a folded black card from his pocket and handed it to Travis. "Don't open that until you're ready. Inside is a long string of random letters, which your counterpart here has already thought. Once you return to *your* end of the tunnel, the Breach will revert to the form you've seen all these years. The plasma channel with entities coming through. It'll stay that way until you unlock the tunnel once and for all."

"And to do that, I just think what's on this card," Travis said, more verifying than asking.

Garner nodded. "It'll work best if you read it aloud—that should keep your stream of thought on track. Other than that, there's nothing to it. You can do it from anywhere on Earth, anytime after you go back. You read those letters, and the tunnel opens for us to come through. Easy as that."

Travis looked at the card. He thought of the disparity between its size and its power. Like a nuclear launch key. He slipped it into his pocket, then looked back up at Garner.

Garner was gazing down through the window again. Watching the edge where stars were continually sliding into view. Travis realized he was waiting for something.

At last the man pointed. "There."

Travis followed his downstretched arm and fingertip and saw a medium-bright yellow star that'd just crept into the frame. At a glance there was nothing special about it. It was all but lost amid the scatter of other stars.

"Is that what I think it is?" Travis said.

Garner nodded and spoke just above a breath. "There's not a day I don't come to this room and look at it. I stare at that little speck, and I wonder if there's anything left of the Ferris wheel on Navy Pier in Chicago, or the Kōtoku-in temple in Tokyo, or Nelson's Column in Trafalgar Square. And I'll never know."

"Can you actually change things?" Travis said. "If all of you come through to 2016, do you really believe you can rewrite history? And if you can, how do you know you'll make it better? Couldn't the same kind of war still happen someday, for other reasons?"

It took a long time for Garner to answer. His eyes and his head slowly turned, tracking the distant pinpoint of light in the endless black. He was still watching it when he began to speak.

"I can tell you about dozens of close calls the world has scraped past, these last twelve hundred years. Any one of those could've ended it. Finally one did. It was a matter of time." Far below the curved glass, the giant gas planet crept back into view. First came one horn of the lit crescent, and then the broad curve. The mostly dark mass of the thing blotted out the stars beyond it like an ink spill. "There are fundamental problems that never seem to go away," Garner said, "no matter how advanced the world becomes. No matter what you invent. No matter what you cure. You never get rid of things like denial, in-group and out-group thinking, cognitive dissonance. The things that underlie every conflict and every war. There are always people who *want* to get rid of those things, and those people get smarter and more capable over the centuries—but so does everyone else: the people who *don't* want those things to change. So the pattern holds." Garner looked up at Travis. "Our arrival in your time would stand some chance of breaking the cycle. We have the interests of the whole world at heart—we know what it's like to lose it—and we also have the knowledge and means to really change things for the better. We're more than just well informed. We're smarter, by a wide margin, than anyone on Earth in 2016. Our brains are physically different from yours, given what we've done to them. Any one of us could complete an IQ test from your side of the Breach perfectly, about as quickly as we could move the pencil."

"But is that enough to change things forever? A few hundred of you, among a few billion?"

Travis watched Garner and saw something in his eyes, flickering beneath the conviction with which he'd just spoken. A vestige of his earlier remorse, maybe.

"No," Garner said. "It takes more than that."

Travis found himself speaking the word even as he thought it: "The filter."

Garner nodded just perceptibly. "How much do you know about it?"

"Almost nothing," Travis said.

Seconds passed. Garner looked away. "A few minutes ago you told me about a computer called the Blackbird. Alien technology that you repurposed in some other timeline. A machine that can make hyper-accurate predictions, even about random events that haven't happened yet."

Travis waited for him to go on.

"We found computers just like that," Garner said, "governing the hubs of this tunnel network." He indicated the massive planet, already slipping back out of view. "You can't see it from here, but there's an object the size of Long Island orbiting just above the cloud tops down there. An artificial satellite. We managed to board it soon after arriving in this system. The best we could tell, it's a way station of some kind, connecting hundreds of these tunnels to one another. The place is filled with old electronics, some of it running down, most of it still working. There's automated maintenance overseeing everything critical, and based on certain timers we were able to decipher, we figure the thing's been abandoned for just over three billion years."

Travis tried to get a sense of time on that scale, but gave it up after a few seconds.

"Huge areas of the satellite are just stores of backup supplies," Garner said. "Including computers. We took one, brought it aboard this ship, and spent about fifty years learning everything we could about it. Learning that it does its computation by interacting with surrounding material. *Large amounts* of surrounding material."

"A whole planet's worth," Travis said. "The Blackbird told me that at the end."

Garner nodded. "Once we understood that part, we realized there was a certain function we could use this computer for, if we ever made it back to Earth through one of these tunnels—back to Earth during your time. This function was very difficult to set up; it's nothing you could've done with the Blackbird. The programming alone took us two decades. Then we ran thousands of simulations of how it would play out in real life once we triggered it. How it would work on Earth."

"How *what* would work? What function?"

"We called it the filter. I don't remember who came up with that name, but it stuck. I guess it made the idea sound clean."

"What does it do?"

Garner remained silent for a while. He didn't look at Travis. Beneath him, the planet slipped away again, leaving only the tumble of stars.

"There's a question philosophers used to ask," Garner said. "Maybe you've heard some version of it. Suppose you suddenly found yourself on a street corner in Europe, in the year 1895, and encountered a six-year-old boy named Adolf Hitler. Could you kill him, right then and there?"

"You're asking?" Travis said.

"Sure."

Travis thought about it. "I really don't know. I'd think I *should*, but that's not to say I *could*."

Garner nodded. "That's a common answer. Let's

say you did kill him. Do you believe World War Two would be prevented as a result?"

Travis shrugged. "I'm sure there'd still be a fight about something around that time."

Garner nodded again. "Same fight, for all the same reasons: broad political and religious ideologies grown out of centuries of ingrained hate; control of primary resources like territory, access to fossil fuel reserves, seaports. *Somebody* would've ended up banging the podiums over it. Different leaders might've been far less cruel, might've conducted the war in entirely different ways, but you could probably swap out the leadership of every country in the world at that time, and the middle of the twentieth century would've still been a nightmare. In which case you might ask yourself if it'd just be a mug's game, trying to change things. Aboard this ship we asked ourselves that question, and not as some academic brain teaser. The answer meant a great deal to us."

Suddenly Travis understood. Or thought he did.

"You and the others planned to bring that computer with you," he said, "back to Earth in 2016. You could use it to identify people who'd eventually be responsible for wars, all kinds of atrocities, long before they took power. Then you could just . . . kill them?"

"We could. And after that we could use the computer again to find out who was now on course to fill their shoes. And if we killed *those people*, we could look for *their* historical replacements, and so on. Beyond a certain point, we'd be killing people who originally wouldn't have done anything wrong. People who might've never ended up in positions of power at all, if we hadn't already killed the first several layers of troublemakers. You can see how the morals of the thing get tangled."

Whoever it affects, Ward had said, *it's not their fault. Not really. Under the wrong conditions, anyone could end up the worst person on Earth.*

"I thought it was about me," Travis said, almost to himself. "I thought I was on track to become . . . someone bad."

"Not you," Garner said. "Others. Many, many others."

Travis looked up at him. "Twenty million."

Garner's mouth seemed to have gone dry. He swallowed with a little difficulty, then nodded. "That's the rough number we came up with, every time we simulated it. If you chose them *very* precisely, the removal of some twenty million specific people from the world population would leave things unusually stable. Conflicts already under way in places like Congo and Sudan would suddenly lack not only leaders and instigators, but anyone able and willing to fill the vacuum left by them. All the suitable candidates would be dead. The same would be true of every saber-rattling regime in the world, including more than a few that don't call themselves regimes. The result of all this would be something uncanny. To any observer who didn't know better, for the next century the human race would seem, by sheer luck, to dodge every potential flashpoint that came along. Every dangerous stare-down between nations would happen to have a JFK or two in the right places to defuse it, instead of the various alphas who'd have normally held those positions. All those aggressive men—and a few women—would've been strained right out of history by then. Filtered."

"Jesus Christ," Travis said. He heard a tremor in his own voice.

"Every one of our simulations showed that a century like that would be enough—would let us get the world on the right track forever. Like a cast for a shattered bone."

"Aren't there easier ways?" Travis said. "If you're taking that computer to Earth in 2016, can't you just ask it, once you're there, for a more benign approach? There has to be something else it could think of."

"There's no end to what it can think of, and many of the alternate ideas would work—but all of them carry even higher death tolls than this one. However you go about it, you're talking about changing the world. It just doesn't happen without conflict. Believe me, we've had time to consider every approach, and the filter *is* the benign one. We're lucky the numbers aren't worse."

"Twenty million people," Travis said. He went silent, listening to his pulse thudding in his ears. Then he said, "How is it even possible to kill them all?"

"That's the function we developed for the computer, taking advantage of how it works: interaction with material at a distance—a whole planet's worth."

"Only at the smallest scale," Travis said. "Elementary particles. Not even atoms. Quarks."

"With the right programming it can do a bit more than that. I told you, it took us forever to set it up. We borrowed a few tricks from the evolution of parasite signals—ways of moving lots of particles all at once."

"To do what?"

"Create simple vibration, mostly—to generate heat. A little point-source of it, about a thousand degrees Celsius, anywhere in the world we choose. Inside someone's brainstem, for example."

Garner saw Travis's expression and continued quickly: "It's painless. They don't even know they're dying. They just drop where they stand."

"All twenty million," Travis said.

"In perfect unison."

A long silence drew out. Travis stared at Garner, then looked away at nothing. He could feel his heartbeat in his chest now. It sounded like drumming in some vast, empty place.

"You see now why your role is central to this thing," Garner said. "It's your decision whether we come through the channel at all. If you do let us through, we're going to trigger the filter the moment we arrive. I tell you that for clarity's sake."

"You didn't have to tell me at all," Travis said. "You could've given me the card and sent me back unaware."

"We debated that. Even voted on it. The outcome was pretty close to unanimous. The way we see it, the Earth at the far end of that tunnel isn't strictly our world. We *had* ours, and we lost it. The world we'd be coming to is *yours*. We couldn't ask you to let us in without knowing the consequences. We believed at least one of you should have the option to veto the idea. I'm sorry it falls to you, Travis. I really am."

Travis thought to ask why it *did* fall to him. Of all the people on Earth in 2016 who had counterparts aboard this ship, there could hardly be a riskier bet to put all the chips on. A young adulthood spent among violent criminals. His own criminal actions and all their consequences. He'd been lucky to reach his forties at all.

But he didn't ask the question. After a second's thought he didn't need to. He recalled the wooded slope outside the mine shaft. The contractors crouched behind their Humvees. The near-total lack of emotion he'd felt, approaching them with the chef's knife.

Necessity pushing remorse aside.

An animal thing from way back.

Something he maybe had more of than he should.

Garner's eyes took on understanding; he could see that Travis had made the connection for himself.

"You're the guy if anyone is," Garner said. He was quiet a beat. Then: "I've said all that it makes sense to say. Go back, and take all the time you need. If you never want this to happen, it never will."

He held Travis's gaze a few seconds longer, then gave him a last nod and walked away, back through the doorway he'd come from.

Travis stared after him, then looked down through the glass floor again. He watched until the yellow speck of Earth's sun emerged once more into the frame.

I really can't get there, he'd said to Paige. *Keep-*

*ing you in the dark about anything at all—I can't
imagine it.*

He still couldn't. Not in this or any timeline. He
could imagine nothing other than going back and
immediately telling Paige every detail. Garner and
a few others, too, but Paige first. He would share
everything with her except the weight of making
the choice. That would be his alone. He could spare
her even the stress of trying to sway him one way
or the other, by simply leaving for a while. Going
off by himself, maybe for weeks. Or months. Or
years. Just thinking it all through, the card folded
in his pocket at all times. He could use it from anywhere on Earth, as soon as he made up his mind.

He thought he knew which side of the choice he'd
eventually come down on.

He imagined Paige would know too.

He thought about all that, and five seconds later
he understood everything: all that'd transpired
between the future versions of himself and Paige.
Why she'd sent her message. Why he'd sent his.
There'd been no misunderstanding at all.

He stared at the distant sun transiting the glass
beneath his feet, and wondered if it was possible to
feel emptier or more numb than this.

He patted the card, deep and secure in his pocket,
and turned to the tunnel's flared entry. He crossed
to it and slipped inside, and began to push himself
back toward home.

SPELLBINDING THRILLERS FROM
NEW YORK TIMES BESTSELLING AUTHOR
PATRICK LEE

THE BREACH
978-0-06-158445-9

Trying to regain his life in the Alaskan wilds, ex-cop/ex-con Travis Chase stumbles upon an impossible scene: a crashed 747 passenger jet filled with the murdered dead. Though a nightmare of monumental proportions, it pales before the terror to come, as Chase is dragged into a battle for the future that revolves around an amazing artifact.

GHOST COUNTRY
978-0-06-158444-2

For decades, inexplicable technology has passed into our world through the top secret anomaly called the Breach. The latest device can punch a hole into the future, and Doomsday will dawn in just four short months—unless Travis Chase and Paige Campbell can find the answers buried in the ruins to come.

DEEP SKY
978-0-06-195879-3

Travis Chase and his covert agency team are in a race back through time and memory to unearth a decades-old mystery that may call down the destructive might of a shadow government.